SHE WAS LIA ANDREWS, WOMAN AWAITING HER LOVER

As she touched a drop of perfume to the hollow of her throat, she paused, smiling. There was a bit of the pagan in the almost ritualistic attention she'd lavished on her body in preparation for tonight.

The rattle of the front-door knocker startled her, and she gave a last glance at herself in the mirror She was naked beneath the flowing white gown The soft folds of fabric fell away at the swell of her breasts, leaving them covered with a single thickness that failed to hide the darker areolas. The taut nipples made no secret of her arousal.

She hesitated a moment, then a laugh rippled up inside her

Fool! she chided herself It's your lover Flint out there!

And she turned to open the door

Books by Jenny Loring

HARLEQUIN SUPERROMANCES
74—A STRANGER'S KISS
129—THE RIGHT WOMAN

These books may be available at your local bookseller.

For a list of all titles currently available,
send your name and address to:

Harlequin Reader Service
P.O. Box 52040, Phoenix, AZ 85072-2040
Canadian address: P.O. Box 2800, Postal Station A,
5170 Yonge St., Willowdale, Ont. M2N 5T5

Jenny Loring

THE RIGHT WOMAN

Harlequin Books

TORONTO • NEW YORK • LONDON
AMSTERDAM • PARIS • SYDNEY • HAMBURG
STOCKHOLM • ATHENS • TOKYO • MILAN

Published August 1984

First printing June 1984

ISBN 0-373-70129-2

Printed in Canada

To Jim Tabilio and Martha Robinson,
who taught me about gambling and casinos,
this book is dedicated with appreciation
and warmest regards.

CHAPTER ONE

FIVE DAYS OUT OF EVERY SEVEN Lia Andrews worked as a blackjack dealer in one of the smoke-heavy casinos that made up Lake Tahoe's south shore gambling enclave. In contrast, the sweet morning quiet of Sapphire Point seemed a breath of Eden. She lay on the beach there, on a towel spread out on pearl-white sand, enjoying the early hours of a day off.

Except for a lone man who emerged from among the trees at the far end of the cove and came sprinting toward her across the water-packed sand, there was not a soul in sight. Chin resting in the crook of her crossed arms, she watched the man lazily through half-closed eyes for a moment before her gaze strayed back to the sparkling waters of Lake Tahoe and the marvelously peaceful scene before her. Across from the Nevada beach on which she lay, a pale haze veiled the California shore. Misty violet mountains thrust up from the pure blue lake in a vast semicircle, their peaks and ridges cutting great jagged patterns into the clear cerulean sky.

For all her ambivalent feelings about her place

of employment, Lia was there by her own choice. If she was not a dealer at a Tahoe casino she would be doing the same thing somewhere else, and if the casino happened to be in Reno or, worse yet, Las Vegas in the Mojave Desert, there would be no Sapphire Point to escape to.

A sudden gusty breeze from the lake skimmed off top sand and dashed it across her face. Blinking, she rolled over and sat up. She flicked her thick lashes with a forefinger and shook her head impatiently to get rid of the bits of grit. The short mop of light brown curls flung a spray of sand back into the wind and sent a few grains of it prickling across her bare shoulders. She had only begun to soak up the first heat of the morning sun, and already it was time to go back to her desk and settle down to the work that was the real reason she was there.

She might as well forget about a dazzling Tahoe tan, she thought regretfully, eyeing her arms and legs with distaste. At such a high altitude the sun could be treacherous later in the day, but in the early-morning hours—the only time she allowed herself at the beach—it gave out a paler heat. After two months her skin was still barely bronzed. What color she picked up on her days off quickly faded under the artificial light at the casino.

Gathering up her towel and canvas beach bag, she reluctantly got to her feet. Her toes curled into the warm sand where she stood, and eyes as blue as the lake they looked upon scanned the white strip that edged the roughly crescent-shaped cove, extending a scant mile from point to point. At either end trees grew down to the water, enclosing and sheltering the sandy beach.

Curiously, she watched the runner as he drew nearer, admiring the performance of the lean, firm-muscled body, the economy of motion with which the man moved swiftly, steadily toward her across the hard-packed sand. After a moment she turned back to the lake. The morning breeze had teased the blue water into ruffles of white-capped waves that seemed to beckon her in.

Lia loved to swim and was good at it. She had, in fact, been the star freestyle contender on her high-school swimming team some years before. Even her bathing suit, a sleek, low-cut jade maillot, was a swimmer's suit, better designed for action than lazing in the sun.

She hesitated. The invitation of the beckoning water tempted her, though she knew the lake was like ice. Old Tahoe hands advised swimming in the afternoon when the sun warmed the shallower reaches near the shore.

But the lure of the water was too strong. Obeying impulse, she stepped up onto the boat dock, which extended a few yards out into the lake, and walked to the end. Dropping her beach bag and towel, she let herself down flat on the rough planks and reached to test the water with her fingers. It was every bit as cold as she'd expected, but its very coldness seemed a challenge. She got to her feet again and stepped back a few paces for takeoff. Steeling herself, she drew in a deep breath and streaked off the end of the dock in a shallow racing dive that barely cut the surface of the water and propelled her some distance into the lake. As she hit, her breath turned to frost in her chest.

It was as if she had plunged headlong and naked into a bank of snow. Her whole body seemed to freeze, and for a moment she was paralyzed. She fought to move her arms and legs, half fearing if she didn't get the blood circulating rapidly at once it would coagulate in her veins. In her best free-style stroke she forged ahead. In spite of the cold that bit into her like shark's teeth, she was in control until a sudden piercing pain stabbed the calf of her right leg, and the muscles tightened into a helpless screaming knot.

"Damn!" she muttered, but without alarm. She'd been a swimmer too long to let a mere leg cramp panic her. The main thing, she knew, was to keep her head and get rid of the small agony before it immobilized her entire body. Forcing herself to relax and unclench teeth clamped tight from pain, she raised her face out of the water, filled her lungs with air and went under in a somersault that put her in position to take hold of the offending leg with both hands. Her fingers groped for and found the charley horse, then began to knead it expertly. The hard knot of muscle that thrust out from the fleshiest part of her calf began to ease. When she could hold her breath no longer, she pushed to the top, letting out spent air as she rose. Surfacing, she drew another full breath, then plunged back to work again on the cramp.

When finally she had coaxed the muscle to relax she broke through the water, flexing her leg experimentally as she went. She felt the same ugly tightening. Impatiently, she ducked under and repeated the treatment. This time the tender muscle untangled at the first firm pressure of her fingers. When a few gingerly kicks brought no new knotting, she pushed up for air, intending to strike back for shore.

As she rose, she was startled by a swift flurry of movement near her and at the same time caught an eerie glimpse of a long shadowy figure speeding toward her through the water. Before she could turn from its path she was caught in a powerful unyielding grip by a creature she couldn't for a single manic instant define. Murky images of the Loch Ness sea serpent crowded into her head as she fought to free herself from the girdling bond, then sanity returned. The sinewy band that circled her upper torso was all too clearly a muscular human arm. For the first time in her years of swimming, Lia was afraid.

A homicidal maniac! It was the first thought that flashed across her mind. She'd rather take her chances with ''Nessie'' than with a madman who went around trying to drown women, she thought wildly, as near panic as she'd ever been in her life. Struggling, she went down. Her shadowy assaulter held fast.

Above water again, Lia fought grimly, bucking and kicking against the iron grip. Then as she was beginning to tire, she suddenly remembered the lone runner on the beach. If she risked her waning energy to scream, would he hear?

She put out her last ounce of strength into her voice and opened her mouth, but her cry for help was lost in a rush of water that filled her throat. In a last conscious moment she made one final impotent move to break away from her captor, and with more amazement than fear faced the awesome probability she was about to drown.

FOR UNMEASURED TIME Lia knew nothing, then gradually she became aware of an outside force pressing her nostrils together, puffing air into her mouth.

From somewhere far above her she heard a rich baritone voice say softly, "Ah, my intrepid lady wrestler. You put up one helluva fight!"

In that instant of returning consciousness Lia knew that she was cold and that a terrible heaviness weighted her body and all her limbs. She imagined she was living a nightmare in which she lay mortally chilled, lacking the power to move, unable even to pull up the covers to warm herself. With a monumental effort she raised her eyelids in response to the voice but saw only a thin sliver of light before they drooped shut again. A part of her mind understood then that this strange state of being was no nightmare and had nothing to do with sleep.

She tried to speak, to tell the hovering giant how desperately cold she was, but no sound came from her throat. Lights flashed and pinwheeled. Strange noises buzzed in her head. Except for the fierce cold that gripped her, she felt remarkably detached from it all. Like the flicker of a firefly, her mind faded in and out.

"Take a deep breath. Deep! Now breathe again."

It was the same sure masculine baritone repeating the same words over and over again in a kind of far-off litany. She wished it would go away. She was too tired for "deep," she thought fuzzily. Shallow would have to do.

But the voice gave her no rest.

"Come on, lovely. I said *deep*!"

From some unknown resource she mustered strength and opened her eyes to find a face directly above her, so near she knew instinctively that but a moment before the wide reassuring mouth had been shaped to cover her own.

In the mistiness of her mind she thought of that meeting of lips as a strange exotic kiss having nothing to do with her, a kiss joined by two other people in another time. Then, in a moment of startling clarity, she understood that it was to *her* the kiss had been given, and that in a very real sense it had been a kiss of life.

Her mind cleared rapidly, and in bits and pieces Lia began to remember what had happened. Some maniac had tried to drown her. The runner had heard her call and saved her life. She was stretched out now on the dock, and the man peering down at her, his weight resting on one knee, was her rescuer...the runner...of course. A giddy senseless laugh rose in her throat.

"That's the spirit," said the man.

Still in a lethargic, half-drowned state she stared back at him, her conscious mind noting dimly the composition of the face above her with such exactitude that later, when she was herself again, she could recall it in perfect detail: the strong chin, the large straight nose, the square forehead crowned with a crop of hair the color of strong black coffee, thick and inclined to curl, the deep-set eyes, which were neither gray nor green but something of both. A single indentation—it was hardly a dimple yet neither was it a scar—marked one lean cheek, lending a faintly rakish look to the face when the man smiled. A half smile plucked at a corner of his mouth.

"I was running on the beach and saw you go off that dock like an Olympic medalist," he told her. "Next thing I knew, you'd disappeared. You'd already gone down three times by the time I hit the water. What happened?"

"Leg cramp," said Lia, and groped to hang on to a transient thought his words sent racing across her mind. "Wait," she whispered hoarsely.

"There's something. ." The thought escaped her as she realized with alarm that she was about to be grossly, disgustingly sick.

Struggling against the heaviness that still pinned her body to the boards, she tried to sit up, only to fall back weakly upon the dock. The man came to her rescue, lifting her easily to the edge of the landing, where he held her head over the water, solidly braced by his arm, and let nature take its course.

"You swallowed half the lake. Get rid of it," he ordered bluntly.

After what seemed an endless time, the ordeal was over and her body fell back against his, shaking as if in seizure, her teeth chattering against each other like hail on a tin roof. There was no warmth to be had in the raw silk beach coat the runner pulled from her bag and slipped around her.

"Hypothermia! My God, we've got to get you warm. Where are you staying?" he broke off to ask abruptly.

Lia waved a wan hand in the direction of Sapphire Point, where a cluster of summer homes were hidden among the trees at one end of the cove a short distance away.

"Up there," she managed to tell him through chattering teeth. "Top of the slope. I'm all right. Never mind...I can make it...." She started to get up, but a new, more-brutal chill grabbed hold of her and sent her crumpling to the dock.

Flinging her canvas bag over a shoulder, the man hoisted her into his arms and set off across the wooden timbers toward the trees. Under the burden of her weight he plowed through the shifting sand at a labored trot. At the top of the slope Lia rallied enough to direct him to the second house on the lake side of the road.

"Do you think you can stand alone?" the man asked when they came to her locked door. Lia nodded. Bracing her shivering body in the circle of his arms, he rummaged in her canvas bag for the key and threw open the door.

Once she was on her own turf and her own two feet, Lia's independent spirit reasserted itself. She brushed past her rescuer and steered an unsteady course across the living room and through the open door to her bedroom, hardly aware that the man was following her. At the bedroom door he halted to watch her rummage in the closet and pull out a long crimson fleece robe with fumbling hands before making her way to the adjoining bathroom. Out of his sight, Lia clumsily peeled off her beach coat and wet bathing suit and wrapped herself in the welcome warmth of the downy robe.

Back in her bedroom she found her rescuer had turned down the covers on her bed. She burrowed beneath them gratefully, accepting without demur the help of the steady pair of hands that interceded and swathed her in blankets until she felt as snug as a larva in its cocoon.

Even so, the cold was so overwhelming she couldn't control the chatter of her teeth, however much she tried. She became increasingly aware of the runner standing at the foot of her bed, watching her tensely from the cool depths of gray-green eyes. A part of her felt compelled to send him away with the assurance she would be all right, but something inside her wouldn't let her give voice to the words.

"Do you have a clothes dryer?" he asked unexpectedly.

Lia looked at him blankly. The question seemed so utterly irrelevant.

"Behind the double doors off the kitchen," she mumbled indifferently, too caught up in her own convulsive chills to be curious as she watched him go. Curling herself into a shivering ball she pulled the covers like a hood over her head and huddled there, oblivious to everything but her own wretchedness until the man returned with a lamb's-wool shawl hot from the dryer. In a few deft movements he pulled back her blankets and wrapped the heated shawl around her over the fleece robe.

Back under the covers, the blessed warmth soaking through to her bones, Lia tried to say "thank you," but her words were no more than a mumble. He pressed his fingers lightly to her lips.

"Don't talk. Save your strength. I'll be back in a minute," he said quietly, then was gone, leaving Lia to revel in the warmth of her newfound chrysalis.

As the chill gradually subsided her teeth stopped chattering, and she felt a return of strength and a fretful wish that her rescuer would come back. Alert now, her senses were teased by a growing curiosity about this man who had again gone off on some mysterious errand of his own devising in her house. Things she'd hardly noticed in her half-drowned state came scrolling across her mind like pictures on a video screen.

There was the man in wet running shorts, browned by the sun and sinewy, his bare torso glistening like polished bronze. Yet not really like bronze, she amended, remembering with a small stir of pleasure the warmth and resilience of that firm flat chest when he lifted her in his arms and carried her up the slope to her door.

She saw again the deep compelling eyes, understanding, alive with humor, and the wide warm mouth. With a sudden awesome gratitude, she tried to call back the moments when his mouth came down to cover hers and fill her with his breath, but they were not hers to recall. They had happened while her conscious mind was closed. The picture she drew in her mind of the man's lips pressed to hers was pure fantasy and had no basis in fact.

Fact or fantasy, her effort to recall the moment kindled a lambent flame within and sent a different kind of tremor racing through her, one that hurried her pulse. For the first time since she plunged into the water she felt warm and full of new life. Suddenly impatient to cast off the invalid role she'd been forced into, she wondered restlessly what had become of the man.

She saw by the digital clock on the nightstand that it was not yet ten. Less than an hour ago she had raced across the landing and dived into the lake. For the first time since she'd opened her eyes to find the runner kneeling beside her on the dock, she began to sort out the morning's happenings with a clear mind.

The memory of the nightmarish encounter in the lake brought an involuntary shudder. Nevertheless, she probed at it doggedly. First there was the cramp in her leg and then the struggle with the madman who was bent on drowning her. Then, just as she was sure she was done for, she'd thought of the runner and yelled. Or had she yelled? She recalled opening her mouth to cry out, but after that all she seemed to remember was water. Had she made any sound at all?

She *must* have yelled. The runner had heard her. Otherwise, why would he have stopped to look? She tried to remember if she'd heard him mention hearing her cry for help. He'd seen her dive off the dock as he was running, he said. Her brow furrowed as she groped for his exact words. When they came to her, she gasped in dismay.

Next thing I knew, you disappeared. You'd gone down three times before I hit the water. Belatedly she grasped the significance that had escaped her when nausea had driven everything from her mind.

The runner! The maniac!

With a shocked gasp Lia sat bolt upright and swung her legs around violently to get herself out of bed. Before her feet touched the floor the runner himself appeared at the open door.

"You...you—" Lia cried out hotly "—*idiot*! You almost drowned me!"

The man's brows arched in surprise. "When I got there you were already doing a pretty good job of it yourself, if I'm any judge of drowning," he said mildly.

"Well, you're not!" snapped Lia. "I wasn't about to drown."

"Then what was all the splashing about—the now you see me, now you don't?" he demanded, his voice beginning to take on heat. "You were bobbing around like a cork when I went after you."

"Of course I was bobbing around. How else do you rub a charley horse out of your leg?" she asked furiously. "I had to come up for air. From the beach it may have looked like I was doing a lot of splashing, but I got rid of the cramp. I was doing fine until you took it upon yourself to get into the act."

For a moment the man appeared so stunned that Lia was almost sorry she'd been the cause of the dramatic change that came over the strongly hewn face.

"I thought you were some kind of a homicidal maniac out to drown me," she reproached him, but her indignation had become tenuous.

He lifted a big brown hand to rub the back of his head in a gesture of helpless dismay.

"It looks like I owe you an apology. I don't really know what to say except that it was a horrendous mistake, and I'm sorry."

"Oh, well. . . really, there's no harm done," Lia said uncomfortably, whatever need she might have had for revenge unexpectedly dissipating.

"No wonder you put up a fight," he observed, still on a note of shock. "I thought for a while you were going to drown us both. If I didn't have a thing about hitting a member of the opposite sex, I probably would have decked you."

"Chauvinist!" Lia accused, and was relieved when he gave a genuine laugh that brought back warmth to eyes that a moment before had looked bleak. But the transformation was only temporary. His face turned serious again, and he eyed her speculatively, as if reassessing their positions in light of what he'd just learned.

"I'd like to have a doctor check you over and make sure you're not going to come up with something lethal, like delayed shock," he said finally.

"That's ridiculous! You can see yourself I'm fine."

The man's face tightened. "Let's hope so. Just the fact that you're still breathing is hardly enough proof." The determination in his voice hinted at a will to match her own. "You may as well know I've sent for an ambulance that'll take you to the emergency hospital. I hope you don't mind."

"Well, I most certainly *do*!" Lia said. "You've got nerve! Just who do you think you are?"

"You've made it quite plain who I am," the man reminded her grimly. There was a stubborn thrust to his jaw, and the single indentation in his cheek deepened ominously. "I'm the guy who 'darned near drowned' you, though I'd already called the ambulance before you pointed that out to me. A near drowning is not to be taken lightly, particularly with excessive chilling. It's an early warning of shock."

"Well, I'm not going into shock," Lia said crossly. "I'm not even cold anymore. The truth is, I'm as warm as toast. I never felt better in my life."

"That's fine. You've still got to see a doctor."

"And if I refuse?"

She saw a flash of anger in his eyes and for a moment thought he was going to pick her up and carry her to the ambulance in spite of herself. She braced herself to resist. Then as quickly as it flared she saw his anger cool.

"Let's face it, my lady. I've got the brute strength to haul you off to the doctor, and you know it."

It was not easy for Lia to let his comment pass, but the hint of humor she caught in his voice caused her to hold her tongue and wait to hear him out.

"Unfortunately, we both also know damn good and well that I'm...uh...temperamentally incapable of following through," he went on half-ruefully. "Manhandling women doesn't happen to be in my bag of tricks." He lifted his shoulders in a shrug that seemed to serve notice he was through being reasonable.

"All right, damn it, I've admitted the whole bloody business is my fault. I've said I'm sorry. What more am I supposed to do?" he demanded testily. "Isn't it bad enough to be cast as the villain without having to worry that you'll develop unpleasant aftereffects? Now, if you'd agree to see a doctor...." He left it there, open-ended and on a plaintive note that suggested he was more sinned against than sinning.

Lia barely suppressed a grin. The man had a certain boyish charm, she was forced to admit as the last of her rancor dissolved. But he was wasting his talents if he thought he could change her mind. It was going to take more than boyish charm to get her into any ambulance today.

Aloud she said firmly, "No doctor. And you might as well quit flogging yourself. I'm honestly all right. I swear!" Then, to show that two could play the plaintive game, she added imploringly, "You'd make it a lot easier on us both if you'd just take my word for it."

"Only if you can show me your medical credentials." Ignoring the fact that Lia had made her position quite clear, he added, "The ambulance is waiting outside."

"I swear, you're as hardheaded as my father," Lia declared in exasperation.

His mouth slanted unexpectedly into a broad, utterly disarming smile that sent Lia's defenses crumbling.

"It isn't every day a man fishes such a captivating catch out of the lake," he said genially. "Can you blame the man for not wanting to take risks with the prize?"

"You make me sound like something to be mounted over the mantel," she said acidly. "Are you sure it's a doctor you're taking me to and not a taxidermist?"

But even as the words were spoken she was aware of a certain lingering shakiness and wondered if she was being too stubborn for her own good. Reluctant as she was to concede the point, it wouldn't hurt to have a doctor confirm the fact she was quite sound.

When the man made no effort to answer her riposte she said none too graciously, "Oh, all right. Since the ambulance is already here. . . ."

CHAPTER TWO

"Your name, please," said the woman.

"Lia Andrews."

They were at the reception desk of the emergency clinic, and a stout, gray-haired woman in white peered out from the admittance window. Clad in checked shirt and jeans, Lia looked back at her from the wheelchair in which she had been deposited, feeling very much the fool. The man—rescuer or nemesis she had yet to decide—stood to one side, a detached observer. He had walked in only a moment before, the ambulance having dropped him off somewhere along the way to pick up his car. Lia saw he had changed from the damp running shorts that had exposed nearly the full length of long athletic legs, to faded jeans and a clean yellow polo shirt.

Watching him covertly from the chair, Lia found little to add to her initial impressions except that his brown hair was lightly shot with silver and his eyes were full of light and shadows like deep pools of a tree-shaded stream. Judging from the lean muscular body and clean vital planes of his face, she decided the man could be no older than his midthirties.

"Employed?" The voice of the nurse broke in upon Lia's thoughts.

"At Stateline—the Goldorado casino," she replied, shrugging off the inner distraction.

"Occupation?"

Lia hesitated, deciding the best thing to say.

"Dealer," she replied. "Blackjack."

Lia could see the lines of the man's dark brows arch in two startled circumflexes and the expression on his face change to one she couldn't read. Surprise? Curiosity? Or was it disapproval? Was it the same look she'd seen not long ago on her father's face?

For a moment her mind carried back to that May morning three months earlier when she'd driven across the Bay Bridge from San Francisco to the family house in Piedmont to tell her parents what she'd decided to do. In a flash of instant recall she heard the roar of her father's voice as clearly as if he was with her there in the emergency room.

"Never mind the circumstances! I won't have my daughter dealing cards...consorting with gangsters. I heard those casinos are run by the Mafia."

And she heard her mother, ever the peacemaker, murmuring as always when Lia and her father locked horns, "Now, Chester, please...."

With a feeling of shame Lia heard herself lose her cool like a spoiled brat and answer back tartly, "Well, in that case you haven't been listening very well. Maybe Las Vegas actually *was* run by the Mafia at one time, but that's not Tahoe, and that's not now. Even in Vegas the mob went out when Howard Hughes came in. Now the casinos are mostly owned by conglomerates. If you looked into it, one of them probably belongs to some company you have stock in. The point is, the employees are as respectable as in any other business, and so are the players. A lot of the dealers are family people who are married and have children. Where I'll be working, for instance, they hire a lot of college kids.''

Her father, not one to give in, had regrouped and counterattacked.

"Which hardly includes *you*, my dear. I don't have to point out that you don't fit either category, Lia. You are a single woman of twenty-eight and no longer a college kid.''

Under the biting tone she'd heard the sound of her father's frustration and hurt.

"I'm sorry, dad,'' she'd said contritely, for suddenly she was. Never mind the lifetime of small wars she and her father had fought. She had a deep fundamental love for the stubborn man, locked in a generation too often at odds with her own. It troubled her greatly when she was forced to defy him to reach a goal that was important to her.

In this case it was her decision to apply for a job as a blackjack dealer. To begin with, her father looked on gambling as a questionable subject for a master's thesis in psychology. That his only daughter expected to do her fieldwork in a casino filled him with fatherly alarm. He managed to make her feel she'd chosen the subject simply to flout his paternal authority.

She was to find a new reminder of her father a short time later in the person of the physician waiting for her in a curtained cubicle down the hall. He was a square, bulldoggish man about her father's age whose demeanor as he went over her with efficiency and dispatch and declared her remarkably sound was not unlike her father's.

"You came in an ambulance. Is that big fellow out there going to see you home?" the doctor asked brusquely when the job was finished.

After all the fuss he made to get me here, he'd jolly well better, thought Lia. Aloud, she said, "Yes, I believe that's why he's here."

In spite of her protests, when the physician was through with her, the nurse insisted on pushing her out in a wheelchair. As they left the cubicle, she was further disconcerted to find the doctor striding along to the waiting room beside her. There her companion in the morning's debacle sat in one of the room's stiff, vinyl-covered chairs, thumbing indifferently through a year-old newsmagazine.

Seeing the tall rangy figure unfold lazily and come to meet her, she felt a sudden ridiculous gladness. An unexpected wave of pleasure washed through her and left her momentarily bemused.

Watch it, Lia! You're overreacting, she told herself wryly. He owed her this much! After all, she wouldn't be here if this character hadn't done his best to drown her.

Uneasily she watched the doctor move forward purposefully to intercept the other man a step away from her wheelchair. Without so much as a handshake, greeting or exchange of names, the physician began to speak about Lia as if she was deaf or incompetent or simply not there.

"Her vital signs are good. I foresee no problems," he said briskly. Lia darted an I-told-you-so look at the runner.

But the doctor had more to say. "You might see that she takes it a little easy the rest of the day. Get her in bed early and keep her there."

Lia met his words with a silent groan. The blasted man obviously assumed her relationship with the stranger to be something quite different from what it actually was. A glance in the runner's direction showed a flash of unguarded amusement in the woodland pools of his eyes, and his mouth slanted in a rakish twitch of a grin.

"It would be my pleasure, doctor, but I . . . ."

Embarrassed and resentful at the cavalier treatment she was receiving at the hands of the two men, Lia brought the exchange to a timely halt.

"I can get *myself* into bed, thank you, doctor," she broke in with asperity. "I don't even know this man. He . . . well . . . I guess you could say he saved me from drowning, but that hardly puts him in charge of my life. If you don't mind, I'll take care of myself.''

Caught in an uncomfortable spot of his own making, the doctor said impatiently, ''I've no doubt you *can*, Ms Andrews. The point is, will you? With all your independence, sometimes you young women don't have the sense God gave a goose!'' With that final statement the physician turned and tromped off down the corridor, clearly washing his hands of the whole matter. To her considerable annoyance, Lia felt like a chastened child.

Wanting nothing so much as to wash her hands of the matter, she raised her eyes to meet those of the tall man standing before her and was grateful to see, along with a truant spark of irrepressible laughter, the sweet balm of understanding in his face. There was sympathy in the slight smile he gave her as he lifted his shoulders in a shrug of dismissal that was oddly comforting.

What a nice man, Lia thought suddenly, *and what a hopeless way to have met him!* Under any other circumstances they might have gotten to know each other—might even have become friends. For the second time she almost wished she hadn't put him on the defensive. Must she have made it so unequivocally clear that the whole wretched mess was his fault?

She gave a nod of helpless consent and permitted herself to be wheeled out to the waiting car. Once inside she let her body go limp against the butter-soft leather of the seat, feeling like nothing so much as a bag of old rags.

She also felt an unaccustomed shyness, uncomfortably aware of the strong male presence at the wheel. Too much had happened between them in too short a time with no shared background of experience to cushion it.

They rode in silence the several miles through heavy south-shore traffic back to Sapphire Point, locked in their separate worlds. She roused enough to nod a greeting to her friend Carrie at the gatekeeper's cottage, who waved them through with a frankly curious stare, but it was not until the car pulled up to the rented lakefront cottage where she lived and the man shut off the motor that Lia forced herself to turn to him with a pale smile.

He studied her quizzically for a long moment, a curious humor in the deep-set eyes. At last he reached a hand across the space between them. A long, blunt-tipped forefinger played gently at one upturned corner of her mouth.

"Nice try...the smile," he said. "Valiant, but hardly robust. At the risk of playing the fool again, I'd be tempted to take you back to emergency if the doctor who assured me you were okay hadn't been such a positive type."

The finger traced the outline of her mouth and moved up the shallow valley of her upper lip to push lightly at the tip of her nose. It was the kind of small playful gesture that usually bespeaks a long-standing affectionate intimacy. Lia's eyes widened in an unexpected swell of appreciation. Quite suddenly she felt wonderfully, vibrantly alive. She concentrated on giving the stranger a new smile that would bloom with health.

The man caught his breath in surprise. "My God, woman, you have a breathtaking smile when you put your mind to it! You're a thing of beauty. You're...." His words drifted into silence and his hand moved to her cheek to pull her face to meet his. Lips came together and clung for a long questing moment.

Somewhere within, Lia felt the rekindling of a half-forgotten flame that had burned at another time for someone else, and she was afraid. Still she let herself cling for one last uneasy moment. It was the man who pulled away, touching his fingers to her cheek again in a gesture of apology.

"Wrong again," he said hoarsely. "Took advantage of the situation. Sorry! No excuse."

Lia felt dazed by a rush of conflicting emotions and was impelled to tell him that she'd been a willing accessory so it would be hardly fair to take offense. Caught off guard by a sudden flurry of inner confusion, she could find no words for what she needed to say. Instead, she unsnapped her seat belt and fumbled blindly for the handle of the door.

Dislodging his long frame from behind the wheel, the man got out and in a few long strides was there to open the door. He reached in and gave her a hand, helping her to step out beside him.

"I take it I'm not forgiven?" he asked, sounding so much less contrite than he had a moment before that Lia found herself laughing.

"There's nothing to forgive. Actually, I rather liked it," she said with an impish grin. Still laughing, she ran the few steps from the car to her front door, where he caught up with her and laid a detaining hand on her arm.

"Wait! Now that I've got you home, my usefulness is over, I know. You made that clear enough in your last remarks to the doctor," he said. "I'll respect that for the time, but you might at least say goodbye."

His words left Lia feeling inexplicably bereft. If she were a man or he were another woman, how easy it would be to say something like "Please stay awhile. I'd like to get to know you." But if she asked the man before her to stay, he would probably read more into it than she wished to convey.

He took her face in his hands and studied her for a long moment, then brushed her cheek lightly with the back of his hand. She understood it to be a gesture of farewell and was dismayed to feel tears well up in her eyes.

"Take care of yourself," he said brusquely.

Numbly she watched him cross the distance to his car in a long easy gait. It occurred to her to call out to try to stop him, but she couldn't think of a single sensible reason for doing so. In the next instant he was behind the wheel and away.

Not until the car passed the point where the road disappeared into the trees did Lia give up watching. With his going she felt an emptiness, as if something that might have been important had just slipped out of her life, and a sense of frustration and regret that she hadn't been able to come up with some acceptable way to prevent it.

Unless she did something herself to bring a meeting about, she was not likely to see him again, she thought, and her pulse quickened with a sudden resolve that was immediately dashed by the painful realization that in all the confusion of the past two hours she hadn't thought to find out his name.

CHAPTER THREE

LIA TURNED BACK to the house and paused in the doorway, dreading the emptiness that faced her. She almost hated to go in.

Sometimes when she came home from an early shift at the casino she let out a small satisfied sigh as she looked across the spacious main room and tree-sheltered deck to the clear blue lake, framed within the perimeters of the sliding glass doors. The house had been built by a friend of her master's professor some years before. Constructed of redwood lumber, now silvered with age, and thermal glass, the house rested partly upon two huge boulders at the top of Sapphire Point's rocky bank, its deck jutting out over the edge of the lake. It was a gem of a house, made up basically of three rooms. The large main room had a beamed ceiling, and a counter-topped island along one side served as a divider from the kitchen. A bedroom of equal size gave up space to a bathroom and walk-in closet, and a smaller guest room with its own bath, like the master bedroom, opened onto a hall that branched off the entryway. Although the house was small and compact it gave an illusion of spaciousness.

Rather too much so, Lia decided now as she stood on the threshold filled with emptiness. When the professor had suggested she take the lakeside house for a nominal rental fee while the friend was away on sabbatical, she could hardly believe her luck. Just the right size for a person who at that particular moment in her life, thanks to her recent and final disenchantment with Toby, was quite content to be alone.

Her typewriter and filing case and her research material fit perfectly behind a folding screen in the far corner where she could look out on the water as she worked. When she'd first seen the house she had viewed it as a private retreat where she could write her thesis in the quiet of her own solitude, away from the razzle-dazzle world where she was obliged to work.

But maybe she had been wrong, she thought disconsolately, as she thumbed through her papers in a listless effort to revive some enthusiasm for the work that lay before her. Not that she missed Toby, her number-one mistake to date. She'd thrown away two years of her life on him. When she had finally broken their engagement it was as if she'd found her way out of a bewildering maze that had threatened to entrap her.

No, she had no wish to share her life with Toby or anyone like him. Even so, today she felt restless and alone.

Maybe the house, as small as it was, was still too big for one person. After all, it had been built for two—the professor's friend and his wife. The place whispered of shared contentment—the man's pipe rack next to the fireplace, a lacy negligee in a bottom drawer, the carved jasper chess set on a game table flanked by two chairs.

She left her papers scattered across her desk and slid back the door to walk out onto the deck. She was experiencing a feeling, utterly foreign to her, of not knowing what to do with herself. At the railing she paused to look across the lake to the distant mountains on the other side—not seeing them; seeing, with her mind's eye only, the clean athletic form of the runner sprinting with piston-like precision along the beach.

How could she have been so stupid? She might at least have found out the man's name.

After a moment she turned away from the railing. Choosing one of the comfortable outdoor couches, she let her body slump dispiritedly onto its plump cushions.

There the morning's ordeal caught up with her. After a minute her eyelids drooped shut, and she fell into a deep sleep. Her dreams were peopled with shadowy figures and disturbed by a recurring horror of black waters closing over her head. She stirred, half waking, only to fall back into the same troubled sleep. When the nightmares had run their course she lapsed into a period of dreamless sleep, only to waken shortly with a bewildering sense of disorientation, wondering for an instant where she was. When she became fully awake and conscious of her surroundings, her thoughts turned back to the circumstances that had brought her to the Goldorado—beginning with Toby. Toby Brasford, real-estate ace. Attractive, devious and too handsome by far.

She'd first seen him in an elevator in the San Francisco high rise where she was a consultant for a family counseling service. He worked for a real-estate brokerage firm in the same building.

Lia was amazed and a little embarrassed, looking back now, that he had managed to parlay a chance encounter in an elevator into a two-year love affair, which for all its ups and downs, was itself not unlike an elevator ride.

Toby was all flash and no substance, a super-salesman who could sell even flawed goods like himself when he wanted to. Lia wrinkled her nose with self-disdain, remembering that at one point she had found him so winning she'd even considered letting him move in with her, something he continually pressured her to do. With a cynicism unlike her, she wondered if they had actually lived together, would she have ever come to a point where she almost married him—something she'd almost done under prevailing conditions.

It was hard to believe that for much of the past two years a part of her had seemed to stand off to one side, watching the affair with dismay. Her infatuation with Toby was not one of the shining periods of her life.

At twenty-eight, Lia had earned a degree in psychology from Stanford University. She had behind her a year of study and travel abroad and two years as an airline attendant for one of the top international lines. She had never suffered a dearth of attentive male friends, and her background of experience had left her knowledgeable and sophisticated where men were concerned.

So why Toby? she asked herself now as she had so many times before. Toby, along with some lesser flaws, was a compulsive gambler, a fact she hadn't realized until well into the second year she'd known him. Enamored though she might have been, the psychologist in her could not ignore the clues.

She'd tried to for a while. Even after guessing the unsavory truth she'd told herself it was a passing thing her professional training would help him to overcome. She'd even let him convince her she was helping him to give it up, and she'd imagined she was succeeding—until the night three weeks before their wedding date when he confessed he'd lost the money they'd been saving together for a honeymoon trip. Lost it in a Las Vegas blackjack game! Lia recalled with disgust.

"Don't worry your little head about it. I know what went wrong. Someone screwed up my counting system. I'll win it all back and a lot more," he assured her, as if it was the most reasonable statement in the world.

And she'd said, "Not on *my* money, you won't, Toby. In case you've forgotten, I was putting money into that account, too."

Toby had given her that look of surprised innocence she knew so well and had fallen for too many times to be fooled by it again, and he had said in that same injured, self-righteous tone she'd heard so often before, "I only did it for you, honey. Now, be honest. Wouldn't you rather spend a fabulous month on the French Riviera than two crummy weeks in Hawaii?"

"You promised, Toby," she'd chastised him. "You promised if I set a wedding date you'd never gamble again."

And he had replied in that aggrieved voice, as if she was being unreasonable and it was all her fault, "I meant it. It's just that I want to give you the kind of honeymoon I can be proud of. Even *you* wouldn't call it gambling when I've got a counting system that can't lose."

"Well, it lost, didn't it!"

"Don't you understand? It wasn't my fault. Now that I've corrected it...."

So that was that. She was through, but Toby wouldn't let go and she'd stayed and listened, though looking back on that ugly night she couldn't understand why she had. It was bad enough to have him argue and wheedle, but the awful part came when he finally realized she meant what she said. His voice took on a whiny note that blamed all the world but Toby for Toby Brasford's failures as he pleaded with her to forgive him. He'd cried real tears. He'd begged her to say she still loved him. Remembering, Lia was ashamed for him. Disgusted and ashamed.

"You've pretty much destroyed any love I might have had for you, Toby," she had said at last.

"You never *really* loved me," he accused, sullen voiced.

And she'd said in complete honesty, "Maybe you're right. I may have had myself fooled for a while. Right now, I don't care if I ever see you again."

It was a good exit line, Lia thought now, wondering why she hadn't turned around then and walked away. But she knew why. She knew that her words, in her own ears, had reverberated, spiteful and unforgiving, like the sound of a sharp slap. It was a sound she couldn't have lived with.

"All right, Toby. I guess I don't really mean that," she'd said in spite of herself. "If you can come to me in a year's time with solid proof you've quit gambling... well, we'll see. Maybe we'll find something between us worth salvaging. At this point I can't promise anything, and don't waste any time coming around unless you've given it up for good."

It was something less than the clean break she'd aimed for in the first heat of anger—though it was not because of anything that had been said to dissuade her. Nor did it have anything to do with love.

"You never really loved me..." Toby had accused. He was right, of course, Lia now knew. If she had, she'd have kept right on loving him even after the handsome disarming facade cracked and showed the sleaziness beneath.

A sharp tap at the front door brought Lia's soul-searching to a halt. Without a notion who might be there, she left the couch in a single eager movement, ready to welcome any interruption to the disquieting pattern of her thoughts. Opening the door, she looked into the round sweet face of Carrie Williams from the gatekeeper's cottage. Carrie peered back at Lia with an expression of combined apology and concern. She carried a covered enamel cooking pot with a cautious hand that warned the kettle was hot.

"You all right?" the young woman asked anxiously, not waiting for Lia to speak.

"Carrie! Come in. I'm so glad you're here," Lia greeted, following her visitor, who had scurried past her and across the big room to set her kettle on a stove burner on the counter island on the kitchen side.

"Hot and heavy!" Carrie explained, blowing on her fingers, then turning the burner on.

"What made you think I might not be all right?" Lia asked curiously when she had her visitor's full attention.

"You look better than a while ago when you drove through the gate with that man," Carrie said. "I was looking for you. I've got a cousin working at emergency. She knows we're friends, so she called me when the ambulance brought you in."

"News travels fast around here," murmured Lia dryly. The whole thing had been so...so ludicrous. It would have been better kept to herself, she thought. She swallowed her annoyance and gave her friend a reassuring smile. "I'm fine, Carrie. A slight case of the blahs, but I'm not even sure that's what caused it."

"Bet you haven't eaten a thing today. That can put you out of kilter. I made you some good lentil soup to perk you up."

At the mention of food Lia realized to her surprise that she was ravenous. She'd had juice and coffee and a piece of raisin toast before she went down to the beach, but that had been hours ago. What a dear Carrie was, she thought warmly, her instant of pique forgotten as she recalled the day the protective barrier of shyness that kept most others at a distance from Carrie had fallen away and they had become friends.

She smiled to herself, remembering the two of them as they'd been that particular morning, the round little person of Carrie scrunched up half in, half out of the cabinet around Lia's kitchen sink, tackling the gooseneck trap beneath with a wrench almost as long as her arm, while Lia hunkered down beside her and peered in to watch with respect. In spite of the young woman's skillful handling of the reluctant plumbing, Lia had known instinctively that Carrie Williams grappled with some greater problem of her own.

When the job was done and they sat down to have coffee, Lia had applied her professional counselling skill to draw out whatever was troubling Carrie. The petite miracle worker served as gatekeeper and watch guard for houses whose owners were away, as well as resident electrician, plumber and general handyperson for the Sapphire Point Residents' Association. In return for these services Carrie received a small salary, and she and her husband, Rick, lived in the gatekeeper's cottage. With free rent, Carrie had told Lia, they could get by on what Carrie made and bank Rick's earnings as a dealer at the Goldorado, looking forward to the time when they'd have enough put aside for Rick to go back to engineering school and finish his degree.

"Sounds like a happy arrangement," Lia had said a bit uneasily. The moment she'd heard the name "Rick" she'd realized Carrie's husband was the dealer she'd heard rumors about. He no longer worked at the casino. The whispers were that he'd left under a cloud. Her remark triggered an unexpected reaction from her companion, who suddenly burst into tears across the table.

"Everything's such a mess, and I don't know what to do," wailed the young woman.

Lia, the cautious professional then, ventured, "Would you care to tell me about it?"

As if held back by some hidden stopper that Lia's words had unplugged, the unfortunate story spilled forth—money shortages in the blackjack pit, circumstantial evidence brought to the manager's attention by some anonymous fellow employee that pointed to Rick.

The manager had been quite decent about it, according to Carrie. When he'd called Rick in to tell him of the shortages he'd expressed personal confidence in Rick's innocence and suggested that if Rick would go on leave of absence until the matter was cleared up in some other way, he could come back to work, and no one would be the wiser. Hurt and angry to find himself under suspicion, Rick had told the manager to go to hell.

Lia had been mildly surprised to learn that Carrie's husband was someone she knew, the subject of recent gossip in the employees' dining room, where it was generally believed Rick had been fired for cheating the house. She'd realized unhappily that she had no supportive words to offer the young woman, but it had seemed all Carrie sought at the time was a listening ear.

Today, shyness forgotten, Carrie's concerns were entirely for Lia and not for herself. She shooed Lia to the round translucent-topped table on the deck overlooking the lake, where she had set two steaming bowls of hearty soup. She pulled up a chair for herself across from Lia.

"What's this about you nearly drowning? You're a terrific swimmer, Lia. What in the world happened to you?" she asked at once.

"Well, you know how cold that water is early in the morning," Lia hedged, willing enough to tell Carrie, yet suddenly not wanting to put the runner in a foolish light. "I got a cramp in my leg." She hesitated as her mind edited.

"But what happened?" urged Carrie impatiently.

"Oh, there was a man running on the beach. He saw me and jumped in and pulled me out," she said, considering it a reasonably accurate account. "I swallowed a lot of water, it seems, and was out cold when he hauled me up on the landing."

"Wow! Were you ever lucky the man was there!"

"We-ell, yes. I suppose," said Lia doubtfully.

"What do you mean, you suppose? He pulled you out, and boy, is he good-looking!"

Lia looked at her in surprise.

"Oh, I took a real good look at him when he drove through the gate with you," Carrie confessed with a grin. "I go for men with that rugged, not really handsome kind of good looks. No offense meant to my Rick."

The description seemed so apt it brought a flicker of laughter from Lia as she recalled with a certain wistfulness her own intimate observation of the not quite handsome face. She glanced up to find Carrie watching her.

"How's Rick doing?" she asked, pulling herself back to the moment.

Carrie was easily diverted. "He's pretty sour," she said unhappily. "He hasn't found a job. The casinos are about the only place around here hiring, and Rick won't even try at any of them. With this Goldorado thing hanging over him, he says what's the use? And he's probably right."

Lia gave a murmur of sympathy.

Carrie was quiet for some moments. At last, as if debating whether she should speak, she said, "Listen, Lia, watch out for Ed Shields, your pit boss. Rick says for sure he's the one who had him fired."

Lia's eyes widened with interest. "He does? What makes him say that?"

Again the young woman across from her hesitated before she plunged on. "Maybe I shouldn't be telling you this, but Rick says there's something real fishy going on in Shields's pit. I don't understand enough to know how it worked, but Shields knew Rick had stumbled on to it, so he framed him to get him out of the way."

"If Rick's so sure about this, Carrie, why didn't he tell Mr. Mansfield, the manager?" Lia asked, trying to keep the skepticism out of her voice.

"Because he didn't have any solid proof. Rick's seen enough to know what's going on, but he was still trying to figure a way to prove it or to get Shields caught in the act. Shields got to Mansfield first. You're my friend, Lia. I'm telling you so you can watch out for him. He's bad news."

"Even as sure as Rick apparently is about this, Carrie, I can't see what trouble Ed could possibly cause for me," Lia protested.

"He's mean and he's sneaky. If he ever decides to use you to save his skin, you'll see!" Carrie predicted darkly.

Hating to ruffle her friend's feathers, Lia said hastily, "I really appreciate your warning, Carrie. I'll keep an eye on Ed Shields."

CHAPTER FOUR

LIA CLOSED THE FRONT DOOR a short time later after watching Carrie drive off in her small car. Her mind tabled her friend's warnings and turned willfully to the disturbing stranger whose life had become so precipitously and briefly entangled with hers. She stood for a moment bemused, feeling again with a small thrill of regret the back of his hand brushing lightly, seductively across her cheek.

"Darn the man!" she muttered Why couldn't he have just kissed her and left? That kind of caress she understood. But how was a woman to forget the poignancy of a strong hand turned gentle passing almost lovingly over the curve of her face?

That's all there is. There isn't any more. She had only herself to blame, she thought scornfully in answer to the growing reproach that she had overlooked the crucial matter of his name.

Not one to squander useful energy poring over something that couldn't be remedied—and for the life of her, Lia couldn't see how to alter this situation—she stepped down the two stairs from the entryway and crossed the big main room to her private lair behind the corner screen. Enough work awaited to keep her mind fully occupied for days to come.

She had discovered long before that small disappointments had a way of getting lost in the excitement of research and discovery, and she welcomed an afternoon of hard work as an antidote for her disquieting thoughts.

As she settled down to her desk to put the remedy to test, her thoughts turned back to that last ugly evening with Toby. With astonishing clarity she finally had the answer to the question she'd been pondering earlier when interrupted by the arrival of Carrie. She understood why she had offered Toby something more than a clean break in that last confrontation.

She realized for the first time that from the moment she'd accepted the fact he had a gambling problem she'd viewed Toby with a certain detachment. She had ceased to think of him as the man she would marry but as a person with an aberration whom she had a professional responsibility to help.

In the final analysis, she saw now, the same curiosity that had drawn her to the study of human psychology and a job in the counseling service where she'd been working when they met, had caused her to leave the small ragged opening when they parted company that final night.

It was the same curiosity that had prompted her

to read everything she could lay her hands on about compulsive gambling, and in so doing to discover that her profession had only begun to focus serious attention on the subject in recent years. She'd been surprised, too, to find a real divergence of opinions among researchers as to why compulsive gamblers were different from people who simply gambled for fun. On only one thing, it appeared, did the experts completely agree: there was no known cure for compulsive gambling.

Not until the night of her breakup with Toby had she recognized the subject as a fascinating ready-made field for advanced study that was not already overworked—something she'd been looking for for a long time. Not unmindful that she owed Toby something for directing her attention that way, she had asked for a leave from her job and returned to university to start an independent study on gambling for her master's degree.

The major casino where she'd first applied for a dealer's job turned her down flatly. They didn't want an employee taking notes on their clients and making value judgments on their activities in a study of any kind, the manager told her. She didn't make the same mistake when she applied at the Goldorado.

The best she could do without actually lying on the application form was to skirt the issue of why she was giving up work in counselling for a dealer's job. She phrased an answer that left the implication she was looking for a more exciting life-style and more money. There was an element of truth in the money part of it. She had been genuinely concerned about how she was to support herself while getting her advanced degree. She'd been independent too long to creep back under her father's autocratic wing and had been vastly relieved to learn that with her salary and tips combined she would earn more as a dealer than she did as a psychologist. Only her parents and her master's adviser knew the underlying reason for what she did.

One of the reasons, she admitted now, acknowledging to herself for the first time that her reasons were not all academic. On the personal side she wanted to find out what made Toby Brasford bent on ruining his life, and with any luck she would learn some things about Lia Andrews along the way.

For instance, why had she let herself get involved with a person as immature as the hapless Toby? The question never failed to bedevil her whenever it came to mind. The psychologist in her wondered if the answer might go deeper than she'd let herself admit up to now.

Toby Brasford had been a flaming issue between her and her father from the very beginning. Was that why she'd made herself champion of a man she'd never, even in her most myopic infatuation, quite been able to admire? Could it be she'd persisted in dating him mainly because her father never missed an opportunity to tell her what he thought of Toby in a voice of scathing contempt?

For a moment there came back to Lia the last instant before she lost consciousness that morning after the water closed over her head, when, by all accounts, her life should have flashed before her.

What she'd seen instead in that moment of clarity was the irony in the fact that she and her father had wasted so many years battling for control of her life, only to have it prematurely snatched out of the control of both. She'd realized then in a flash of understanding that she'd fought as hard with her father over things that didn't matter as for what she cared about most, sometimes even when she'd known for a fact she was wrong.

The strange new insight told her that if she'd tried, along the way she might have come to terms with her father, whom she loved, without compromising herself. In that last instant before she blacked out she was sad.

Lia prodded now at the morning's self-discovery before turning her full attention to the material she'd gathered to date. She closed her mind resolutely to all intrusions—the disturbing stranger she was unlikely ever to see again, the events of the morning, the beauty of the sylvan scene beyond her open glass door—and settled down to her notes, typing and assembling them in orderly, color-coded files.

She worked with the same total concentration that had earned her a degree with honors at graduation, not aware of time passing until late afternoon, when a brisk breeze whipped through the open door from the lake, carrying a hint of the snow still on the surrounding mountaintops. It stirred the papers on her desk and sent a shiver of cold across her shoulders, reminding her of the lateness of the day. Even in mid-August at such a high altitude the air grew chilly when the sun dropped behind the western mountains.

Gathering her papers together, Lia rose and pulled shut the sliding glass door, her body suddenly cold. Her chilliness brought back unpleasant memories of the morning, and she went into the bedroom to change into something warmer than the thin, short-sleeved T-shirt and shorts she'd put on when she came back from the emergency hospital. Rummaging through her closet she brought out a bright red velour jump suit that zipped all the way up the front and hugged her body cozily from ankles to collarbone—an extravagant whimsy she'd always been glad she'd bought. At times like these it warmed her spirit as much as it warmed her body.

She touched a match to the wood in the living-room fireplace, and after making a second meal of Carrie's hearty soup she arranged herself cross-legged in front of the blazing fire, feeling, in spite of the jump suit, uncommonly depressed. For all her effort she couldn't call back the afternoon's pure concentration and found herself staring blindly at the pages of the open book in her lap as the print dissolved into the image of the runner and his warm, wonderfully appealing face turned gently sardonic by that curiously slanted smile.

It might have been pleasant to have gotten to know him, she found herself unwillingly thinking again.

A sharp *tat-tat-tat* of the front-door knocker brought her meandering thoughts to a surprised halt. It seemed unlikely that Carrie would be stopping by again—not at this hour. Lia knew no one else in the area who might be apt to drop in on her unannounced. Curiosity as much as caution directed her to peer through the peephole at her caller. She drew in her breath sharply and stood for a moment composing herself before she reached for the doorknob. She was much too relieved to see the tall lean figure of the runner on her doorstep to wonder what he was doing there.

"I happened to be in the neighborhood..." he began as she opened the door, then he broke off to embrace Lia with a lazy, self-deprecating smile. Lia's pulse played a quick grace note, then righted itself and hurried on steadily at a somewhat faster pace.

"That's not exactly true," he confessed shamelessly. "I was actually clear over on the west side of the lake some miles from here. I drove around to make sure you're all right."

"Thanks, but I'm fine. You needn't have," said Lia, feeling as if she had to stop and catch her breath.

"You're wrong. If you rescue someone it's up to you to keep an eye on your rescuee from that point on. Everyone knows that."

Lia resisted the temptation to remind him just who it was that had put her in need of his noble rescue. The momentary recollection of those nightmarish moments in the water brought an involuntary shiver down her spine.

"See!" the man said, picking up on it instantly. "You're still cold. How about finishing this inside?"

Half teasing, half serious, suddenly heady at the admission he intended to stay for a bit, Lia hesitated.

"Not as long as we don't know each other's names."

A note of puzzlement in his voice, he said, "But I know your name, Lia Andrews," confirmation that he'd listened closely to her answers at the emergency admittance desk. "Lia Andrews," he repeated, then finished grandly, "It's engraved on my brainpan as with a diamond stylus, never to be erased."

"Don't try to distract me with your pretty rhetoric," Lia said smartly. "If you really want to be invited inside you'd better tell me yours."

The dark wings over his eyes arched quizzically until a look of dawning comprehension lighted his face. An instant later came the easy embracing smile of apology.

"I'm Flint Tancer," he said. "I live and work

on the peninsula south of San Francisco. I'm staying at the Goldorado at present and have just come from having dinner at the summer place of relatives between Meeks Bay and Homewood about halfway up the west side of the lake. I'll be glad to show credit cards, medical history and furnish any further references you may require. *Now* will you let me in?''

"Flint Tancer,'' Lia repeated thoughtfully. Flint. Brittle...hard. Somehow it didn't suit him. "How did you come by the name Flint?''

"It's my honest-to-God given name, not a nickname,'' Flint told her. "At the risk of disenchantment, I confess when applied to me Flint doesn't necessarily mean lighter of the flame. Much more mundane. My mother was Mary Flint.''

Though Lia was not prone to blush she felt a sudden rush of heat to her face. For a moment she was at a loss.

"Look at it this way,'' he said soothingly, "she might have been Mary Puffenwhacker.''

"I suppose I might as well let you in,'' said Lia, recovering.

Stepping back into the entrance hall she nodded toward the open fire and stood aside for him to pass by her. He crossed the threshold, closed the door behind him and stopped. Lia was uneasily aware of how near he was to her—so near she could determine the exact spot where her head would fit between chin and collarbone, should he reach out and pull her into his arms. It was strange and a bit unnerving to Lia, a rather tall young woman accustomed to viewing male acquaintances at slightly above eye level, or, in some cases, a little below. With this man she must raise her chin to look into eyes that surveyed her with an unabashed admiration, which once again brought the feeling of heat to her cheeks.

Not curbing the overt appreciation in his voice Flint said, "That red...foofaraw...that romper thing you're wearing...." He stopped, clearly groping for a more suitable name for the garment.

"Jumpsuit," Lia supplied, and was rewarded with a marvelous rakish grin.

"That's it," Flint said. "I like it. Is that what you wear to bed?"

"Of course not," Lia said, bridling, immediately on guard.

"Then how about getting into some bedclothes."

"Talk about a direct approach!" sputtered Lia.

Opaque eyes gazed down at her with an innocence that strengthened her guard.

"Direct? Maybe. But you might have thought I was trying to pull something if I'd used a more roundabout way to tell you," he said reasonably.

"Tell me?" repeated Lia. "Tell me what? As if you've left any doubt what you have in mind!"

"Tell you I'd come to carry out the doctor's orders."

"And what is that supposed to mean?"

"You heard the good doctor this morning.

Didn't he say to get you to bed early and keep you there?'' he reminded her. This time the innocence in his face was no mask for the underlying devilment.

"Well, of all the.... Good night, Mr. Flint Tancer,'' Lia flared. "I read your intentions loud and clear.''

The hint of playfulness suddenly disappeared from the man's eyes, leaving his face quite serious.

"I swear I didn't arrive on your doorstep with any ulterior motives,'' he said with such sincerity Lia had no choice but to believe him. "Having half drowned you this morning I'll be damned if I'm looking to top my own oafishness by trying to seduce you tonight. I just wanted to make sure you were okay after the manhandling I gave you, and it occurred to me all that thrashing around in the water with a mad killer might make you uneasy tonight, in which case a little well-meaning company and a hot toddy to help you sleep might be in order. I've got stuff for the toddy here. I'm sorry my intentions were misconstrued.''

"*You're* sorry? *I'm* sorry!'' said Lia, and continued ruefully in her own defense. "I don't often come on so skittish, but that doctor routine was too much! When a man starts talking about getting a woman into bed it hardly ever means he expects her to go there alone.''

"I'd be a liar if I said the thought of sharing yours never entered my mind, but I rose above it,'' Flint admitted wickedly. "As for the doctor, I'd forgotten all about him until you appeared in that smashing red garment made like my sister's kids' sleepers, without the feet, and reminded me.''

Lia gave in with a laugh. "A toddy sounds great. You make it, and then come in by the fire."

"Glad to see I'm forgiven," he remarked dryly.

"Don't you believe it," she said with a grin, but she followed him into the kitchen and leaned against the counter to watch him make the promised toddy. He then poured a splash of the very good brandy he'd brought to make it with into a wineglass—in the absence of a brandy snifter—for himself. As he worked she took pleasure in the easy movements of the lean supple body and the square competent hands.

Soon they were settled in front of the fireplace, the lazy flow of their talk moving on—inconsequential, amusing, unrevealing talk meant not to challenge or disclose but simply to please.

The small fire Lia had built burned to embers as she savored the last of the toddy's liquid heat and felt it burn a fiery path down her throat. She sat curled up in a plump, dark green corduroy-covered chair, heavy eyed from the warmth of the room and a lovely indolent inner heat that came from the toddy. She savored, too, the presence of Flint Tancer, slouched comfortably in the matching chair on the other side of the lamp table, the wineglass cradled in one hand to warm the brandy he sipped. She watched him tip the glass to his lips to empty the last drops of amber liquid and felt her pulse quicken in anticipation as he placed the glass on the table and righted himself to get up. Her breathing shallow, Lia waited, wondering what kind of a leave-taking lay ahead.

As he was about to rise, his eyes came to rest upon the book she had left open facedown on the table when she jumped up to answer the door. Picking it up, he examined the cover, then thumbed through it lightly.

"Hmm. About gambling. I didn't know dealers were expected to do homework."

"They aren't. I...well...I thought I'd like to know something about the kind of people who... get a kick out of it," Lia said lamely. The toddy was potent and had left a fuzziness around the edges of her mind.

"Well, you won't learn anything about them from a book like this. This book's about compulsive gamblers. They don't gamble because they get a kick out of it. They gamble because they don't know how to quit."

"The book's all right," Lia said without enthusiasm, reluctant to get into the subject with him. "Basically, I suppose there are only two kinds of gamblers, anyhow—the compulsives and the people who just do it for fun."

"I think you're wrong, Lia. There are as many kinds of gamblers as there are gamblers. As many kinds as there are kinds of people. You haven't been dealing long?" It seemed more of a statement than a question.

"A little over three months."

"That explains it. You still have a lot to learn."

Putting down the book where he had found it, Flint rose abruptly and a step later stood looking down at her where she sat curled in the chair. The lamp highlighted his strong high cheekbones and cast a bronze glow across the suntanned cheeks. On his face was a curious searching smile. Looking up at him, Lia could imagine an almost magnetic force between them. Without willing it, she uncurled herself and moved to get up.

"Christmas in August," Flint said.

Still seated, her feet positioned to stand, she paused to stare up at him, mystified.

"You look like a Christmas card in your red jump suit and the green chair," he said, reaching down to take her hands and pull her to her feet and into his arms. She could hear the hard percussive beat of his heart next to her ear, feel her own answering pulse racing to match it. She felt his kisses upon her head. Mindful of the unmistakable response of his body to hers she lifted her face, her lips moist and waiting. But when he lowered his head it was not to join her mouth to his but to close first one of her eyelids and then the other with a kiss and let her go.

She swayed a moment where she stood, as much from the wave of disappointment that swept over her as from the liquor's heady aftereffects, and his hands steadied her.

"I'm going to leave you now as I said I would,

Lia Andrews, but God knows, I'm going to need all the help I can get,'' Flint said huskily.

For a moment Lia wondered muzzily if she really wanted to help him. She liked this man. But even as she acknowledged the liking, she acknowledged too, in a clear-eyed flash, that she knew hardly anything about him—his name, where he came from, his present base. Liking wasn't enough. Casual intimacy might work for others, but a certain fastidiousness that ruled Lia Andrews made it unworkable for her.

But she did like him. Or was the promise she imagined she saw in Flint what she liked, perhaps even more than the man she hardly knew? A promise she liked so much she dared not risk it, though she wasn't even sure what the promise was. She only knew instinctively that if for an hour of unguarded passion she lost whatever it was, her heart would never let her forget.

Without a word she turned away from the man and led the way to the door. There he kissed her, touching only her lips, softly, lightly, and stepped out into the night.

CHAPTER FIVE

LIKE OTHER MAJOR GAMBLING establishments on the Nevada side of Lake Tahoe, the Goldorado Hotel-Casino trained its blackjack dealers at a house-conducted dealer school. It was at one of these concentrated midsummer sessions that Lia learned the professional techniques for shuffling and dealing and spotting the card combinations that add up to twenty-one.

It had taken less than a week on the job to discover the importance of reporting for a shift on time. One late worker could throw the whole operation out of sync and incur the wrath of the person responsible for work-station assignments, the one known among the dealers simply as the pencil man. Nor did tardiness make points with punctual co-workers, who were put out by unnecessary delays.

It was understood that when the fall layoffs began, the chronic ten-o'clock scholars would be the first to go. Lia couldn't afford such a risk if she was to stay on at the casino for as long as the thesis study required. She had no intention of being banished from her research field before she was finished for any cause as preventable as being late.

Perhaps to convince herself of her own fitness that first morning back after her near drowning, she pulled into the employees' parking lot at the casino in her small car some minutes earlier than her usual early arrival time and hurried across the lot and under the huge cantilevered marquee that covered the main entrance as if she was already late. The automatic double glass doors, one of three matching pairs, hissed open at her approach and she stepped inside.

"Late again," Reilly, the stout, balding bell captain, greeted her heartily from his station next to the line of registration windows to her right. It had become his regular morning quip during her first weeks on her new job, his personal comment on the fact she was usually the first of her shift to arrive.

Lia grinned to show she appreciated his joke and glanced at her watch, dismayed to find how ridiculously early she was.

"Looks like I really outdid myself today," she said, shrugging aside a momentary annoyance at her own poor timing. She might as well get a newspaper to read while she waited before going upstairs to check in.

With a parting wave of her fingers to Reilly, she walked across the hotel lobby with its enormous native-stone fireplace laid with artificial gas-burning logs, past the bank of elevators that carried guests to the Goldorado's five hundred hotel rooms occupying seventeen floors, past a row of flashing video games to an arcade of shops that linked the hotel and gambling casino to an eight story annex of a hundred luxury rooms overlooking the lake. In one of the shops she bought a San Francisco daily paper and was given three quarters in change for a silver dollar. The heavy coins forever made her feel as if she was carrying an anvil. She couldn't remember the last time she'd been handed a dollar bill. In a gambling casino that featured a solid row of dollar slot machines, which could only be played with "hard" money, a paper dollar was a rare commodity.

As she left the lobby Lia paused under the gilt framed horseshoe-shaped archway that led into the glittering casino to survey the scene, both fascinated and amused as always at the awfulness and opulence of the decor. It looked as if it might have been decorated by the madam of a gold rush bordello

The background of the rich carpeting that cov ered the acre of floor was fire-engine red, pat terned with interlocking chains of huge gold coins The carpet was visible in its full flamboyance only upon the broad passageway leading to the keno lounge and the restaurants and bars along one side; it was nearly obscured elsewhere by the machines and gaming tables that crowded the casino floor. A thousand clear light globes set in diamond-shaped patterns overhead bathed the arena in a relentless incandescence, and these were abetted to some degree by three chandeliers the size and shape of oversize hot tubs, from which dripped hundreds of crystal prisms that cast frenetic fragmented rainbows across the ceiling.

In the entire casino there was no window through which a patron could catch a glimpse of the world outside, which might draw him away from gambling pursuits. Nor, by the same rationale, was there a clock of any description to remind a gambler of the passage of time.

Much of the big arena was given over to a forest of slot machines set one against another in rows. Between the rows were alleys wide enough to accommodate players back to back with additional space to allow for the restless shifting of people from machine to machine and row to row.

A large clearing was set aside for the gaming tables—or pits. These were made up of the blackjack tables, at one of which Lia would shortly take her place to deal, the craps and roulette tables and the money wheels. Majordomo over each group of tables was the pit boss, whose job it was, among other things, to watch for errors the dealers might make and for any cheating on the part of players or dealers.

It was only midmorning, but already the machines were busy with the firstcomers of the weekend crowd. At the far end of the casino where the charter buses from the Bay Area and the Sacramento and San Joaquin valleys pulled in, a stream of people poured through the revolving doors, dispersing noisily in all directions. By late afternoon the casino would be milling with customers. By this time the next day players would be jostling one another for places at the slot machines.

As Lia crossed the casino toward the stairs that led up to the room where the dealers checked in, the pit boss, Ed Shields, came around a bank of machines a few steps ahead of her. Seeing him brought to mind her conversation with Carrie the day before. Carrie had seemed so sure Rick was the innocent fall guy in some kind of complex scam masterminded by Shields. Lia eyed the man curiously, wondering if there could be anything in what Carrie would like so much to believe.

Ed was a sallow-faced man with thin lips and a nasty tongue whom Lia didn't particularly like, nor did she mind believing him capable of such a thing. But common sense told her no. Considering the eye-in-the-sky surveillance of the pits from overhead—a round-the-clock, closed-circuit television watch covering the entire casino gambling floor—she found it hard to believe Ed or anyone else could get away with any large-scale rip-off. More likely Rick had been paying off short and got caught.

She gave the pit boss a nod and a word of greeting before moving on. Toying idly with the three quarters still in her hand after buying the paper, she wandered between the rows looking for the "right" machine

In the belief she could not lend full authority to her thesis on the psychology of gambling without ever having gambled herself, Lia made a practice of dropping whatever loose change she had with her each morning into one of the slot machines as she crossed the casino on her way upstairs to check in. She stayed clear of the gaming tables. There, in a few minutes of academic research, she knew it would be quite possible to lose a month's rent. In the same amount of time on the slots she could gamble every day and lose no more than a little small change.

She never lost much, but except for a winning cherry or two or three oranges that occasionally rolled up on the display space, bringing a few coins clattering down into the pan, she didn't win much, either. Nor, after two months of this daily indulgence, was she any nearer to understanding what caused people to ride hundreds of miles and run the risk of bursitis to pull the handles on a roomful of slot machines.

Feeding the gods of chance each morning had become a discouraging and increasingly tiresome exercise for Lia, but she continued to pursue it dutifully in the stubborn hope that it would one day pay off—not in the form of money but in a sudden, revealing insight into the seemingly hypnotic force that drew people into the gaming sphere.

Halfway across the casino floor on a diagonal course she stopped in front of a triple-pay machine, dropped one of the quarters into the slot and watched the first pay-off line light up. She was about to pull the handle that activated the machine when she paused to consider. If she put in the two remaining quarters to turn on the other two pay-off lines, she stood to win far more than triple the amount she'd win on the single quarter, which would pay only the amount shown on the first line of the display. On the other hand, she'd be betting all her change on one pull of the handle, whereas if she played her quarters one at a time, three pulls of the handle, she had three chances to win or lose.

After a moment she shrugged and emptied her hand, following the first coin with the second and the second with the third. All three lines on the display board in front of her lit up like a Christmas tree.

She pulled down on the handle and visualized the headline: "Last of Big Spenders Risks All on a Single Pull of the Arm!" The display drum rolled. One by one the lines fell into place. Even before Lia recognized the winning combination, a red light on top of the machine flashed, a bell began to ring, and before her astonished eyes quarters came clattering out of the bowels of the machine from some hidden trove within. Into the receiving pan they poured in a noisy stream until she wondered if they would ever stop.

Overcome with a sudden frenetic excitement her eyes darted up to the display board to see how much money was on its way down. She chortled with delight and astonishment. Seventy-five dollars! She could scarcely believe her eyes. Never had she seen so many quarters in one pile. In the entire two months since she'd started playing the slots, she couldn't have lost more than ten or fifteen dollars altogether, she thought exuberantly, and laughed softly to herself as she gloated over the unexpected return on her investment. And still the quarters rolled out. No money that had ever come to her, not even her first paycheck, had intoxicated her as this did.

Over the clatter of the dropping coins as the machine disgorged the last of her winnings, she heard an amused voice behind her say, "Well, if it isn't the lady of the lake on a busman's holiday!"

Lia turned in surprise to find her visitor of the night before standing a few steps away. She gave a small outcry of pleasure.

"It's you! I just won a whole bunch of quarters. This is my lucky day," she exclaimed, making no secret of the fact she was glad to see him.

"So I see," said Flint. "Do you play the slots often?"

Still full of the excitement of her win, Lia laughed. "Oh, yes. I play them every day," she replied honestly.

"Oh?"

Did she detect a sudden cooling in the dark laughing eyes? In her exuberance she refused to worry about it but hurried on in a rush of words.

"I thought you were here for a convention. I really hadn't expected to see you in the casino."

"You don't mind that I'm here, do you?"

Lia laughed. "I'm delighted, of course. It's just that somehow I didn't expect to see you *here*."

"Why not? You must have guessed by now that it's not the sailors and sun worshippers who keep these multimillion-dollar casino-hotels afloat."

For no reason she could justify, Lia felt strangely let down. "You're here for the gambling?"

"I expect I'll do some gambling while I'm here," he answered with an evasive grin. "May even take a lesson from you. Are you always this lucky?"

Looking down at the pile of coins that filled the pan of the slot machine beside her, Lia swallowed a new laugh as it rose in her throat and said smugly, "Well, I manage to stay ahead of the game."

"Spoken like a true gambler!"

"Oh, but I'm not a—"

"Gambler?" Flint finished for her with a skeptical laugh. "That's what they all say. I've known a lot of gamblers, but I've yet to meet one who says he *is* one. And they're always ahead of the game."

His words filled her with a sense of frustration, but she made no further effort to correct the wrong impression she could plainly see had taken shape in Flint Tancer's mind. She knew that further denial would merely confirm what he already thought. At the same time it occurred to her that

in view of what he'd just said, he might be knowledgeable enough about gambling to be a good research source for her.

"You seem to speak with authority on the subject of gamblers," she remarked, and then asked
innocently, "Do you plan to be here long?"

His answer came slowly, and when it did he
seemed to have settled some sort of conflict within
himself. His mouth curved in an engaging off-
center smile and the coolness in his eyes that she'd
detected a moment before warmed.

"Long enough to buy you a cup of coffee," he
said with a nod toward the Golden Urn, a casino
coffee shop nearby that featured breakfast around
the clock.

A glance at her watch told Lia she was due in a
few minutes to check in upstairs for her shift.

"Sorry, but thanks anyhow. I have to report for
work in about five minutes," she said regretfully.
"I wish we had time to talk. Another time, I hope.
Right now I really must go." She turned, about to
leave, but was stopped short when he reached out
and laid a detaining hand on her arm.

"Wait. You're not going off without your ill-
gotten gains, are you?"

Lia turned back in confusion, aware that she
who never blushed was blushing again. The
amusement she saw in Flint's eyes was doubly disconcerting to her. She could hardly believe she'd
let herself get so rattled by his appearance that she
completely forgot the winnings she'd been so ex-
cited about two minutes earlier.

Struggling to regain her composure, she dropped her eyes to survey her spoils, realizing for the first time what a pile of coins seventy-five dollars in quarters made.

She gasped. "Good heavens! I can't begin to stuff all that in my purse."

"Wait here. I'll get you something to put them in." Flint headed for a nearby change booth and returned in a moment with a large waxed cardboard container into which he scooped the quarters out of the bowl of the slot machine.

"What in the world am I going to do with a bucket of quarters?" she cried in dismay as he handed her the nearly full container, heavy with coins.

"I believe the idea is to feed them back into the machine."

Lia glanced again anxiously at her watch. "I'm serious," she said. "I've got to go in a minute. Any quick ideas about taking care of this blasted money? I certainly can't carry it around with me all day."

"Cash it in at the banking window."

"If I have to wait for them to count it, I'll be late for work," she moaned.

"Then I'll cash it for you. That is if you'll trust me with that much loot."

"Here. Take it," she said, thrusting the heavy container into his hands with relief.

"I'll meet you in the lounge when your shift ends. No. Better yet," he said. "Let me pick you up at your house. I'll take you to dinner to celebrate."

"I should take *you* to dinner!"

Flint groaned. "Wait a minute! You're not going to turn out to be one of those women who keeps tally of every miserable penny to make sure it's all split fifty-fifty right down the line?"

"Not really," she said amiably. "I just don't like to take advantage of anyone because I'm a woman, and by the same token I hate for anyone to take advantage of me. Right now it hardly seems fair for you to do all the work and for me to have all the fun."

Flint grinned down at her slyly. "Don't be too sure about that, my lady. One never knows. I may want to collect a commission. We'll see."

"For nearly drowning me?" Lia asked tartly, ignoring the implications she saw in his grin. "Come to think of it, you owe me a couple. You can cash my winnings *and* pay for my dinner—services I've more than earned." She smiled. "Now, I really must go."

A few steps away it occurred to Lia that perhaps she really didn't want him to convert the whole seventy-five dollars into paper money, as he undoubtedly was about to do. Why shouldn't she keep a few dollars of it in quarters? Five...maybe ten. Maybe as much as fifteen. She really wanted to try that same machine tomorrow when she came to work. She remembered noticing that the jackpot figure, recorded at the top of the display, was in the neighborhood of fifteen hundred dollars. If she kept putting in three quarters at a time as she'd done just now, maybe....

She was about to turn back and tell Flint to save some of the quarters she'd won when she was struck by a sudden sobering recollection. Research studies had determined compulsive gamblers often became compulsive after a large win or an extended winning streak. It was as if, in certain predisposed persons, the thrill of winning triggered a sudden sense of power that clouded reason and caused them to believe, even when they were losing, that if they continued to play they would win.

Instead of changing her course she walked on, strangely shaken. Winnings forgotten, she considered briefly the question of her own vulnerability and shrugged it off. Although she rose to the challenge of games of skill, she quickly tired of games of chance.

Which still left her, as a researcher, with an unanswered question.

Why did they keep coming back? Not the compulsive gamblers, the ones the hard-core gambling world called degenerates. Not those, but the others—the solid, responsible people who made up the great majority of the casino crowds. Those people looked on gambling as no more than a favorite diversion they indulged in from time to time. She visited with them whenever she could. From them she'd learned that most came to the casinos with preset limits on the amount they'd let themselves lose. When that limit was reached, they quit.

Unlike the compulsives they were realists, for

the most part, who came expecting to lose. On the whole they seemed rather less concerned with winning and losing than with how much action they could get before they reached the funding limit they'd set themselves.

She thought of the answer she'd overheard one winner of a hundred-dollar jackpot give to a curious bystander when asked what she planned to do with her haul.

"Why, play with it, of course," the winner replied, as if the question was absurd. "I'd gone through most of my gambling money. If I hadn't won this I'd have had to quit. Oh, I'll put it all back in before I leave. They don't call these things one-arm bandits for nothing," she finished with a contented chortle.

These were the people Lia had come to think of as the fun players—the amiable pleasure-seeking patrons who gambled with gusto yet knew when it was time to quit. The fun players took time away from their gaming to snow ski in the winter, water ski in the summer and visit the fine restaurants and star-studded shows the casinos staged in their vast dinner theaters year around.

Moving on up the broad carpeted stairway to the room where she was to check in, Lia paused and turned back to look out over the arena until her eyes found the tall figure they looked for, weaving his way through the alleys between the slot machines, her bucket of quarters balanced carelessly in the crook of one arm. The day before she'd been so sure she would never see him again. Then last night he had come to see her, and now there he was, and they were going to have dinner together that night.

She watched him a moment as he crossed the main passageway toward the row of banking windows on the far side, moving with that athletic grace she'd noted and admired on the beach, and her mind turned to their bizarre first encounter. Assaulter-rescuer, she mused. She barely suppressed a laugh as she saw for the first time a certain zany humor in the circumstances of the previous morning.

Her eyes lingered on the broad shoulders for a moment with a feeling of intimacy, as if the ridiculous charade they'd played out together had given them unguarded glimpses of the two private selves within and made them something more than strangers.

For a moment she saw the dynamic face as she had when she'd peered up at him through half-opened eyes from her supine position on the landing—the warm, potently sensuous mouth so near her own, the deep pools of his eyes peering down at her with concern. At the memory a small shiver of pleasure raced up her spine.

Straightening her shoulders she turned away and walked resolutely on up the stairs, reminding herself again that she knew only his name, where he was staying and where he came from—and one more fact. He was there to gamble.

CHAPTER SIX

STANDING BETWEEN TWO ROWS of slot machines, absently balancing the bucket of quarters in his hands, Flint watched her go. She seemed to hesitate and slow down for a step or two, and for a moment he thought she might turn around. He waited for a parting glimpse of her face—that petal-fresh triangle notched by a widow's peak that made it resemble the shape of a valentine heart. Unexpectedly, instead of turning, she quickened her pace and moved away from him.

There was something strangely unsettling about the straight back as she walked and the slight sensuous movement of firm, neatly rounded buttocks under the snugly tailored black pants of her dealer's uniform; something about the tapering of her thighs into a waist so small he might almost encircle it with his two hands—an idea he found too inviting to immediately put aside.

He liked the confident set of her shoulders beneath the oyster-white silk of her shirt, the natural lift of the short-cropped curly head. To him they spoke of an independent spirit he found strangely appealing. Yet for all this manifest freedom of spirit she was pure woman. devastatingly female...and as feminine as a whiff of French perfume.

He watched her mount the stairs and in his mind saw again the elegant rise of her breasts under the scrap of cloth that passed as a bathing suit. Breasts made to fit the curves of a man's two hands. He thought, too, with a sudden hot rush of blood through his veins, of the same slim body dressed in that ridiculous red jump suit.

Seeing again the velvety frontal sweep of her torso toward her breasts, the tapered and curving thighs, he felt a certain sheepish pride in the self-restraint that had kept him from making even more of an ass of himself than he had in her presence.

"Hey, mister, you gonna play this machine?" A brash voice broke in upon his thoughts, erasing the picture. Tancer looked around with annoyance to see a bearded fellow in jeans and a Stetson eyeing him impatiently.

"If you're not gonna, I wanna try it. I seen it pay off for your lady friend, and I mean, mister, it's hot."

"Be my guest," said Flint laconically, moving away with Lia's bucket of coins.

He headed for the banking counter to get rid of the cumbersome burden. He watched a teller count out the three hundred quarters, asked for currency in exchange and was given two twenty-dollar bills, three tens and a five. He tucked these into a separate pocket of his wallet to turn over to the winner when he saw her again that night.

At the Golden Urn café a few minutes later he picked an end seat at the L-shaped counter and ordered a cup of coffee. Sipping the hot bitter brew his thoughts turned again to Lia Andrews, seeing her now as she'd first appeared to him the other morning when he was running on the beach.

The lissome figure in a scrap of green bathing suit that fit like skin had caught his eye and brought him to a sudden stop. He'd watched as she moved across the dock with a splendid leggy grace and lowered herself to trail a testing hand through the water. Then she rose to her feet again, and he saw her bend her knees in the slight crouch of a racing diver and push off. When the sleek body cut into the icy lake as smoothly as a young sea otter a shock ran down his spine and he could almost feel the chill of the water closing in around her. That was when he should have headed off again and not looked back, he thought sardonically.

Instead, he'd just stood there watching her, mesmerized until he realized with horror she was in trouble. At least, he'd *thought* she was. He'd been so sure!

Flint didn't relish the picture of himself as a latter-day Don Quixote. Had he jumped to the rescue too impulsively? But he knew he hadn't. From all appearances she was a swimmer about to go under for the last fatal time. Under the same conditions, even at the risk of playing the fool, he knew he'd respond exactly as he had.

Once she was on the dock and he was pressing his mouth to the soft cold lips, breathing air into her lungs, she began to revive. He would never forget the incredible exhilaration that shot through him when, with almost his first breath, she began to respond. Even if he'd known that if he couldn't bring her back, her drowning would be on his head, he couldn't have been more jubilant, he realized now. He'd felt like grabbing the lovely young woman and giving her a big hug.

It wasn't much like the way he'd felt the other time he'd given mouth-to-mouth resuscitation to revive someone, he recalled derisively. It had been a long time since he'd even thought of it, yet strangely enough, as he dived in after Lia, that other utterly worthless life he'd saved had come in a flash to his mind. How ironic, he'd thought then, if he should fail to save this beautiful woman whose life, if appearance was any measure, seemed so unequivocally worthy of being saved.

That first rescue had happened in his eighteenth year. He remembered because it was the summer he played blackjack in a casino until it was discovered he was a minor and he was kicked out. That time it was not drowning but smoke inhalation, and the victim was a small-time hood who had stolen Anitra from him. Hating the man with the full force of adolescent hatred, Flint had pulled him out of a burning car. Every breath he breathed into the wretch was delivered with a curse.

Sipping coffee at the café counter some eighteen years later, Flint felt a surge of gratitude toward that young Flint. There had been nothing to stop him from simply walking away and letting the bastard die, but he knew now that if he had, Flint Tancer, the man, would still be living under the shadow of that terrible default long after the cause of his hatred was all but forgotten and the hatred itself dissolved.

It was a guilt he'd been spared, simply because something had kept the boy he'd been then blowing air into that other mouth, knowing all the time he was doing it that if the guy lived, he'd probably take off with Anitra—which two days later he did. Flint hadn't seen either of them since.

How long had it been since he'd even given Anitra more than a passing thought, he wondered now in astonishment. In the callowness of his new threatened manhood there'd been a stormy time of black rage and wounded pride when he couldn't think of anything else. Now, at the distance of two decades, he thought of her with a certain wry affection and a measure of sardonic tolerance.

She was the "older woman" a man sometimes has in his life; at thirty-six—his own age now—she'd been just twice the age of the young Flint. She was a cabaret singer at a Vegas casino and had the fairest skin and breasts as round and smooth as honeydew melons—and a heart of gold.

A hazy memory of her intermittent presence stretched back through most of his teenage years. His first vague recollection of her was when he was fourteen, after his mother died, and after his small sister, Rozlyn, was sent to live with their mother's sister.

Flint was left in his father's charge. Lucky Tancer had been a traveling salesman for a company that manufactured restaurant and bar equipment. At least ostensibly that's what he was. Actually, he was an unregenerate gambler, though he never admitted to the appellation. He called himself a salesman. Even after the death of Flint's mother, when he quit the company and turned to cards full time, that was still what he said he was. From then on until he died, Lucky did nothing but move from casino to casino, following his luck at the gaming tables. Inevitably, he and Flint were often in the same place at the same time as Anitra, who sang and pranced in the casino bars.

There had been times when Lucky was in the chips and Flint was sent to a private school in Arizona, sharing luxury suites in casino hotels with his father at vacation time. There'd been weeks in Monte Carlo and Puerto Rico, the Bahamas and France, and assorted other foreign gambling spas. Other times they lived in a battered camper in trailer parks on the outskirts of Vegas, and Flint went to whatever school happened to be within walking distance of the trailer park.

Whether it was the camper or a penthouse suite,

he remembered, Anitra was often around. He'd liked her well enough, though he never paid much attention to her until one day he realized she'd quit treating him like a kid and was treating him like a man.

That was when he fell in love with her, with the terrified, senseless hot-blooded fervor only a teenager in love for the first time can know. She took him to her bed and taught him—among other eroticisms—ways to please a woman, letting him discover on his own the mystical personal adventure of knowing how. It was a part of Flint's education he never regretted, even when she went off with her small-time gangster and left him to find out for himself that a broken heart was not a killing disease.

Sitting now at the counter of the Golden Urn, watching the lights on the keno board above him flash on and off yet not really seeing them, Flint thought maybe the experience with Anitra had been the most valuable part of what education he got during those awful adolescent years. School in those days had been pretty much catch-as-catch-can for him, and what he learned from Lucky's scene was how to win from the amateurs at cards and how to use a reasonably reliable system of counting cards at the casino blackjack tables.

It was a combination that paid his way through four years of college after his dad died. He won his tuition from all-night poker sessions with rich boys on fraternity row. The rest of what it cost him to live he picked up at casino tables during vacation breaks. Until, on the day he graduated, he finally admitted to himself that he hated everything he'd been doing and said to hell with it. He took his college degree and went to work, swearing he would never walk into a casino again, much less count a card.

As for that other part of his education, not the least of the lessons he'd learned at the bosom of Anitra, he reflected now, was to keep his skepticism well-honed where women were concerned. It was a bit of wisdom that had saved him from any long-term entanglement but gave him some passing concern that it might work against him should that mythical "right woman"—the woman with whom one might be tempted to share one's life—happen to come along.

On the other hand, he didn't need a refresher course to remind him that the women he'd known in gambling casinos were hardly fireplace-and-slippers types. In Lucky's day there'd been no women dealers, but there were other women— chorus girls, cocktail waitresses, change girls. Many of them were there for no reason but to make a decent living, he realized now, but the ones he'd been around with Lucky were all cut out of the same material as Anitra. Some of them attached themselves to the high rollers or, worse, the underworld toughs much in evidence before the state of Nevada stepped in and cleaned out the Mafia.

Flint hadn't been in gambling environs for fifteen years. He was quite willing to concede that the casinos had become respectable since big business replaced the mob, but the casino scene from his adolescent years was embossed on his memory, lending a certain narrowness to his perspective, he supposed. He was pretty damn sure that Rozlyn, his sister, would never have been found working in a gambling joint.

So what about Lia Andrews?

An old cliché popped instantly into his mind: *What's a nice girl like you doing in a place like this?*

He groaned inwardly. Lia Andrews, a casino blackjack dealer who, by her own admission, played the slot machines every day. From his years of experience as a bystander he knew it could mean only one thing: the woman had gambling in her blood.

But what difference did it make? Pulling someone out of a lake didn't imply any long-term commitment. Who was he to kick a gift horse in the teeth? He'd been as sour as an old bottle of wine with a bad cork until Lia Andrews appeared to brighten the scene. Why should he care how she chose to earn a living, or what she did with her money or spare time?

But he knew he did care, and it had little to do with her beauty—there'd been more beautiful women in his life—or with the ineffable charm that set her apart from other women in his mind.

It had to do with the rescue. In some strange way it was as if nearly drowning her and then saving her life had given him a preemptive interest in what she did with it, which, in turn, gave him the right to disapprove.

He saw this rationale for the nonsense it was and abandoned it at once with a derisive grunt. Looking up from his cup of coffee he found that one of the comely girls in a brief swirl of skirt who collected customers' marked cards for the next keno drawing had stopped beside him.

"You playing keno, sir?" she asked.

When he smiled and said no, the woman moved on. Flint glanced at his watch and finished the dregs in his cup in a gulp. He paid the cashier and left the casino for the parking lot.

LATE MORNING found Flint stretched out on the deck of a Tahoe summer home on the west side of the lake some miles to the north, pulling absently on a dead pipe caught loosely between his teeth. Beside him lounged his brother-in-law and sometimes business partner, Aaron Burney. Before them the blue lake shimmered in the morning sun, but the two men looked out across its bright surface, not seeing it, as they dug into a hugger-mugger of problems relating to Burney's most recent investment—the Goldorado Hotel-Casino.

"Here you are, Aaron," Flint said at last, handing over to his brother-in-law the detailed list of recommendations they'd spent the last hour discussing. "I've given the hotel and restaurant operations a complete check-over this week. The place can use some reorganization, but as far as I can see there's nothing basically wrong."

"They're not showing a profit. That's what's basically wrong!" Aaron reminded him gloomily.

"Don't worry about it. It's not a resort inn you're running, it's a gambling establishment. The hotel end of this business isn't necessarily going to make money," said Flint. "You ask any longtime casino-hotel manager. He'll tell you the hotel and the restaurants and bars are just the etceteras. Your main business is the casino. The etceteras are for keeping the gaming public from straying away from your games. You don't have to worry about your patrons unloading their money at your competitors across the street as long as you give them the best accommodations—food, drink, entertainment, rooms—and be sure that for the high rollers it's all on the house."

"It goes against every principle of sound business practice, Flint—having sixty percent of the floor space given to operations that just barely pay their own way," Burney argued. "The partnership would never have made it if we'd run any of the other companies we took over like you tell me to do this."

"But this one's different, take my word for it. Here it's the tail that wags the dog, and to keep this kind of tail wagging, it better be a big healthy dog."

Though Burney grunted his disapproval, when next he spoke his voice contained respect coupled with affection. "I'm not arguing with you, Flint. You know what a dud *I* can be where gambling's concerned!"

Flint managed to suppress a grin. He knew exactly what a "dud" Burney could be. At the same time his own affection and respect for his sister's husband would not let him point out that Burney had bought the failing Goldorado against all Flint's advice.

"I had my fill of the gambling scene when I was growing up, Aaron. Leave me and the partnership out of it, please," Flint had said unequivocally. "You'd be better off to forget it, too."

Later he'd tried again to dissuade Burney from buying it. "I think you're making a big mistake to sink a pile of money into this casino, Aaron. What the hell do you know about running a casino?"

Too late he'd seen that his tactlessness had touched a sore spot in the other man.

Burney had responded huffily, "I know a little something about running a business, wouldn't you say!"

And Flint had hastened to make amends. "I'd say about as much as there is to know, Aaron. You know that! My only point is that business is one thing. The business of gambling is something else."

The conversation had taken place more than eight months earlier, but Flint's opinion hadn't changed about the casino—or about Burney's gambling skills. Burney cleared his throat uncomfortably and gave his brother-in-law a sheepish glance.

"We-ell, damn it, Flint, I wouldn't have coerced you into coming up here to do my troubleshooting if I hadn't been up a creek without a paddle," he said in his own defense. "I need your help."

Sooner or later Flint knew he would have been obliged to come to the rescue even if Aaron hadn't "coerced " him. They were in-laws, partners, friends. There were too many ties between them to sit by and watch him fail.

"Forget it. It's no big deal," Flint reassured him brusquely. "As a matter of fact, I'm enjoying it."

It was a well-meant lie, intended only to temper his brother-in-law's self-reproach, but the image of Lia Andrews sprang before Flint's mind. For a split second he imagined the silken-soft feel of the lithe body pressed close to his and knew what he'd told Burney was true. He was glad to be on the scene.

Until that morning he'd carried on his work in the hotel environs without setting foot in the gambling arena, dreading the moment he'd have to start checking the casino, reluctant to risk dusting off the frustrations and sorrows of adolescence locked in the attic of his mind. Now all that seemed irrelevant.

He'd said to Aaron it was no big deal. Well, it wasn't. Small enough, certainly, when you considered it was Burney who'd come up with the money that got their successful partnership started. Without Burney, Flint doubted he could have made it.

Looking across now at the suntanned handsome face, the balding head, the square body grown slightly paunchy from too much of the good life, Flint saw in its place the youthful, free-spending postgraduate Aaron Burney who'd been one of the poker-playing fraternity crowd whose regular late-night sessions paid Flint's way through college.

An overgenerous trust had kept Burney drifting aimlessly back to campus to enroll in random classes three years after he'd officially graduated, making him more affluent and at the same time somewhat older than the other well-heeled "brothers." His was the most readable poker face ever to be found across a green baize table, Flint recalled.

After he quit school and went to work in the management end of Widnick and Company, Flint might never have seen Burney again had they not run into each other quite by accident in downtown San Francisco one day two years later at a time when each happened to be at a personal crossroads. Flint had just learned that Widnick and Company, a small tool-manufacturing concern, was being forced to liquidate, and Burney, tired of playing the perpetual sophomore, was groping to make a place for himself in the real world.

Because he liked Burney—what could anyone find *not* to like about this generous amiable man—but also because he'd always felt a little guilty for having taken money from such an easy mark in those fraternity-house poker games, Flint had suggested Aaron join him for lunch.

That lunch had turned out to be a remarkable occasion, Flint thought in amused retrospect. Neither of the two was a midday drinker or prone to be bibulous at any hour, yet lunch began with two very dry, very double martinis, and though they had never known each other except across a poker table, their meeting that day ended with an an agreement between them to form a partnership and rescue the dying firm of Widnick and Company from bankruptcy court. Burney was to provide the collateral. Flint had already figured out how to get the business back on its feet. It was a partnership that remained in good health after more then twelve years.

In light of the magnitude of Burney's financial contribution to the partnership and the paucity of his own, Flint, common sense askew from the second martini, had promised to turn Aaron Burney into a winning gambler.

As far as Widnick and Company and the newly formed partnership were concerned, thought Flint, looking back now, it had proven a lucrative venture—even in the earliest days when Burney and Tancer were known to take a chance on any shaky enterprise that looked as if it might be salvaged for resale at a profit. They'd revived everything from a failing mattress factory to a badly managed chicken-processing plant. Over the long haul it was money from operations like these that got them into the first of certain promising new research and development companies in the field of high technology. In high tech, the partnership's returns had been nothing short of phenomenal.

Flint had found, somewhat to his own surprise, that in addition to more than his share of business acumen, he had a kind of sixth sense that told him when and what to get into and what to do with it once he was in. It was a factor Flint attributed to luck, and he was highly entertained to find the media referring to it as ''the uncanny judgment of the youthful venture-capitalist'' and crediting him with a kind of ''wizardry in getting to the heart of problems and meeting them with ingenious solutions that seem to work.''

They could call it what they liked, thought Flint sardonically; it was Burney's money that had given them the blast-off that put the partnership in orbit.

As for himself, he hadn't even held up his end of the bargain. In spite of his promise and his best efforts to teach Aaron how to gamble without losing his shirt, he'd never made it. Aaron himself finally admitted he had no card sense and gave up gambling for good. It was Flint's private opinion that the frustrated gambler in Aaron had made him unable to resist the Goldorado when it came up for sale.

"Dammit, Flint, you aren't even listening!"

The reproachful voice of his brother-in-law from the nearby deck chair brought Flint's wandering thoughts to heel.

"Sorry, Aaron. You were saying?"

"I was talking about the casino. You'll be checking it out next, I suppose."

"The casino? Yes, of course. Tomorrow," said Flint. "But you borrowed Les Mansfield from the firm to take over the management right after you bought it, so it's my guess he's got everything under control, if I know Mansfield."

"Well, as a matter of fact, he has. Les is a good man. He walked in on a terrible mess. Sloppy management from day one! No security to speak of, bad accounting practices that brought in the IRS. It's no wonder the business went down the tube," Burney told him. "But Mansfield's about got all that straightened out."

"Good for Les. Then there's not much left there for me to do."

"Well, there are other problems," Burney said with seeming reluctance. "We're not making the kind of money we should on the blackjack tables. Mansfield is sure one of the employees is cheating the house but he can't put his finger on who. He got a tip pointing to one of the dealers, but nothing conclusive. When he tried to talk to the guy he got mad and quit.''

"Are you still coming up short now that's he gone?''

"Things have pretty much leveled off, but Mansfield had a player barred from the casino about the same time, a player who had a suspiciously long run of incredibly good luck, so it's hard to say.''

"What does Mansfield think the fellow was up to?''

"That he'd either perfected a detection-proof card-counting system or was in cahoots with an employee who's cheating on the house.''

"I doubt if anyone can figure out a system for counting cards that can't be spotted reasonably quickly,'' said Flint. "It sounds like cheating to me. What makes you think he and the dealer weren't in it together?''

"Les is satisfied the dealer was innocent. It bothers him to lose an honest dealer, particularly when he thinks we still have someone on the payroll we can't trust.''

"So?''

"He's sure one of our employees had a scam going with the player he kicked out and is lying low for a while. He predicts that one of the pits will start showing short again one of these days.''

"Just what has all this got to do with me?'' Flint asked uneasily.

Burney was slow in answering. When he did, his

voice was full of apology. "I hate to ask you to do this, Flint. I know you're not going to like it, but Mansfield says it's the only way."

Flint eyed his brother-in-law with open rancor. "I can see where this is leading, Aaron, and I don't like it," he said coldly. "The answer is no."

"Now wait a minute, Flint. All I'm asking you to do is play blackjack on house money and keep an eye open for what's going on. As far as the dealers and the rest are concerned, you'll be just another gambler."

"I don't like it, Aaron," Flint repeated in a level voice. Then, in an effort to be reasonable, he asked, "How long were you thinking you'd want me to keep up this charade, supposing I agree?"

"Mansfield says greed will win over judgment. He says he'll be surprised if whoever it is isn't back in business with a new partner in a week or two."

"And if he isn't? If Les is mistaken and you've already got your man, you could have me playing blackjack at the Goldorado for the rest of my natural life," Flint pointed out, his ire rising again. "Just how long are you going to want me to hang around the casino pretending I'm Sam Spade?"

"I know, Flint, I know," Burney said with such distress in his voice Flint's resistance began to crumble. "If the whole idea goes against the grain with you, I wouldn't want you to do it, of course."

Flint, saying nothing, waited

After a long moment Aaron said 'Not if you really don't want to.

Still Flint said nothing. He waited for the other shoe.

"I wouldn't want you to do it,' his brother-in law repeated "Not even for as short a time as two weeks.'

Flint gave a snort of exasperated laughter. He knew when he was being had. Well, Aaron was asking for it!

"Thanks, old man. It's damned decent of you to see it my way," he said silkily, and enjoyed a moment of wicked satisfaction at seeing the wily Aaron suddenly rendered speechless

Luckily he'd finished all the other work, thought Flint. Now he could throw his stuff in the car and be back in San Francisco by evening Burney could get a pro to do his sleuthing. It was out of Flint's line.

He was about to say as much to his brother-in-law when he remembered he'd asked Lia Andrews to have dinner with him and knew he would have to postpone his departure until the following day. He resisted a thought that he might leave a message for her saying he'd been called back to the city. For one thing, he'd told her he'd give the money to her in person, so it might as well be over dinner. He couldn't very well walk up and hand it over to her at a casino blackjack table. An exchange like that could be misconstrued by the security people watching through their eye-in-the-sky.

But that, he was obliged to acknowledge uncomfortably, was only half the reason he didn't want to cancel the dinner. The rest was Lia Andrews herself, who would fade gradually into his past after he went back to the city. Was there anything wrong with wanting to see her one last time?

His brother-in-law was still eyeing him with disbelief, but Flint saw he was rallying his forces for another go at wearing him down. Flint rose quickly to his feet.

"I've got a few things to do before I leave for the city in the morning, so if you don't mind I'm going back to the Goldorado now. I'll talk to Les about the casino problems before I take off," he said. "Sorry I missed Roz and the children. Give them my love. Tell her I'll be around to say goodbye before I take off tomorrow."

"Hey, Flint! Don't go. Wait a minute," called out Burney, finding his voice. He hoisted himself heavily out of his chair, but it was too late. Tancer, in strategic departure, was on his way through the house and out the front door before the other could catch him.

CHAPTER SEVEN

OF ALL THE CASINO SHIFTS, the one she was currently assigned to was the one she liked the least,
thought Lia, suppressing a yawn. The first hour or
so more often than not was painfully slow. It was
against her nature to sit there doing nothing like a
wallflower at the prom waiting to be asked to
dance. She felt trapped, waiting for players to
come to her empty table.

This was the midmorning lull. Even the casino
seemed to yawn. The all-night players had drifted
away in the predawn hours to grab some sleep. The
name-tagged conventioneers who had swarmed the
gambling arena the afternoon before were now in
conference rooms on the mezzanine in order to
justify their presence on their income-tax returns.
The early-morning bus crowd had vanished into
the coffee shop and rest rooms or had dispersed
among the alleys of slot machines. The steady
flow of foot traffic along the passageways had
dwindled to no more than a trickle, and only a few
of the blackjack tables that were kept operating at
this hour had customers.

Lia's eyes roamed restlessly over the half-empty

gambling arena, past the craps tables, where a few die-hard gamblers hung out at all times of the day, past the now-idle roulette tables and the wheel of fortune. Not until they came to rest on the banking windows did she realize she'd been canvassing the place for a glimpse of Flint Tancer, who was nowhere to be seen.

He intended to gamble, he'd said, but he hadn't said when or where. Would he come to her table? she wondered with a flicker of anticipation. But then maybe blackjack wasn't his game. Maybe he preferred his gambling in another form—baccarat...roulette...six-card stud. For all she knew he was a craps shooter. There was something very physical in the way certain men rolled the dice, something sensual in the body language that went into the throw, in the witty coaxing talk a player used to woo the small spotted cubes as they left his hand. Yet when she tried to picture Flint at the craps tables she couldn't. Somehow craps didn't seem his style.

But was blackjack? What challenge would the facile mind of Flint Tancer find in a simple game like blackjack? The jargon of the game—split, stand-off, soft seventeen—and the mechanics were almost harder to learn than the game itself. For instance, when a player wanted another card from the dealer, instead of asking for it in the normal way, he brushed his cards lightly on the table. If he asked in words, he said he wanted to be "hit." It was this window dressing that lent a certain mystique to an otherwise simple game.

"Excuse me."

She broke off her idle musings to turn her attention upon the stout gray-haired woman wearing a maroon pantsuit and a determined face who had come to her table.

"I want to learn to play blackjack," the woman said. "My husband says 'stick to the slots. Blackjack's a man's game. Women don't have the minds for it,' he says." A sudden resentful note crept into the woman's voice.

"I'd be glad to help you prove your husband's mistaken. It's casino policy for the dealers to help beginners learn to play when we have an empty table. I'll teach you whatever I can," volunteered Lia.

With a shrug of acceptance the woman seated herself at one of the high chairs around the empty table. Lia shuffled the cards and began.

"The idea of the game is to aim for a series of cards that will add up to twenty-one, but no more. Anything over, you lose," she explained quickly. "Kings, queens and jacks count ten. All other cards count their face value except for aces, which can count eleven or one, whichever is to your advantage. The object is to reach a total closer to twenty-one than the dealer draws."

The woman interrupted, shifting restlessly in her seat. "I know all that stuff. I have a blackjack and I'm an instant winner if the first two cards you deal me face down total twenty-one. I'm a loser if I draw a card and it puts me over twenty-one. Isn't that right?"

Lia looked at her, puzzled. "You already know the game. There isn't much else to teach you. It's really that simple."

"I picked that much up watching my husband play, but there's a lot more to it than that."

Lia laughed. The woman was right, of course. You couldn't dismiss the game with a breezy over-simplification. It could be as simple or as complicated as the player wanted to make it.

"What I want to learn is all the other stuff," the woman went on stubbornly. "You know...how to keep track of the cards so you can improve your odds and bet high when you know the cards are right."

"Oh. Now we're talking about card counting. That's something else," Lia said in sudden enlightenment. As a dealer she'd learned to watch out for counters, those mathematical wizards who devised mind-boggling systems for remembering each card in the deck after it had been turned up, but she knew little about the various techniques for doing it. There was nothing simple about it. Some counters devoted as much time and effort working out formulas to beat the game as she had set herself for earning a master's degree. Those who perfected the art could tell at any point in a game what cards had been played, what cards were still to be dealt. By counting they bettered their own odds against the odds of the house, and, in theory at least, the number and amount of their winnings. It took skill, intelligence, persistence and a punishing concentration to count. A photographic memory didn't hurt.

Smiling, Lia shook her head to reply to the woman across the table. "I'm afraid you've come to the wrong place to learn about card counting," she said pleasantly. "It's complex, I understand. I don't know any dealer who could teach you, and in any case the casino would certainly disapprove. If you're really interested, there are a lot of 'how-to' books written by counters. You can find them in most any bookstore."

The woman slid out of the chair. "I might just do that," she said. "Thanks."

Lia felt obliged to venture a gratuitous word of caution.

"I wish you luck, but I think I should tell you that very few counters ever win dazzling sums at the game, and if they do, they have trouble forever after finding casinos where they can play."

"You mean it's illegal?"

"No. Counting's not against the law, but a casino has a right to bar a player from its tables, and most of them do, in the case of known counters."

The woman shrugged and moved away with a perfunctory nod of farewell, leaving Lia alone at her empty table. After a few idle moments, her rambling thoughts reeled back to her father, who had often been in her mind since the morning before in the emergency room.

Whether from seeing him in the person of the doctor or seeing herself with a new clarity after the mishap itself, she had discovered within her a nagging yet wistful desire to resolve her prickly relationship with her father. To resolve it completely was more than could be hoped for, she feared. She was too much of a realist to imagine there weren't matters on which the two of them were always bound to tangle. But it was becoming increasingly important to her to find some better way to deal with their differences than to square off at each other like two feisty terriers.

A sudden wave of homesickness for the contentious man who was her father swept over Lia. It occurred to her that since Tahoe was no more than a four-hour drive from San Francisco and her father was semiretired from the firm he owned, there was no good reason her parents shouldn't come up for a visit, if only for her mother's sake. Her mother would love it, and it would be a real challenge to get her father to admit, at visit's end, that he'd enjoyed it in spite of himself.

She decided to write her parents a note inviting them to spend a few days with her at her rented lakeside house. Maybe she'd call her mother, she thought with a measure of cunning, and tell her what she had in mind. If she talked to her alone before the letter arrived, her mother could try to soften her father's rigid attitude toward the casino and Lia's work there.

Further thought of a Camp David meeting between herself and her father was cut short by the arrival of a somewhat rumpled-looking gentleman who hoisted himself up on one of the tall chairs at her table. Muttering something about a long bus ride, he laid a twenty-dollar bill on the table for playing chips.

Down the stairs from the mezzanine the conventioneers had begun drifting into the casino, and in a matter of minutes the passageways were filled with milling people. As they came, they peeled off from the mainstream to stake claims on slot machines, preempt positions at the craps tables, and ease into the high empty chairs around the half-oval blackjack tables. The tempo of the gambling arena accelerated; the atmosphere sparked with an electric charge. Lia turned her full attention to the assortment of players who had stationed themselves around her table and began to deal.

BECAUSE OF THE ABSOLUTE concentration required by the job, casino dealers were on duty only forty minutes out of every hour and were replaced during the other twenty minutes by a rotating break dealer. Lia snatched a late-morning break to write her invitation to her father and mother. In the early afternoon she took advantage of another break to leave the gambling arena for the hotel lobby to give the letter to a desk clerk who would see that it went out with the rest of the mail.

As she walked through the archway away from the cacophony of the casino into the quieter environs beyond, the sight of the tall athletic figure of Flint Tancer standing before one of the windows at the desk brought her to an abrupt halt. Only quick footwork on the part of the woman walking directly in back of her averted a pileup of others coming from behind.

"Sorry," murmured Lia, her pulse pounding hard and fast. She hardly noticed the angry glares beamed her way as she hurried to step out of the stream of movement into the relative shelter of a tower of potted greenery at one side.

More than once that day she had caught herself scanning the casino for a sight of the man who had plunged so precipitately into her life the morning before, but at the moment she was totally unprepared to come upon him unexpectedly at the hotel desk where she was headed. He was receiving an assortment of mail from the clerk. Lia hesitated, half-tempted to step forward and let her presence be known, but she was held back by an unaccustomed shyness she was at a loss to understand.

In that moment of suspended movement she watched Tancer turn away and walk slowly across the lobby away from her, his eyes on the sheaf of envelopes he thumbed through as he went. He stepped into the maw of an open elevator, the doors closed, and before Lia had completely recovered her aplomb, he was gone.

Behind the screen of leaves she let out a deep breath of disgust. Now, what in the world was that all about? she asked herself derisively. Wasn't the time in her life for unexpected coyness long past? Feeling a bit foolish she peered around to see if her impetuous retreat had been observed, then stepped out into the passageway again and moved on in the direction of the reception counter with a fine show of nonchalance.

She was glad to see that the clerk at the mail desk was Clara, whom she'd had lunch with in the employees' dining room a few days before. Clara knew everything that went on under the acre of roof covering the Goldorado, and there were those who said she lived primarily to talk about what she knew.

Lia gave Clara the letter along with money for the necessary stamp and heard the latest bit of house gossip. Then, about to go, she turned back, her voice carefully tailored to convince the other woman that the question she was about to ask was no more than an afterthought.

"Oh, by the way . . . that man who picked up his mail just now. . . ."

The clerk lifted a naughty eyebrow. "You too? How 'bout that!" she said. "Now there's a man! I'd let him snap my garter any old time he liked. Actually, he's not what you'd really call handsome, but then who cares about *handsome* with a man like that? His name's Flint Tancer."

"I know, but where's he from? What does he do?" asked Lia, forgetting her disinterested role.

Clara riffled through the registration file before her and pulled out Flint Tancer's card. "He's from Burlingame, it says here. That's down on the peninsula from San Francisco."

"I know. I know," Lia said impatiently.

"Investments," continued Clara.

"Investments?"

"Investments. Self-employed. That's all it says." Clara held out the card for Lia to see. "Except for this. Look. He's staying in one of the luxury penthouse suites. See that gold star in the corner? You know what that means?"

Lia shook her head.

"It means he's a guest of the house."

"Are you saying he's a high roller?" asked Lia in disbelief.

"What else? The Goldorado wouldn't be keeping him up there in that penthouse suite at their expense if he didn't have a track record. They know he bets big and can be counted on to come out a heavy loser—maybe not this time, but the next time he comes or the next. He'll eventually pay for every time he's stayed in that penthouse—with interest. Plus a good fat profit for the house."

"So the sucker pays for his own bait," Lia commented cynically.

"The casinos all do it. Besides, nobody's getting baited," said Clara. "It isn't as if the big-timers like Tancer don't know what's going on. It's a kind of side bet for them. They know the casinos expect them to lose a lot more than the price of a suite, but the gamblers are betting they won't. The casinos know the high rollers are going to gamble *somewhere*. They give them the freebies to help guarantee where they'll gamble."

LIA RETURNED TO HER TABLE and took up her job again, blind to the action around her. An inner listlessness replaced the first wave of sick disappointment that had washed over her with the desk clerk's words.

She accepted the fact she had no right to blame Flint Tancer for what he was. It wasn't as if he had deceived her. In all fairness the one thing—the only thing, in fact—he'd told her about himself except for his name was that he gambled.

He'd told her, but she wouldn't listen. She'd seen the strength, the warmth, the intelligence, the self-effacing humor in the wonderfully not-quite-handsome face, and something within her had refused to listen. Flint Tancer was so utterly unlike Toby. Her mind had only half heard the words with which he told her that he shared Toby's unacceptable flaw. Half heard, and less than half accepted. So what if he did intend to gamble while he was at the Goldorado? That hardly made him a hard-core gambler, she'd told herself.

With the unarguable evidence from Clara that he was a high roller, Lia was forced to accept the unwelcome correlation: Flint Tancer was, in fact, a hard-core gambler, one of those who spent a considerable share of his life in pursuit of Lady Luck.

While a part of her composed the note saying she would not have dinner with him that night, or any other night, a note she planned to leave at the hotel desk at the end of the day, another part of her obstinately refused to go along with the ultimatum.

How could she deny the special flavor of his company when the thought of seeing him again sent a small glow of anticipation skittering through her? How could she deny that when she looked back on those two unique encounters with Flint—the wildly slapstick rescue he'd pulled off the morning before and their electric parting at her front door last night—she found a certain sense of adventure, a hint of mysterious, unplumbed depths in the man, unexpected ingredients that somehow added new exhilarating dimensions to her life?

Wasn't the fact he was a hard-core gambler irrelevant, after all? He was the same Flint Tancer she'd thought wonderfully engaging until she'd listened to Clara. Except now when she thought of him it was with the dull sense of loss that comes when something of value has been damaged beyond repair. For a moment she felt a stir of resentment toward Clara. Reminding herself that Clara was only the messenger, she was ashamed.

What are you afraid of, Lia Andrews? that dissenting part of her jeered. After all, he'd asked her only to spend a few hours with him, not the rest of their lives. By the following week he'd be gone. High rollers never hung around for long.

And still the inner voice taunted: *You're afraid. Afraid if you see him again it will only make it harder when it comes time for him to leave for good.*

As the afternoon progressed she performed her chores with the precision of an automaton, eyes following the cards as they fell, mind sizing up the players, hands moving swiftly, efficiently, to take in the money, give out chips, shuffle, deal, rake in the spoils, undeterred by the continuing debate that went on within.

Are you going to believe a gossip like Clara? Clara's been known to be wrong.

Not this time. It's right there on the registration card.

The card didn't say he's a hard-core gambler.

A guest of the house in a penthouse suite. It's all the same.

So the silent argument raged. Only once, when a pair of well-built shoulders passed by the corner of one eye, causing a quick intake of her breath, did her attention falter from the job of dealing the cards. Her eyes strayed for no more than an instant before they swung back, but it was just long enough. The stout, red-faced, slightly inebriated loser in the far right seat at the table brushed his cards impatiently on the baize, the signal for her to deal him another card.

In her moment of distraction the man's movement was seen but scarcely noted by Lia. Almost at once she reined in her wandering attention to find herself in the spotlight of the irate player's glare.

"How long do you have to wait for a card at this table?" he demanded. "Hit me! Hit me, I said."

Lia swallowed a retort that rose to her lips and gave the player another card facedown. He stared at it sullenly for a moment before slipping it under the other two facedown cards he toyed with on the table.

"Gimme another," he said harshly, and before Lia could comply demanded, "Hit me. I said hit me again."

If only I could, mister, Lia thought. Aloud she murmured meekly, "Sorry." When she dealt the fourth card she had her own moment of satisfaction. The player sputtered an expletive and slammed his cards down on the table to expose a count of twenty-four. Lia raked in the losing chips on the betting line.

But her anger was less at the irascible player than at her own undisciplined self for having let her attention wander. Resolutely she closed her mind against intrusive thoughts and gave her undivided attention to the deal

AT HOME AT THE DAY'S END. Lia towel dried her hair after a steaming shower. A short time later she stepped into her favorite dress, its silken perfection pleasing her hands as she eased it gently up over the swell of her thighs and breasts and slipped her arms into the short sleeves.

The dress was the color of the lake and her eyes and clung to her like a caress. Below her knees it ended in a swirl of motion. It was sophisticated and at the same time deceptively simple. Lia

CHAPTER EIGHT

HIDDEN IN EVERY MAN, Flint strongly suspected, was a covert belief that somewhere a mythical right woman was waiting for him, and Flint was no exception. Whether a girl like the girl who married dear old dad or a *Playboy* centerfold was a matter of individual taste.

By the time he reached the front door of Aaron Burney's home on his way out that afternoon he knew exactly why he had no intention of breaking his dinner date with Lia Andrews. She was not like any other woman he'd met. He saw intimations of that very rightness in her. It was as simple as that.

Since he had left her the night before, after pulling her out of the green chair and into his arms, he'd been in a kind of limbo. Now the odd uncertainty that had plagued him since he'd left her was gone.

He'd seen in her eyes that she had wanted him to stay, but taking him at his word, she'd made no effort to hold him there. When he saw she was not going to, he had a moment of surprise, then frustration, then impatience because he'd blown it. It was that moment, in sudden recollection, that had thought of it as an honest dress. Somehow it made a statement about her that she knew instinctively was true.

She did not keep Flint waiting when he arrived on her doorstep at the appointed time. She let him ring only once before she answered the bell and stood in the open doorway, a smile of greeting on her face. For the moment she felt at peace with herself.

By an act of sheer stubborn will she had managed to cram the ugly doubts that had tormented during the afternoon into a holding cell of her mind. While never entirely free of their presence she made herself pretend for tonight they didn't exist. She knew they would eventually come out—as soon as tomorrow, maybe, but not tonight.

Tonight the gambler Flint Tancer was nothing more than a figment of Clara's imagination.

Tonight belonged to Lia. To Lia and Flint, the man.

decided him. He had a driving need to find out what had gone into Lia Andrews to make her seem so right to him. It was this that set her apart, the thing he'd looked for but never found in any woman.

The improbable Anitra had introduced him to the mysterious affinity of man and woman before he was old enough to consider the nature of the other gender or give thought to what kind of a woman he might wish to spend the rest of his life with. When a "right woman" later took form in his mind the model was neither Anitra nor his mother, though there was a little of his mother in her and a little of Anitra, too.

After Anitra, his experience had not been barren of women or of love affairs. There was a pretty vivacious sorority queen he'd been more than a little in love with for a time, and again, when he was twenty-nine, an account executive who was bright and beautiful. There had been others, but not even in the most fatuous moments of these infatuations had he ever imagined a continuing relationship with any of them.

In recent months these failures had begun to disturb him. As he approached thirty-five he'd begun to look on the aging bachelor as an unfinished man. A possibility plagued him from time to time that in order to complete his life, and in the absence of one who was *right*, he might be obliged to content himself with someone out of the crowd.

A sudden insatiable hunger to know all there

was to know about Lia Andrews—not just what could be learned in two hours across a restaurant table at dinner—possessed him. He couldn't simply walk out and let it gnaw at him and bury itself in his subconscious to pop out and plague him at unlikely times.

Somewhere between the Burney front door and his car Flint decided not to go back to the city the next day as he'd told his brother-in-law he intended to do. He would stay on awhile and look into the casino problems. It would make Aaron happy and give him a plausible reason for not going back.

She was not a simple woman, this Lia. It could take time. It might take a month…or a year. Or the rest of his life.

BACK AT THE GOLDORADO he took the elevator to the second floor, the location of the hotel-casino's business offices, where he'd held forth while looking into the affairs of the hotel and its peripheral operations for Burney. Since there was a strong possibility he was about to deal himself back in the game, it occurred to him this might be a good time to get a clearer picture of what was going on at the casino.

The manager's secretary greeted him cordially. "Mr. Mansfield's out, Mr. Tancer," she said. "He'll be back shortly, if you'd like to wait."

"I'll wait," said Flint. Meanwhile, he might as well start checking the background of some of the casino employees, he thought. "Mind if I take a look at the personnel files?"

The first folder contained the record of a change girl, Dorothy Abbott; then Mike Afton, busboy; Kenneth Akers, dealer; Cheryl Albright, waitress. Then a pit boss, Ames; then Lia Andrews.

Lia Andrews! There, between Ames and Asher, right where it belonged. The name jumped out from the file folder at Flint as if in letters three feet high. He stared at it numbly for a moment, holding it in his hand, wondering why he hadn't realized that it would be there.

He slapped the folder back into the file drawer as if it stung his hands. He wanted to know everything about Lia, but damned if he'd do his learning as spy for his brother-in-law.

His hand moved on to take out the Asher file, but his mind stayed with the other. He looked back at it uncertainly, filled with an overwhelming desire to read what the file contained. Perhaps he was being overscrupulous. In her case his motive was not to entrap. All he wanted from the file were simple facts he might have heard from her own lips had the circumstances of their meeting been less bizarre.

In such spirit he went back to Lia's file. Not to ferret out something negative but looking, with an almost boyish eagerness, for something substantive to reinforce what instinctively he imagined he saw in her.

Californian. Parent's home address, Piedmont.
Flint was well acquainted with the old, affluent,
upper-middle-class hillside community on the east
side of San Francisco Bay. Father, an executive in
a successful accounting firm Flint had dealt with
and respected. So went the facts, telling him nothing that really mattered to him one way or another
about Lia. He moved on hurriedly.

*Two years at Stanford University, another
traveling in western Europe, two as a flight attendant for an international airline, then back to
Stanford for a bachelor's degree in psychology.*
Nothing to warm Flint's heart. He imagined he
saw a pattern of restlessness emerging that troubled him vaguely.

*Employed as consultant in family counseling
service. Quit four months ago to take job as dealer
at Goldorado.* Feeling somehow let down, Flint
put the résumé aside and picked up her personnel
form, skimming through essentially the same
material, filled in on dotted lines. It wasn't until
his eyes reached the question: *Why did you leave
your last employment?* that the bomb fell.

"A casino offers a working environment filled
with color and excitement, in contrast to the pas-
sive nature of the counseling field in which I am
currently employed," Flint read. "It also pays
better. A dealer at the Goldorado makes considerably more money than a psychology consultant who has no more than a bachelor's degree."

Excitement and money. In the final analysis

that's what Anitra had wanted, wasn't it? And Buffy, the sprightly coed. And Erica, the elegant career woman, come to think of it. These were the three he'd known well enough to find out for sure what they wanted from life. Maybe that's what most women wanted. Maybe it had something to do with their struggle to break out of the servile role male tradition had pushed them into. It was hardly a fair shake. You couldn't blame them for rebelling.

Still, excitement and money! A shallow pair of goals for a woman of twenty-eight. Flint let out a deep sigh of regret. The right woman had just left.

He put the folder carefully back in its place between Ames and Asher and closed the file drawer. Walking into the office he had used during his stay, he spent some time getting books and papers in order, separating what was to go into Goldorado company archives from what he would take with him when he went back to the city the following morning. Mansfield had not returned by the time he was through. He left word with the secretary that he would talk to the manager before he left, as he'd promised Aaron he would do.

He took the elevator up to the penthouse suite and spent the next half hour packing. There was nothing to stop him now from going back to the city. He wished he had gone that afternoon as he'd first intended.

If he'd gone then, he would have carried away with him nothing more disturbing than the illusion that if he'd stayed and given himself a chance to know Lia Andrews, she might have turned out to be that elusive perfect woman for him, the one he had tucked away in his mind.

An illusion wasn't something to keep a man warm on a cold night, but it was better than learning how wrong about her he'd been, the damning evidence tatted out by her own hand on the same daisy-wheel electric typewriter he'd seen yesterday morning on her living-room desk. It was better than knowing that this woman he was beginning to regard as special was no different in a matter of considerable importance than other women he'd known in his life. It was better than the return of the nagging concern that there might never be a woman who was right for him.

All the way over to the Sapphire Point house that evening Flint thought of turning back to the ridiculous penthouse suite Aaron had put him up in at the Goldorado and calling to say he couldn't make it for dinner. He had to leave for the city on business at once, he could tell her. Something like that. He'd leave her slot-machine winnings with Mansfield at his office. She could pick up the money in the morning when he was gone.

Why the hell hadn't he left today after he told Aaron he wouldn't play sleuth, instead of sticking around and doing on his own what he'd declined to do for good old Aaron? If he'd gone, at least it would have saved him from snooping through the casino's personnel files and finding out more than he wanted to know about Lia.

Excitement and money. The words were etched in his brain. But more deeply etched was the memory of her piquant face, her questing eyes, the warm curved column of her body that fit, as if they were two parts of a puzzle, so perfectly in his arms.

It was a fit that even now drew him back to claim what her eyes had told him was waiting for him to take last night. And after he had taken it?

He was in front of the house, easing the car next to the curb. There was still time to drive off, and he considered it, but only for a moment. He reached over instead and lifted the bottle of champagne cushioned on the soft leather seat beside him, taking care not to stir up the bubbles.

He'd bought the bottle after he left the casino that morning in anticipation of making dinner with Lia a kind of celebration—of what, he couldn't exactly say. At the time he bought it, it had seemed important to bring something worthy of her, the best the wine cellar had in stock. He eyed the bottle of Dom Pérignon sourly. For what he now had in mind it didn't take the most expensive champagne in the house.

On the slate landing before the door he stopped a moment, not yet ready to lift his hand to the knocker. In fairness he knew he had no right to feel resentful toward the young woman waiting inside. It could hardly be considered her fault he'd wanted her to be someone she wasn't. And since she wasn't, the sporting thing tonight was to give the person she'd turned out to be a farewell evening to her liking.

For starters there was the Dom Pérignon. She could taste money straight from the glass, he told himself cynically. As for excitement—well, he'd made reservations at Reno's most glittering casino for a dinner show that he hadn't seen but was said to be a combination of the Ziegfeld Follies and the Parisian Folies-Berg6ere.

He straightened his shoulders and reached for the door knocker. Before he could rattle it a second time the door opened quietly, and she was there before him as straight and slender as a taper, her dress the rich violet blue of wild larkspur, no bluer than her oval eyes.

He was not ready for this quick unexpected appearance, nor for the almost physical impact he felt when the door swung back. Reeling inwardly, he stood quite motionless for a moment, unable to break free from the incandescent enchantment of her smile. Previously he'd seen a gamine quality in her, which for all its charm hadn't prepared him for the self-contained, sensuous, utterly captivating woman who stood before him in the doorway.

What was she trying to do to him? The dress was overt seduction, he thought with a new surge of resentment, but an innate balancing factor within him that forever monitored his judgments told him that the dress could hardly be called immodest by any standard. It offered no frills, no enticements, no flaunting décolletage. Nothing but an honest length of fluid fabric cut to follow faithfully the planes and curves of a body as perfect as any he'd ever seen. The seduction was implicit in the body, not the dress.

But the danger was not in the body. The danger was in the eyes; those slightly uptilted eyes that tonight lent a certain exotic aura to her face. Eyes that reflected the spirit—direct, humorous, independent, wise. Unlike the dangers of the other, which, thanks to Anitra, had never held any fears for him, this danger had nothing to do with sex. Nothing and everything to do with it, he amended with a soundless groan. The body and the mind— so intertwined who was to say which was which and which played what part in love?

Flint Tancer, who had once been awarded a commendation for bravery after single-handedly rescuing an aging woman from four full-grown juvenile hoods armed with bicycle chains, was suddenly afraid.

She spoke to him—said something that simply didn't register. A greeting of some sort, he supposed, yet still he stood on the flagstone landing outside her door, stupefied for a moment by a swell of warring emotions within. Not one to suffer his own fumbling gladly, Flint reacted with a helpless, almost petulant anger at Lia for being the unwitting cause of his discomfiture, but even more at himself for the fact he was there.

"Aren't you going to invite me in?" he asked querulously.

Lia's eyebrows raised in surprise. There was a touch of the gamine in the grin she gave him.

"I hadn't really planned to," she said warily.

Flint now had himself in hand. "I'm sorry. I guess that sounded a little abrupt," he apologized with some grace. He held out the bottle of chilled champagne for her to see. "What I meant to suggest was a glass of this before we move on, but if you'd rather—"

Lia didn't let him finish. "Champagne! How did you guess it's my favorite indulgence, and the one most seldom indulged?"

"Good. We'll stay. It always seems a waste this time of day to miss the best show in town."

"Show?"

"The show that people who hide away in windowless casinos and restaurants never see. The one the sun puts on over Mount Tallac to the west the last hour before dusk."

She hesitated, studying him with her eyes, as if debating whether to take exception to the slightly snide tone that had crept into his voice. Then she said, "Well, won't you come in?"

She stepped back to lead the way into the house. "There's smoke drifting up from the valley on the other side, so there should be magnificent reds and oranges. We can have our wine on the deck. I usually watch the sunsets from there while I have dinner when I don't have to work."

Flint detoured to the kitchen and began to pull away the foil on the bottle.

"Mmm," crooned Lia, wrinkling her nose with pleasure. "I love it. And Dom Pérignon! My, we *are* elegant! I should tell you, though, you shouldn't waste pure gold bubbles like this on someone who can be made happy with a bottle of any cheap wedding champagne. I have the palate of a peasant.''

Flint released the cork with a deft hand. "You have any of that brandy I brought last night?" he asked.

"I should hope so! In case you've forgotten, you left almost a full bottle." She brought out the brandy from behind a door over the wet bar and handed it to Flint, who poured a generous splash of the amber liquor into the bottom of one of the tulip-shaped crystal glasses she'd given him for the champagne.

"Hey, what are you doing?" she cried out in alarm.

"Ever hear of a French Seventy-five?" asked Flint, looking up as he was about to give the second glass the the same treatment.

"You expect me to say no, don't you?" she accused, flashing him a smug grin. "Well, as a matter of fact I have. Two ancient gentlemen on their way to a convention of World War I veterans told me how to mix French Seventy-fives for them when I was a flight attendant. Said it was named after a big French gun and bragged it was every bit as lethal.''

"I'll bet the old boys weren't drinking them for their lethal qualities," Flint said, his mouth slanting in a sardonic smile. "The soldiers in the First

World War considered the drink an aphrodisiac, I've heard.'' He moved the bottle to pour brandy into the second glass.

"The same is said of eggs and oysters,'' Lia said with a sniff. "I find it hard to believe you would need any of them, Mr. Tancer.''

The larkspur eyes gazed at him innocently. Silken lashes lowered and hid the eyes for a moment. When they looked into his again they were as bland and sweet as the smile on her face.

"In any case, would you mind doing your experimenting on wedding champagne?'' she asked, the tone of her voice belying her words. "No one but an insensitive clod would adulterate Dom Pérignon with brandy anyhow. Pour mine back in the bottle. Champagne's enough for me.''

Flint arrested the champagne bottle over the second glass as he was about to pour. He shrugged and with a lazy movement dumped the brandy from the glass down the sink.

She was right, of course. The last thing he needed in the presence of the lovely Lia was an egg or an oyster or a French Seventy-five.

AFTER A LINGERING good-night kiss to Tallac's bald pate, the sun exited flamboyantly, leaving the champagne drinkers in the amethyst shades of early evening. They had positioned themselves at opposite ends of a cushioned porch swing on the deck.

Flint had a chip on his shoulder the size of an

admiral's shoulder boards, thought Lia in dismay. Between them she sensed a kind of electric current, which, though not exactly negative, was certainly not the positive charge that had sparked the air around them the night before.

Considering her discovery that the man was a confirmed gambler, there was reason enough for her own feeling of constraint, but for the life of her she couldn't imagine why Flint was acting so strange. Could it be a reflection of the change he sensed in her? she wondered. If so, he chose an odd way of showing it. He acted almost as if he had learned something unsavory about her instead of the reverse.

Long before the sun went down in a last blaze of glory she began to wonder what they would talk about while they finished their drinks. The beauty of the lake, the merits of the champagne, the sunset; when these subjects were exhausted the silence closed in around them. Neither made any effort to break it, though as silences go it could hardly be deemed companionable.

To her surprise, Lia did not find herself chafing under its strain. The situation struck her as rather absurd, and she realized uneasily that she was dangerously close to giggling—she, who was not a giggler either by temptation or by inclination. At the same time she became aware of a fuzzy edge to her thinking and knew that the divine Dom Pérignon had cushioned her sensibilities against the discomforts of the evening's realities. With this revelation the wine suddenly went flat for her. She'd be darned if she'd let it become an escape from an evening that was rapidly turning into a disaster.

Champagne's enough for me! Hadn't she said that to Flint just before she proceeded to drink half a bottle of the lovely stuff? She should have known her stopping point and quit. Even with champagne there were limits.

Toying with the crystal stem of her nearly empty glass, she studied the closed face of Flint Tancer through her winey haze and wondered how things could have gone so awry in the short time between morning and night. She regretted the instant intimacy that had somehow sprung up between them after the craziness in the lake, lulling her into a false notion that she knew him, when in fact she hardly knew him at all.

There was something flip and brittle in the man beside her, and this was as surprising to her as her discovery that he was a hard-core gambler. The man who had gathered her into his arms the night before and embraced her this morning with his eyes had vanished as if he had never been. Except for an occasional flash of wry humor, even the gray-green eyes held little of this morning's warmth. They were cool and impersonal and in the fading light the color of gunmetal. They told her nothing. Nothing at all.

She had seen that closed untelling look someplace before, but she couldn't remember where. Then, watching him, suddenly she knew. It was the expression worn by six-card stud players in the poker arena at the casino. The shock of recognition cleared away all vestige of fuzziness from her mind leaving a smoldering, clear-eyed wariness in its place.

What a hypocrite the man was, sitting there like a poker player chesting his cards when she'd openly shown him her hand! He'd been the last person she would have suspected of turning on charm to disarm a woman and then turning it off when it was evident she'd been taken in by it He'd done such a good job of convincing her he was true-blue she hadn't even felt the need to hide the fact she found herself irresistibly drawn to him

Thanks a lot, Flint Tancer, for wearing your poker face tonight, she thought acidly. Thanks fo. putting her on notice that any openness between them was over. It was a game she too could play.

Interrupting her dour thoughts, Flint raised his tulip glass in salute. His mouth slanted in a suggestion of a smile—whether self-mocking or simply mocking, Lia could not be sure. She lifted her own glass in return

"Cheers, he said, but there was little cheer in his voice. Lia did not respond

They drained their glasses. Flint took Lia's and put it with his on a low table near the porch swing at his side. Then, unexpectedly, he closed the distance between them until he sat so near she could feel the warmth of his body through their light summer clothing The soft wool of his blazer brushed lightly against her bare arm as he settled beside her.

"So, Lady of the Lake," he said, "let's see what excitement I can pleasure you with tonight." Though his voice was ingratiating she sensed a certain note of reproach in the words, and this unnerved her a bit. His face was half-hidden in the shadows of gathering dusk, but she knew it would tell her nothing even if she could have seen it.

"Excitement?" she repeated, stalling for time.

He lifted a hand and let two fingers trace a soft pattern across a cheekbone to the hairline, where they stopped to play with one of the short curls framing her ear. It was an exquisite distraction Lia was in no mood to permit. She shook her head lightly and brushed at his hand with hers, only to have her hands captured and held fast.

"I understand there's a spectacular new show at one of the casinos in Reno. Cast of thousands, million-dollar costumes and sets," he said. "We can take a ride over the hill and have dinner there. Maybe you'd like to play a little baccarat or roulette after the show, or the slots, if that's what you like." The words were spoken absently, as if they had nothing to do with some other more important occupation of his mind. His voice was quiet, but there was something almost libidinal in it that made her acutely aware of her own sexuality and of his. He raised her hands and filled her palms with kisses.

The change in his manner, even more baffling

to Lia than the covertness of a moment before, did nothing to restore her confidence in him, yet no amount of mistrust could quell her body's wildly sensual responses to his blandishments.

"No. Not Reno, please. I don't even know how to play baccarat or roulette," she said unsteadily, moving deeper into her corner of the swing, determined not to let any hint of capitulation be telegraphed to Flint. "Not any casino, if it's all the same to you."

"Whatever you say, but if Reno's not your idea of excitement, would you mind telling me just what you think is?"

Belatedly, Lia's ear caught the recurring theme.

"I had no idea excitement per se was such a thing with you!" she said, forgetting herself for an instant in her surprise.

"I want you to enjoy yourself," he said.

"Then you can forget about Reno and casinos. After all the time I spend in casinos. . ." She left the sentence in midair.

Then she was in Flint's arms. Gently he nuzzled her neck, moving up the slope of her chin to taste the lobe of an ear.

"Stop it, Flint," she whispered tensely, fighting against the yearning to give in to the man as much as against the man himself. "Flint, I said st. . . ." But his mouth covered hers and her words were smothered. She struggled to break free.

Then, in spite of herself, her own mouth softened and clung. For an instant she felt the same as she had in the water the morning before, struggling against his grip; she was experiencing that same sense of helplessness. As if giving in to the inevitable, she let her mouth feast hungrily with his.

There was a quickening deep within her as his hand slipped under the curve of one of her breasts. The arc formed by his thumb and forefinger lifted the breast in a gentle upward movement, caressing the small erection that rose in response out of the firm mound and strained against the silk of her dress.

In the next moment she was lost to everything but the gentle yet ever-insistent, ever-more-daring insinuation of his body upon hers. She was lost to everything but his erotic plundering and the urgent answering throb in a deep chamber within herself. She knew nothing of time or reality. Whatever had sent her into the corner of the porch swing was forgotten, and she left the corner for the pleasures of his arms.

At first she hardly noticed that the swing had not been designed for a love couch, its seat too narrow for two lovers in reclining embrace. Then, as she lay pressed against Flint's body, his mouth drinking deeply of hers, some small part of her mind worried that their locked bodies teetered precariously on the swing's edge. Yet still they clung there, until at last his lips pulled with seeming reluctance away from hers.

"Oh woman, woman, what you do to me! If

you only knew...." His words were almost a moan. Then unexpectedly he disentangled himself and rose to his feet, pulling her up as he went.

"Come. Let's go in," he said quietly, urgently, the honey of unsated passion in his voice. She blinked at him, catapulted into reality.

He had broken the spell. For a time there—had it been no more than a minute...as much as an hour?—her own sensuous nature had betrayed her. Her lips even now were moist and engorged from his kisses, her body ripe with desire. Only a moment before she could have given herself to the man, and a moment before that, he was someone she didn't know.

Her mind reeled. Did she know Lia Andrews any better than she knew Flint Tancer? she wondered in a wave of panic. For the first time in her life she seriously considered that her father was right in believing she wasn't to be trusted to manage her own life. Then, like a camera coming in focus, her senses cleared, her pulse slackened. She was herself again.

Remembering his abrupt withdrawal the night before, she wondered irritably if cutting his romantic overtures short was a part of Flint's regular routine.

Struggling to leave his arms she said, "You're right. It's getting cool, and we should be thinking of dinner."

Flint laughed softly. He pulled her more closely to him. The flats of his hands moved slowly, sensually down the length of her back to curve around her hips and press her hard against him, letting his body make known to her the full extent of his desire.

"Lia. Oh, Lia. You are driving me wild. About the last thing I have on my mind at this moment is dinner. You must know that," he said hoarsely, his lips close to her ear.

Lia's body went still. She was barely aware of Flint's lips playing at her earlobe. She listened to an inner voice that intruded upon her consciousness, and her throat filled with the dull constricting ache of disenchantment.

She said levelly, "Would you mind telling me what you *do* have in mind?"

"I want to make love, Lia, and so do you," Flint murmured into her ear, his voice heavy with desire. "I want to go someplace away from this damned skimpy swing and make love. Oh God, how I want to make love just once to your beautiful body before we say goodbye."

"Goodbye?" she repeated dully. "You're leaving?"

There was a drawn-out moment of silence. The shrill of a night bird pierced the darkness.

"In the morning," he said at last.

"So that's what you came for, Flint?" Her voice was a shard of ice. She wrenched herself free from his arms and stood glaring into the darkness at his shadowy form. She sensed rather than felt his hand reaching out for her and shoved it away.

"That's all you came for, isn't it?" she said softly. "Last night I mattered. Tonight you don't give a damn. That pretty euphemism that has nothing to do with love is what you came for."

"Lia...."

"If what you're looking for is a quick tumble in bed, you've come to the wrong house," she said tonelessly. As indignation turned to outrage, her voice rose. "I won't be treated as if I'm something I'm not! Ever since I opened the door tonight I've had this strange feeling you resent me, and the joke of it is I haven't the ghost of an idea what I've done to cause it."

"Lia...."

"Well, let's get one thing straight, Flint. No matter what ugliness you've got festering in your mind, I'm the same woman you treated with decency and respect last night. The difference is all in you."

She heard a sound out of the darkness, a soft wordless murmur of protest, and felt his hand on her arm.

"Don't touch me. I don't even know you," she said evenly. "I don't know what became of the decent, funny, open man I was beginning to think I might almost care about. But I can tell you this, Flint Tancer—" her voice broke, but she went on "—he's not you!"

She turned blindly toward the darkness of the house and slammed through the door, bumping hard into a chair a dozen steps in. A few paces behind her Flint fumbled for and found a switch. They stood where they were for a moment, blinking in the sudden flood of light. Lia didn't wait for her eyes to adjust, but moved quickly on. She wanted to escape before he could see her face wet with tears. She'd gone only a few steps when Flint's hand caught her arm and turned her around to face him.

"Wait, Lia," he said, and though she tipped her head forward to hide her face he grasped her chin. Against her resistance, he tilted it up until he looked directly into her tear-drenched eyes. The tears crested and spilled down her cheeks.

"Lia, we've got to talk," he pleaded urgently.

She twisted herself away. "Not really. You're a stranger to me. I don't know you, and at this point I think I'd rather not. It's just not worth the effort," she said in a tone of defeat, the flame of her anger spent.

"I hope you don't mean that," Flint said quietly.

Lia steeled herself against the sadness she heard in his voice.

"Oh, but I do," she said. "I'm not the good-times girl you're looking for. If we keep on like tonight, you'll drown me this time for sure."

"Lia...please, Lia."

"Go," said Lia wearily. "Just go!"

CHAPTER NINE

SHE SHUT THE DOOR behind him and leaned against the doorframe, the sound of his retreating feet on the slate landing outside pounding like drumbeats in her ears. She pressed her head to the cool surface of the door and closed her eyes. She couldn't remember a time since the first grade when she'd pulled another little girl's hair in some long-forgotten quarrel that she had been so out of touch with her own actions or so disturbed with herself. She heard the car door open and close, the rasp of the starter, the motor purring to life.

When the car had pulled away in a rattle of tossed-up gravel, Lia straightened and opened her eyes. Her cheeks felt tight from the salt of the tears that had bathed them, and her nose could use a tissue, she realized with a sniff.

When she'd taken care of the offending nose in the bathroom and splashed water on her face, she peeled out of the blue dress and hung it back in her bedroom closet. She kicked off the slim-heeled gray kid sandals and poked in the closet for a T-shirt dress to put on, reached for it, then put it back.

In a sudden violence of motion she flung open a bottom drawer and pulled from it a bedraggled gray sweat shirt and running pants, tugging the one on over her head, the other up over legs and hips, and tying the drawstring at her waist. From the back of the closet she retrieved an old pair of tennis shoes and slipped them on. As she headed back to the other part of the house she caught a glimpse of herself in her mirror. The sorry sight brought a reluctant grin to her face.

If Flint Tancer could see you now! she said grimly to the image. The psychologist in her wondered how much her choice of the baggy sexless garments, by no means her usual leisure wear at home, was a defiant message in absentia to the man she had verbally thrown out of her life a few minutes earlier.

In the living room she shuffled through her eclectic collection of records, which ran the gamut from Beethoven to Scott Joplin, looking for cheerful relaxing sounds to drive out the sweet seduction of Flint Tancer's voice as it insinuated itself persistently upon her mind.

How I want to make love to you . . . he'd said.

She put one of her favorite mood lighteners, a late recording of "Take Five" by the Dave Brubeck jazz quartet, on the stereo. The easy fluid beauty of piano and saxophone were no match for the pervasive memory of Flint's caressing voice.

Paralleling the repetitive flow of the record, his words whispered over and over again through her mind: *make love...make love...make love to that beautiful body just once before we say goodbye.*

Once before we say goodbye! Those were the key words, the stunning indictment off Flint's own tongue. What a fool she'd been, worrying that she might be heading for a serious commitment to yet another confirmed gambler when all he'd had in mind was a one-night stand!

She brought the empty champagne glasses in from the deck and set the kitchen's small disarray in order. The Dom Pérignon, which had given her its own effervescence a short time before, had turned to flannel in her mouth. Behind her temples there was a dull suggestion of pain, a queasiness in her stomach, a loneliness in her heart.

With dinner no longer in the offing and no appetite for it if it was, she made an indifferent survey of the refrigerator and brought out a carton of milk. Pouring a glass, she carried it into the living room, where she shed her shoes and curled up in one of the green corduroy chairs. There she tried to give her attention to her thesis notes, then to the afternoon paper from the city, and finally to a new paperback suspense thriller she'd picked up at the casino newsstand a few days earlier for in-bed reading. When she found herself starting the same paragraph for the third time, she let the book tumble to the floor.

It wasn't as if Flint Tancer was the first man

who'd ever tried to make love to her or that she hadn't thrilled to his ardor with a passion she hadn't guessed was there.

Up to this point she had done her utmost to circumvent the painful truth she had closeted away like a family skeleton, refusing to acknowledge it was there. Now, in the cold light of returned sobriety, Lia at last admitted she'd put on a very bad show.

Not surprisingly, the psychologist in her came to the fore again. *Let's talk about it, Lia,* said the psychologist. *Let's find out what the histrionics were all about.*

Why, for instance, had she torn herself from Flint's arms and stomped off like an outraged virgin when he put his intention openly in words? probed the cool, analytical voice within. Couldn't it almost be said the intention was shared by her?

No! Lia protested. *Not the intention!* But the voice bore down. Not the intention, but what about the desire?

And what made her think, persisted the voice, that Flint had come tonight deliberately bent on seduction, knowing full well he was going away, not intending to see her again? That was the callousness she'd accused him of, but had she actually believed it herself?

Even at the moment she'd flung the words in his face, hadn't some small part of her known that what she said wasn't true? Hadn't she really understood from the moment of his arrival that he had come armed with a firm resolution *not* to let himself be beguiled? Hadn't she seen it in the closed face that told her he was on guard, in the breezy brittle manner she'd never seen in him before?

She'd realized from his first bristly words after she opened the door that he was steeled against her. Was that why she'd suddenly wanted to hurt?

Or was it the stunning cataclysmic understanding that the most promising beginning of her life was about to come to an abrupt, unreasonable, unexplainable end?

Some psychologist you are, she told herself with disgust. *All you come up with are questions. How about an answer or two?* Whatever the answers, in retrospect her own behavior in the stormy scene just past looked foolish and overplayed, she admitted with regret and embarrassment. He hadn't said anything like goodbye forever. She'd provided that dark prediction herself. But she'd acted like a Victorian maiden scorned. All he had said was that he was leaving in the morning. That was all! He hadn't said he wouldn't be coming back, she reminded herself with a sudden pale rush of hope.

Of course he'd be coming back! High rollers always came back, she told herself, but her sense of relief was diluted by the grim recognition of the irony intrinsic in pinning her hopes on his weakness for gambling, a weakness she'd bitterly deplored that afternoon.

He hadn't said goodbye forever. He hadn't said.... He hadn't said *anything*, she realized in sick recollection. In her surfeit of self-righteousness she had never given him a chance. Looking back with disbelief, Lia wondered what Flint might have said if she had shut up and let him talk.

He hadn't said goodbye forever, but after her bravura performance it was hardly necessary.

Because he was a high-roller Flint would undoubtedly come back to Tahoe's gambling community another time, but it was a sure bet he'd do his gambling at some other casino, she brooded sorrowfully. It was hardly likely he'd deliberately risk another exposure to a tongue that could turn virulent as quickly as hers had.

The persistent clatter of the front-door knocker brought Lia blinking into consciousness, surprised that she'd dozed off in her chair. She was even more surprised when she glanced at her watch to find she'd been asleep for almost an hour. She had a distinct impression the knocking had been repeated more than once. Only half-awake, she untangled her legs and sprang up from the corduroy chair. Her foot met the floor like a lead pincushion. A thousand electric needles shot up her ankle and calf. Moaning, she flexed her foot for a moment before she hobbled barefoot to the door.

Too drowsy to give thought to who might be there at that hour, she remembered to look through the peephole only the moment before she pulled open the door. What she saw held her frozen in disbelief.

It seemed less a person than a walking floricultural display—roses, delphiniums, glads, stocks, snapdragons and other rarer beauties, some of which she couldn't identify. They burgeoned in a panic of color from a loose conical paper wrapping that was fast losing the battle to contain them. Except for elbows and an arm and a pair of long trousered masculine legs, a cascade of foliage and flowers was all Lia could clearly identify.

Someone in the neighborhood must be giving a party, she thought. She hoped for the sake of the host that this was an unreasonably early delivery for an affair the following day and not a very late one for that night. In any case they'd come to the wrong house. She pulled the door open, intending to set the delivery man straight, but before she could open her mouth a familiar baritone voice spoke out from somewhere behind the flowers.

"I hope you haven't been worrying about your money," Flint Tancer said, and from over the top of the huge bouquet peered the most exciting face in the world. He wore a tentative, lopsided smile and a beseeching look in his eyes that would have disarmed her had her state of mind not already been far more amenable than when she had closed the door to the sound of his departing footsteps more than an hour before.

"Money?" Lia stared at him blankly for a mo-

ment. Then she remembered her morning's winnings. Something inside her did a flip-flop, and
she was forced to call on every ounce of self-
restraint to hold back the burst of laughter that
rolled up within. The man was either quite mad or
she was Wonderland's Alice. She'd practically
thrown him out of her house, and he had come
back—with flowers, yet—to find out if she was
worrying about the easy-come quarters she'd won
on the slot machine.

"Worry? Me worry?" she managed to say as
coolly as she could. "I naturally assumed you'd go
out and buy flowers with the money."

A red rose spilled out of the loosely contained
bundle and fell on the landing before her She
eyed it curiously but didn't bend down to pick it
up, still bemused by the dreamlike quality of the
scene. "Where on earth did you find   ? It's
crazy! This time of night   "

"It's a long story. First let me apologize for
being late. Let me in. Then I'll tell you about it,"
Flint coaxed.

"Late?"

"For our dinner date. Come, come. Surely you
haven't forgotten that."

Another rose, a pink one now, dropped down to
join the other. Its falling at last brought to Lia's
attention the bareness of her feet. With that
awareness the moment of fantasy dissolved. Traveling up the length of her body, her eyes deplored
her homely genderless attire—the baggy gray

sweat shirt, the sag-bottom pants. Then, spanning the small distance between them, her eyes met the amused gray ones peering over the absurd mountain of flowers.

"Don't think of changing for dinner. You're adorable just as you are. It's turned a bit chilly, though. You may want to put on shoes." Flint's voice was quite serious, but there was a hint of laughter in his eyes. Whether with her or at her, Lia couldn't be sure.

She stared at him in dismay. Surely he didn't think he could walk in as if the evening was just beginning when, in fact, it had already ended earlier.

"Look here, Flint. . ." she began with asperity, but before she was even certain what she was going to accuse him of, she was distracted by a sudden shift in the armload of blossoms. A portion of the huge bouquet broke loose from the fragile paper cornucopia that held it and slid down in a jumble of stems and petals to land on the already fallen roses.

"Not that I mind throwing roses at your feet, but are you extracting some kind of a penance?" Flint asked plaintively. "I thought you might like them in vases around the house."

Lia capitulated in helpless laughter. What could you do with such a man!

"Much as it pains me, I'll forgo the gratification of having you throw them at my feet. They are truly splendid. Do bring them in," she said. "I don't think there are enough vases in all Sapphire Point for this many flowers. Buckets are what we need.''

She bent and gathered the fallen flowers into her arms, then turned back into the house with a nod to Flint to follow. She dipped her head as if to breathe in the fragrance of the blossoms she held, though she was hardly aware of their scent. The movement was far more a protective gesture against the stunning charisma of the man. If he caught a glimpse of her face he would see in it a reflection of the chaos that stormed within her. And she couldn't have that.

While her heart cried, *Why did you come back, Flint? What do you want of me now?* the voice of the latent psychologist demanded, *You, Lia? What do you want with Flint?*

Questions. Always questions. Questions she needed answers for in the ten seconds it would take to walk from the front door to the kitchen. Otherwise how would she know what she was to do when they got there? Should she send the man packing before he completely ravished her silly heart? Or was the brief euphoria of one last evening with Flint worth the emptiness of all the tomorrows?

In the kitchen, still without answers and of half a mind to pose her questions directly to Flint, Lia came to an abrupt halt and turned to confront him. Clutching the conglomerate of blossoms and greenery, which seemed to have taken on a kind of mobility of their own, Flint sidestepped her and reached the sink, where he dumped the whole magnificent mélange with a sigh of deliverance. Behind him extended a trail of flowers leading all the way to the door.

"It was a lovely gesture," Lia couldn't help saying softly, though she hadn't intended to. Flint rewarded her with a smile that stole her breath.

"It was a hell of a lot of trouble," he said with a fine show of modesty.

"At nine o'clock at night, I'll bet it was," Lia said dryly. "Considering all you've been put through, would it seem rude if I asked what message you hoped to convey?"

She thought she caught a certain fleeting uneasiness in his eyes, but it quickly passed.

"We'll talk about that over dinner. If you have a couple of buckets or something big that'll hold water I'll stuff these in. You can do what you like with them tomorrow."

Tomorrow. Tomorrow Flint would be gone.

At that moment Lia came to a decision. She was through asking questions—questions she'd never pin the man down to answer even if he should stop peppering her with distractions that kept her from asking them.

She brought out several large containers and retrieved the loose blossoms Flint had strewn on his way in. She gave no outward sign that when he was through cramming his flowers into water she was going to bid him a noncommittal goodbye. A dull feeling of emptiness came with the thought of what she was about to do, but she saw no choice. After tomorrow he would be gone. Why postpone the inevitable?

His voice interrupted her thoughts. "If you want to change for dinner, you could while I finish up here, but don't do it on my account. You're enchanting enough as you are. Whenever you want to, we'll go."

Now was the time to tell him, thought Lia. A few well-chosen words. But before she could come up with them, Flint was talking again, and her ears, having somehow grown attuned to the changes in his voice, heard a new seriousness beneath the overlay of playfulness that had characterized his return until now.

"Would you mind putting on that blue dress again?" he asked, and there was something almost wistful in the way he said it that brought a bittersweet ache to her throat.

"I don't know," she hesitated. She tried but failed to mask the small tremor that crept into her words. "Last time I wore that dress I didn't have a very good time."

His hands were still cold from the water, still slightly damp as he took her face and tilted it up until they looked into each other's eyes. She could smell the pungent woodsy odor of the chrysanthemums freshly clinging to his fingers. Her heart beat so hard she was afraid he could see the slight movement of the rise and fall of her breast beneath the ugly sweat shirt. The gray-green eyes searched hers deeply, hungrily, a small smile playing at his mouth. The strong face spoke of a collage of feelings beneath, his expression questioning, tender, beseeching, regretful, even a little sad. Watching, Lia forgot to breathe.

"This time will be different, lovely Lia," he said, and there was no doubting the seriousness in his voice. "It will be good. This time I promise it will."

CHAPTER TEN

Away from him she could hear—even listen to—
the voice of caution that told her she must go out
there and bid him a final goodbye. Away from
him, she even imagined she could do it.

She stepped back into the blue dress and applied
a touch of color to her cheeks and lips, still not
sure she intended to go with Flint. However reluctant she was to put an end to the sweet disturbing
attraction that had sprung up between them, she
knew that if she did it now she would get over it. A
few hours in the heat of that devastating charm...
well, she wasn't sure.

What has he done to you? she asked the troubled
face that looked back at her from the mirror, seeing
in it an uncertainty that rankled. This was not the
decisive Lia Andrews she knew herself to be before
Flint Tancer half-drowned her and kissed her back
to life.

Outrage at the lack of resolution she saw in
the image before her squared her chin and shoulders and sparked a fire of determination in her
eyes.

"That's more like it," she muttered. Turning

on her heel she marched out to face him, to tell him he'd have to go.

A few steps down the hallway, at a point where she could see into the living room, she stopped with a sudden catch of breath and braced herself against the spell of the man she saw waiting for her.

He stood facing the window, gazing off into the darkness, the tall, graceful, athletic body poised half sitting against the back of one of the large upholstered chairs, obviously unaware he was being observed. From her vantage point Lia could see much of his face. A feeling of wonder coursed through her as she recognized the troubled uncertain look in the rugged countenance and realized it was a match for the one she had just seen in her own mirror.

An almost adolescent longing to seize the moment drove out any concern for her own capriciousness. She moved toward him, her pulse accelerating madly as he turned and came to meet her, hands outstretched, embracing her with his eyes.

If she imagined he intended to take her in his arms she was to be disappointed. He took only her hands, turning them over to look into the palms as if appraising some remarkable objet d'art, lifting them in turn to lay a kiss at the beginning and end of each heart line. When he released them, Lia let her hands fall loosely to her sides. As if held by some strange enchantment she stood motionless before him, their bodies not touching, yet so close to each other she imagined she could hear the soft irregular soughing of his breath.

For a long still moment his eyes moved hungrily up the length of her body as if to record it faithfully in his mind for another time. Between his thumb and first two fingers he caught a bit of the dress's full swinging skirt and played softly with the larkspur blue silk. Sweeping it up, he pressed it to his cheek for an instant with a kind of artless reverence that at the same time was infinitely sensual. Deep within her a latent flame sprang to life. To her eyes came an unexpected welling of tears. Flint's eyes meeting hers spoke of some hidden inner yearning, a poignant unrequited need. The smile that warmed his face held a trace of wistfulness.

"You are beautiful," he said huskily. "Thank you for wearing the dress."

THE RESTAURANT was a quiet spot on the California side of the lake some miles away, far from the gambling scene. The dining room had been broken into a number of small dimly lit areas on various levels, the tables discreetly screened from each other by greenery or decorative devices, a setting designed to give diners a sense of privacy. Lia welcomed it, but couldn't help feeling a certain uneasiness as to what such exclusive togetherness might bring forth between her and Flint.

The questions Flint had bewitched her out of

asking were still burning in her mind, and Lia stubbornly refused to shelve them. Whether or not he chose to answer them, they were still going to be asked. She'd made up her mind to find out everything she could about Flint Tancer tonight. When their time together came to an end she had a right to know whom she was saying goodbye to.

She bided her time. Conversation was as light as the freshly caught lake trout with watercress and the minted sugar peas they ate. But when they'd finished the orange soufflé and were lingering over coffee in the shadowy enclave, it was Flint who started the questioning.

"What made you decide you'd rather be a blackjack dealer than an airline flight attendant?" he asked bluntly without preliminaries.

Lia glanced at him in surprise, then she remembered she'd mentioned her stint with the airlines to him earlier in the evening. "Actually, I've never really compared the two," she said agreeably. "When I applied for the dealer's job I was a psychologist with a family counseling service in San Francisco. I quit flight work several years ago to go back to Stanford and get my degree in psychology."

"I see," said Flint.

But he didn't see. She knew with a sense of frustration that he didn't see at all. His next words convinced her of this.

"I shouldn't think psychology would be all that dull," he said in a level voice.

"Who said it was dull?" Lia replied, bridling. "It's fascinating. I can't think of anything that intrigues me more than the study of human behavior...the human mind."

"Then why in blazes did you quit what you were doing to take a job as a dealer?" Flint demanded rather bluntly, then backed down. "Not that there's anything wrong with dealing. It's good work for bright people who don't have anything they like better to do, people who don't mind the monotony of going through basically the same movements hour after hour, day after day. But, Lia, you say you have a deep interest in the field you're trained for! Don't tell me you're so hungry for excitement you'll give that up for the casino razzmatazz?"

"You're the one who keeps talking about excitement, Flint," said Lia a bit testily. "Once and for all, could we get this straight. I didn't come up here for excitement. On a list of things I'm looking for in life, excitement doesn't even appear, and if it did, a casino's not where I'd go to look for it. To be perfectly honest with you, I don't find casinos all that exciting."

For a moment she imagined she saw a spark of satisfaction in his eyes. But in the next instant it died.

"Then you came here for the gambling," he concluded dully. "Lia, if you're here to gamble, you must realize—as a psychologist—that you are in big trouble! Quit *now*—that is if you can."

"Wrong again. I'm not a gambler. I've never received any kind of a kick out of games that depend on luck rather than skill to win," Lia told him with asperity. "That bucket of quarters this morning was a fluke. I dropped some change into a machine as I was passing through and all that money rolled out. I'd never won before, and I don't expect to keep trying on the hope I'll win again."

"Then would you mind telling me why you *are* here?"

It was on the tip of Lia's tongue to say something flip...something like "Why, Flint, hadn't you guessed? I came here just to meet you." But flipness wasn't the impression she wanted to convey. She wanted to tell Flint exactly why she was there, at least as much as she could without jeopardizing her study. She had no idea what kind of rapport he had with Mr. Mansfield, the casino manager, but as a favored gambler and a guest of the hotel he might feel an obligation to the host establishment. What if he saw it as his duty to report to management the fact that one of their dealers was a psychologist working incognito at the Goldorado to study the gambling phenomenon—and without their consent? The manager might simply say, "What of it?" On the other hand, he could say to her, "Out!" And that would put a definite end to her fieldwork, not just here but at any other casino. It was common knowledge that when it came to security there was a network of communication between the otherwise competing casinos.

"Well, one thing you should know, it isn't the lure of the fleshpots—an impression you seem to have picked up," she said at last. "In a way, though, it's not surprising for you to think the glitter and excitement are what brought me here. When people hear the word *casino* they immediately think excitement. Come to think of it, that's one of the reasons I gave when I applied for the dealer's job."

"But...why?"

Lia hesitated. She said, finally, "The real reason is a bit complex and hard to explain on an application form. I was afraid if I gave it, it might actually keep me from getting the job."

"It beats me why you'd put in the work to become a psychologist and then chuck it to go work as a casino dealer."

"Who said anything about chucking it? If I wasn't a psychologist, I doubt if I'd be here at all." Again Lia hesitated, not sure how much more she dared say. After a moment she went on. "Someone I...I...knew...someone I thought for a while I cared for, turned out to be a compulsive gambler. I'd never known any gamblers, and it suddenly seemed important to find out what goes on in their heads. A casino seemed the logical place to begin."

"So that's it. You fell in love with a degenerate. That's what they call them in the trade, you know," said Flint scathingly. "You think you're going to discover some magic way to cure him. Well, forget it! You won't."

"That isn't it, Flint. I don't even know where he is, and I don't much care. What I had thought was love was never anything quite so fine. If it had been love, I wouldn't have quit loving him when I discovered what he actually was," explained Lia earnestly. "As for cures, I suppose you're right. I've found out enough to know that the only one who can cure a hard-core gambler is the gambler himself."

"If you're not in love with the guy and don't expect to come up with a cure, why keep on with it?"

She hesitated, debating what she should say. "You might call it intellectual stubbornness. My father would, I suppose. I have to know what makes the compulsive gambler different from the one who just plays for fun. The only way I can hope to find out is to get to know all kinds of gamblers, talk to them—as many of them as I can. I want to know what motivates different people to gamble. The ones who can't quit until they've brought ruin down on their heads...well, there must be a way to get through to them."

"Not if they don't want to quit. Take it from a man who knows," said Flint grimly. "My dad was a gambler. He married my mother and quit for the fifteen years she was alive. He was a salesman. Six months after she died he went back to gambling and never sold a thing from then on. I was four-teen. I grew up in casinos and gambling joints. He gambled to the day he died.''

"Flint, I'm sorry," Lia replied softly, seeing the young Flint in the kids she saw every day jostling one another around the computer games or simply milling idly around in a state of boredom, waiting for their parents to come out of the casino. Some-times she'd see one of them there when she came in at the beginning of her shift, and he'd still be there when she left at the end. It seemed a forlorn way to have to grow up.

But Flint declined to be pitied. Unexpectedly he grinned. "It wasn't all bad. Unlike the true de-generates, my dad was a real pro. He always quit before he got completely wiped out. Sometimes he was in the chips. We lived poor a lot, but other times we were rich, and by the time I was eighteen I'd seen most of the world's great gambling spas."

There was a sudden hint of wickedness in his eyes, a cynical twist to his smile. Lia's curiosity was titillated.

"I learned a lot in those years that they don't teach in the public schools," he said musingly, clearly lost in recollections he didn't propose to share. Lia discreetly swallowed the questions she was burning to ask.

He gave a slight lift of his shoulders as if to divest himself of that past and returned to Lia with such a look of homecoming her heart seemed to lift like a bird in flight. What a complex character was this man who leaned across the table toward her now, the large-boned face marked with a quiet inner elation that gave it an almost luminous quality. Gone from his smile was the cynical twist of a moment before. His face looked strangely vulnerable.

"Tell me I haven't screwed it up beyond repair, Lia," he said, suddenly grave.

She could have pretended she didn't know what he was talking about, but she didn't. "I was mad at you, but when I cooled down I was mad at myself," she admitted truthfully. "I overreacted. It was rotten to accuse you of coming for a quick tumble in bed—I believe that's what I said—when I knew it wasn't true. But it was obvious that between morning and evening you'd picked up some mistaken ideas about me. Would you mind telling me where...and if you still believe them?"

Flint groaned. "Believe them? No, I don't. I swear! I've been secretly afraid if I never met a woman like you my life would be...oh, hell! I was a stupid ass to build a case...."

"On what evidence, Flint? What led you to think I was some kind of a...a...an elderly teenager who never grew up?" The question seemed to add to his discomfiture. He was quiet for a time. Then he reached across the table for her hand.

"Don't ask me. Not yet. It was out of context and would only complicate matters. Trust me in this, Lia. I'll tell you, but not now, please."

With his words she remembered the source of

the dull ache she'd kept hidden within her since she'd stepped into the living room two hours before and seen a loneliness and uncertainty in Flint's eyes that was as great as her own.

"Since you're leaving in the morning, that hardly seems likely," she said crisply.

"Oh my God! I forgot all about.... Come on. If you're through with your coffee, let's get out of here."

So now it was out in the open—the fact of his impending departure. It had put a blight on their relationship from the moment he'd let it slip. With a dull sense of defeat she watched Flint rise and come around the small table to pull back her chair. What difference did it make? Words, said or unsaid, didn't alter the circumstances. They had been simmering inside her all evening, waiting to boil over. It was just as well they were out.

But the words, whether spoken or unspoken, couldn't alter her response to the caressing touch of his hand on her bare arm as he curved it lightly beneath her elbow to lend a slight leverage as she got up from her chair. As she rose, the edge of the strong graceful fingers grazed the curve of her breast, and beneath the blue silk she could feel her instant response, half hoping that he felt it, too. She wondered what it was like for him to feel the taut bud, a signal of invitation against his hand. She steeled herself against the light tingling shock of arousal, against the moment when they would reach the privacy of the car and Flint would begin to play his overture to their last goodbye. Or had she already heard the opening strains? she wondered dryly.

Not that she didn't believe he regretted his wrong judgment of her. She was sure he did. Or that he regretted the scene that had taken place between them on the deck. She was even sure he had sincerely wanted to make amends when he returned loaded down with a houseful of flowers. But she was equally sure, whether he realized it or not, that somewhere—perhaps tucked away in Flint Tancer's subconscious—the goal was still the same. To make love just once before he said goodbye.

The arrival of the waiter beside them interrupted Lia's thoughts.

"If you'd like to wait at your table, Mr. Tancer, I'll call you when the parking attendant brings up your car."

"I'd appreciate it," Flint said. Handing the other man the ticket, he turned back to the table, but Lia had already slipped quickly into her chair, giving no chance for further physical contact between them.

They waited, the air heavy with the unspoken, and Lia was only minimally aware of the two men who passed by their alcove. Seeing only their backs in the dimly lit room, she absently watched them walk on and disappear in the direction of the door

Still, there'd been something familiar about one of the men, and it kept nagging at her mind. Sure ly she'd seen him somewhere before. She was sure if she got a good look at him in decent lighting she could make the connection. There was something. . . was it his walk?

When she saw the waiter approaching a moment later she put the matter out of her mind, hurrying to her feet before Flint had time to move around the table and pull out her chair for her. Outside she all but raced him to the car, hoping to forgo the courtesy of his help getting in.

"Hey, what's the hurry?" he called out with a laugh. He was a few steps behind her, then, turning the situation into a contest, he quickened his pace and overtook her before she reached the door. He grabbed her in a quick lunge that threw them both momentarily off-balance and sent them reeling against the side of the car. They teetered there, and Lia laughed in spite of herself until Flint's warm sensuous mouth covered hers and smothered the bubbling laughter.

Then, in stark realization that the end lay directly ahead, Lia willingly gave herself over to her senses for one last mindless moment. Under the ravishment of their mouths, she breathed in deeply the faintly musky scent of the man, letting her fingers play across the gently abrasive surface of the recently shaved cheek. She let her body go. It melted and conformed to his long muscular planes and discovered the full extent of his arousal. Somewhere within her burned an ember that set her senses aflame.

She gave a deep sensual shudder and made herself pull away. Shaking her head lightly, she began to free herself. Slowly, reluctantly she pressed her palms against his chest and gradually withdrew from the kiss. But neither seemed able to make the parting of their lips complete. They plunged together again, hungering, tasting, feasting in a kind of wild tormented seeking as if they might gain fulfillment from their mouths.

It was the honk of a horn that brought them finally apart to find themselves spotlighted in the bright circle of a car's headlights. There was a nearly soundless moan from Flint as Lia tore herself from him. In a single quick movement she flung open the door and sank into the seat of the car, yanking the door closed with a slam behind her. The other car pulled out around them and with another breezy honk went on its way.

Breathless, her pulse pounding heavily, Lia ached with the pain of lost rapture. Nor was she happy about having other eyes witness such a profoundly intimate scene between her and Flint. For the sake of her own integrity and self-respect she knew she couldn't be a party to a repeat performance. It had been their final goodbye. She could not bear to think it was nothing more than a moment of voyeurism for strangers.

To her relief, Flint took his time about walking back around to the driver's side, allowing her to compose herself before the door on the driver's side opened quietly and he folded himself in behind the wheel and started the engine. Before he set the car in motion he turned to her.

His voice heavy with emotion, he said, "Lia, we've got to talk, but not here. Not in the car. If you don't trust me enough to let me back in your house we'll find someplace else, but I promise you this time there'll be no problem."

"No, Flint. Not my house. Not any place. We've already said goodbye. Please just take me home."

"My record's against me, I know, but damn it, Lia, what happened just now doesn't count. You know yourself it...it just happened. It was as much your doing as mine."

Lia didn't reply, knowing guiltily that what he said was true. In the silence between them the car motor purred impatiently.

"We've got to talk, Lia," Flint repeated. "There's still some straightening out to do between us. Would it make any difference if I told you that I'm not going anyplace in the morning?"

Lia sat straight in her seat and turned to stare at him in disbelief.

"You're not just saying that?"

"Of course not. I'm not going anywhere, I swear."

She still had to be sure. "If not tomorrow, then when?"

Flint groaned. "You drive a hard bargain, my

darling. Not tomorrow, not the next day. Not next week. Who knows when? A lot depends on us both. That's what we've got to talk about.''

"Then what are we waiting for?''

CHAPTER ELEVEN

ALL THE WAY BACK to the Sapphire Point house Lia's mind was a circus of questions, but the one in the big ring was what Flint had meant by that last enigmatic declaration of his: *A lot depends on us both.*

The ride that had passed quickly earlier that night now seemed endless to Lia. She was impatient for Flint to clarify whatever he'd intended to imply in those few words. Secure in the knowledge he would be around for a while, she deemed it the better part of wisdom not to press him for answers until he was ready to talk.

At last they reached the house. As he opened the car door for her, he turned his eyes up to the fat round moon and drew in a breath of satisfaction.

"What a night! Look, it's as light as day. I'll bet the moon's made a path across the water deep enough to walk on. How about going down to the beach? We can sit on the boat landing and look at the moon from the lake."

Stepping out of the car, Lia looked down at her high-heeled open sandals dubiously.

"Not in my sitting down shoes, I'm afraid."

"Got anything against changing them?"

"Not a thing. Besides, I'm a little dressy for the beach. If you don't mind, I'll change all around. It'll take a minute. Maybe you'd like to come in."

Flint hesitated. "I'll wait out here, thanks. If I go inside I'd just start thinking how much I want to make love to you."

"Very flattering," Lia said, suddenly heady.

"But I don't especially care to get thrown out again! Besides, right now I want to talk."

"Well, that's a switch!"

"Lia...you're not making it easier." He caught her and kissed her breathless, but this time the kiss was an end in itself. When she pulled half-reluctantly out of his arms he made no move to detain her, and she darted off down the walkway and through the front door.

She emerged shortly, dressed now in an old pair of soft corduroy pants, a heavy cotton sweater and canvas shoes. Flint greeted her with an appreciative whistle.

"How do you do it, lady?"

"Do what?"

"You'd look sexy in combat fatigues."

They started off together toward the beach. When they had gone some hundred yards and Flint showed no signs of launching their projected talk, Lia's patience reached the end of its tether.

"Tell me, Flint," she prodded. "When did you change your mind?"

"You mean about leaving?" He was still for a

moment. She could hear the quiet crunch of their feet in the deep sand as they trudged on.

"It just happened. There wasn't any deliberate mind changing involved," he said finally. "I forgot about it after I left your house the first time. Until you brought it up at dinner a while ago, I didn't think of it again. When you did, I knew without giving it any thought that I wasn't going to go."

"Why, Flint? Nothing had really changed."

"Nothing but my perspective." He reached out and took her hand, and they walked on in companionable silence. Flint appeared to be sorting out his thoughts.

"I had intimations from the first that you were an authentic gem. I should have listened to my instincts. My only excuse is that my experience with that mysterious other sex has been too limited for me to recognize quality when I see it."

"Somehow, I rather doubt that."

"It's true. The casinos, in my growing-up days, were not like the Tahoe casinos today. The women I knew after my mother died were mostly those who gravitated around my dad when he was in the chips. I was old enough to notice they didn't hang around when he was down on his luck."

"But there've been other women, Flint. Women who've meant something to you?"

"I can't deny that. I got fairly serious about a couple, but none of them was really...for me. I don't mean to put them down when I say that.

They were fine women, all of them, but they just weren't right for me. I'd almost quit thinking there was a right woman—until you came along and put her back in the running again.''

Lia glanced up at the man in sudden apprehension. ''You mean you've got some kind of ideal woman you're looking for?'' The question brought an abashed laugh from Flint.

The white sand shone silver under the moon. They had crossed the beach and walked the length of the dock, hardly aware of their own passage. Now they stood together gazing absently across the path of bright water laid down by the moon while Lia listened with a growing sense of depression to Flint tell her about the ideal woman that he and his fellow men imagined would someday walk into their lives.

''It does sound a little presumptuous as I tell it, I suppose,'' he finished defensively.

''You're darned right it's presumptuous—and arrogant and patronizing and...and offensive, and I can think of a few other words I could use. What right have you, Flint Tancer, to expect some perfect, tailor-made doll to walk into your life and the two of you live happily ever after?''

''Now wait a minute, Lia. It's not like that. I suppose all I'm really looking for is a real authentic woman—someone I can love—not some alabaster Madonna. I want her flawed. I'm flawed, God knows. If she didn't have a full quota of flaws, how could she put up with me?''

It was quite a speech, thought Lia with grudging admiration, spoken with some passion and without rancor. She could see his features clearly in the moonlight. A slow smile touched his face.

"My only stipulation is that her flaws are ones I can live with—not insurmountable, that is... and that she has a certain built-in tolerance for mine."

"Not completely unreasonable," said Lia, "but I'm still not sure I like the idea of being held up for comparison to some figment of your imagination. Luckily, all men don't whip a model woman out of their minds and check every new woman who comes over the horizon against her."

"Don't you believe it. Universally, every man carries around with him an idea of a unique right woman who's waiting exclusively for him. Women do it too, I'll bet. Don't tell me you don't have a picture of what your kind of man is like."

Lia gave him a sheepish grin. Raising herself on tiptoe, she kissed him lightly on the cheek.

"I think maybe I just found him."

And then they were in each other's arms— laughing and rocking together in a kind of jubilant celebration, showering each other with wild joyous kisses. Then as quickly as they had come together, they separated as if by unspoken mutual consent.

"I was kidding, of course," Lia said quietly. "It's crazy for either of us to think we've learned all the important things there are to know about each other in less than forty-eight hours. There's no such thing as love at first sight, Flint.''

''I don't know what it is, Lia. I'm afraid to put a name to it. All I know is, there's something good going between us. . . and it's something more rare and invaluable than the man-woman thing, though God knows we've got more than enough of that.'' He gave a groan of frustration. ''Just saying it makes me wild with longing. I want to bare our bodies and lie down and make love with you here on the dock, under the eyes of that big melon moon. I want to bury my head between your breasts and drown in the softness of your flesh.''

''Flint. . .'' Lia's breath was almost a gasp. ''No, Flint! No. We need time.''

Flint drew a deep breath and dropped down to sit on the unfinished boards of the dock, reaching up to draw Lia down beside him.

''You want it too, Lia,'' he said as if she was betraying him somehow. Under the pressure of his hand she allowed herself to be pulled down, unresisting, and let him position her in front of him in the vee formed by his outspread legs on the rough planks. She shivered under the touch of his hands as they slipped underneath the ribbed edge of the bulky sweater and moved up over the plane of her belly toward her bare breasts.

He inched her body closer to him across the boards and a sharp prick of pain brought her up to her knees. ''What the devil!'' Flint exclaimed.

"Splinter," said Lia shortly, exploring the surface of her buttock with her fingers. "I can feel the end of it but I can't get hold of it."

"Blazes! I've done it again," moaned Flint, up on his knees beside her, his fingers joining hers to probe for the offending bit of wood.

"You've done what?"

"Bodily injury to you, dammit. Here it is. It's as big as a toothpick," he said, bringing it around for her inspection. "We'd better get you home and get something on the wound."

"Really, it's nothing," Lia protested. "These pants are as tough as shoe leather. It didn't go in far. Just enough to let me know it was there."

She was almost glad for the interruption now that the moment was over. Their rampant sensualities had been about to lead them down a long road, one with no easy turnaround. There was little doubt in her mind that the time would come when they would be ready to take that road, but tonight was too soon.

They perched on the edge of the dock, dangling their feet above the water, watching the moon's silver path on the lake.

"About this 'something good' we've got going between us....?" Lia ventured at last.

Flint's voice was serious. "I wouldn't have said that if I hadn't been so sure you feel it, too." Then his tone became somewhat anxious. "You *do* feel it, don't you, Lia?"

And Lia took his hand, as earlier he had done to

hers, and laid a kiss in his palm. "Oh, Flint, I do. I do."

He breathed a deep sigh of contentment and moved closer to tuck her gently within the curve of his arm.

Her head on his breast, Lia said softly after a moment, "You thought I might be the right one for you? That's why you decided not to go?"

"That's exactly why, my love. Maybe we're *not* made for each other, but we'll never know if we don't stick around and find out. I've been waiting too many years for someone like you to leave just when the goal seems to be in sight."

She knew his hand was back under her sweater. She thrilled to the power of its seduction against her bare skin for a moment, then reluctantly removed it and placed it lightly on top of the sweater again, anchoring it with her hand.

"Well, Mr. Tancer, may I remind you of the old saying, 'What's sauce for the goose...'?" she said wickedly. "I expect equal time to find out if you're *my* kind of man—your phrase, not mine! All I really know about you is that I find you pretty hard to say no to, but that's not love."

Flint shifted restlessly. "I'm not sure where this conversation is heading. I'm not sure I like it."

But Lia forged stubbornly ahead. "We are talking about love, aren't we? Then I believe first things have got to come first. This...well... physical attraction between us is so...*overwhelming* it throws everything else out of focus. Don't you see, Flint? If we let it take over it can't help but color our judgment about whether we care for each other in all the other ways that count?''

"You're telling me that if we go to bed together before we've established the fact of love, it'll put a blight on it?''

"No. I'm not even sure that's true,'' she said slowly. "Maybe it's not, for you.'' She thought about it a moment before she went on earnestly, "You know, you're not the first attractive man to send a shiver up my spine, Flint. I mistook physical attraction for love once, and it left scars. I don't want to risk it again. Maybe *my* insurmountable flaw is that I can't be casual about it. This time I've got to be sure it's really love.''

After a moment Flint's arm left her waist. He pulled his feet to the deck and stood up. Well, what could she expect? thought Lia with a sense of disappointment, almost regretting she'd been so candid with him.

"What time will you leave in the morning?'' she asked dully.

"Leave?'' She could see his moonlit face above her. It was cast in its own shadow as he bent his head to peer down at her. Then he laughed. He leaned down and brought her up beside him, folding her in his arms, burying his face in her hair.

"It'll take more than that warning to drive me away, Calamity Jane,'' he said tenderly. "Even couched in your psychological jargon, I can't quarrel with your stand. As a matter of fact, I'd hate like hell to think of you giving yourself to all those Burt Reynolds prototypes who send a shiver up your spine.''

From somewhere in the region of his collarbone, Lia said sweetly, ''It's only fair to say there haven't been all *that* many.''

In the circle of each other's arms they rocked lightly back and forth on the balls of their feet.

''What you've said is probably right, but that doesn't mean I buy it,'' Flint said at last. ''It could be that *my* insurmountable flaw is a hopeless inability to keep a rein on my libido where you're concerned.''

''Hey, that's *my* jargon you're using!''

But Flint wouldn't be teased. ''It's not going to be easy. I'll need help,'' he said seriously. ''Most of the time when we're together, I'm thinking how much I want to make love to you. Just don't ask me to promise to stop trying!''

His hands came down and he circled her waist between the arcs of thumbs and forefingers to hold her slightly away from him so they stood looking into each other's faces—the tall woman and the taller man, eyes locked in a silent pact. After a moment, he bent down and touched his lips lightly to hers. The kiss deepened and lingered, yet still did not bring their bodies into contact. Then Flint broke away.

''Let's get out of here,'' he said, his breathing ragged. He seized one of her hands and started running across the dock. After the first few steps he adjusted his pace to hers and they ran together along the hard-packed sand at the edge of the water and on up the wooded rise to the house.

By the time they reached the slate walkway leading to the door, Lia, who by choice was not a jogger, was winded. She stood for a moment in the shadows panting, leaning back against him for support as her breathing slowed to normal.

"Come out and run with me every morning. I'll get you back in shape," Flint challenged.

"I'm not that crazy about running. Swim with me in the lake and you'll see who's out of shape."

"I swim only in the heated pool at the Goldorado. I learned to swim in hotel pools, and that's where I've swum all my life. There's no way you could get me into that arctic water."

"I wish you'd felt like that yesterday."

"I did. It was that beautiful body that got me."

He tilted her head up from her shoulder and leaned his own down to play kisses along her hairline and nip gently at her ear. For a while there was no more banter between them, no more talk of any kind. His hands came around her from behind and found their way under her sweater and up to enfold her breasts lightly with an unbearably exciting brush of his palms across the naked flesh.

"Flint," she gasped. "You said...."

"I told you I promised nothing," he reminded her huskily, but he let her go.

Lia pulled herself together and walked away from him, down the walkway to the house, Flint following a few steps behind. Her heart was beating as wildly again as at the end of their run, her thoughts and emotions running apace. She was the one who had laid down the rules. He'd promised nothing but to continue to do what he'd been doing all along. Which was fair enough, she supposed, since that was the way he felt about it, but it left it all up to her. As Flint had said, it wasn't going to be easy. She just hadn't expected it to be so hard.

She didn't invite him to come in when they reached the door. She didn't dare. She didn't trust her will to resist him. They both needed a cooling-off period. They were too much on fire. To her relief—relief tainted by an instant of regret—Flint appeared to agree. He gave her a warm, firm, almost impersonal good-night kiss and loped off up the slightly inclined walkway to his car.

Long after he was gone, he stayed with her. In the moment before she buttoned herself into the creamy silk tailored men's shirt that was her favorite sleepwear she stood naked before the room's full-length mirror and tried to see her body through the eyes of the man. The thought of his eyes watching her sent a small electric thrill racing through her. A bit ashamed of her drift into such deliberately provocative fantasy, she turned her back on the mirror and slipped quickly into the shirt, loving its silken caress. She couldn't think of anything she would rather have around her, except Flint Tancer's arms.

As she was drifting off to sleep a truant thought intruded upon her euphoria. If only he wasn't a gambler. It lasted but an instant. On its heels came a new thought that brought her sitting bolt upright in bed.

Gambler! That's who the man was—the man whose back she'd glimpsed as he walked away from her in the dimly lit restaurant. She couldn't mistake that slightly offbeat, awkward gait that made him hard to walk beside. It was Toby. Toby Brasford, of course. If she hadn't been so absorbed in Flint she would have known him at once.

ONLY THE HAZARDS of nighttime traffic and the narrow shoulders along the interstate highway he'd be obliged to use kept Flint from leaving his car and sprinting the distance between Sapphire Point and the Goldorado. Drunk with exhilaration, he wanted to turn handsprings, jump high hurdles, scale buildings, fill his lungs to bursting with sweet mountain air, shout out his satisfactions to the world.

Instead he climbed sedately behind the wheel and drove back to the casino and his penthouse suite, saluting as he passed the twenty-four-hour florist shop next to the round-the-clock wedding chapel by the roadside, just two miles beyond the Sapphire Point gate. He grinned, remembering the look on the shopkeeper's face while he'd moved around filling the order.

"I want about ten dozen..." Flint had been about to say roses—weren't roses every woman's favorite flower?—but it occurred to him he wouldn't be doing a fool thing like this if Lia Andrews was the average woman. He'd been astonished to realize he hadn't known her long enough to know even such a simple thing as her favorite flower.

"Just give me ten dozen or so—every kind of bloom you've got in the house," he had requested, while the shopkeeper eyed him as if he was quite mad. "And stick in a lot of that green stuff to go with it."

Lia would never have let him back in the house if he hadn't thought to camouflage himself with that horrendous bouquet, Flint thought now. All the time he'd stood out there on her doorstep playing the fool for her, a voice inside his head kept saying, "Tancer, why in *hell* didn't you keep your nose out of that file this afternoon!"

And when he came to his senses and saw how his quantum leap to conclusions had maligned her, he just hadn't had the guts to tell her he'd been reading her personnel file—at least not until he could explain by what right he had access to it. At the moment there'd been too many other things to straighten out between them. It had hardly been an auspicious time to go into his relationship to the Goldorado's owner and why he'd been rummaging in that file. In any case, he was none too sure she would approve of his having looked into her file without her consent.

He also didn't know how Aaron was going to feel about telling Lia of his family connection with the casino. There was always the possibility his brother-in-law might be opposed to having one of his employees know that the casino had been operating on shaky financial ground or that Flint had been called in to troubleshoot.

Like it or not, Flint thought, Aaron was going to have to get used to the idea, because the first thing he intended to do in the morning was to get his sister to invite him and Lia to dinner at the Burney house the following night. He wanted Rozlyn and Aaron to meet Lia. He wanted Lia to like his family—he wanted her to fall in love with Roz and the kids when she got to know them.

Lia. Oh, Lia. Oh, Lia.

The name sang like the strain of a flute in his mind, evoking the sweet taste of her mouth, the scent of her flesh, the clear bright music of her voice.

Oh Lia, Lia, how long will you keep me waiting to cup your satin-soft breasts in my hands? something cried out from within. *How long before you let my eyes feast on your glorious unclothed body and cover it with kisses? How long until we come together in an act of love?*

CHAPTER TWELVE

"IF YOU WANT MY OPINION, Flint, you'll be doing the young lady a disservice if you tell her you're there to keep the casino under surveillance, especially when she's a dealer in one of the very pits we expect to watch. I'd say you'll be putting the young woman in a helluva spot," said Aaron Burney. The two men were seated across the table from each other in the Burney breakfast room, finishing the last of the morning coffee.

Flint eyed him broodingly over the top of his cup.

"She hasn't been with us long. How does she feel about the other dealers?" Burney asked.

"That's not exactly one of the things we've gone into in depth," Flint said dryly. "Still, it's both her nature and her profession to be interested in people. I have the impression she's definitely interested in the people with whom she works. She's remarked to me that for the most part she finds the dealers an unusually smart personable lot. She's become quite friendly with two or three of them in her pit."

"How's it going to set with her, then, knowing

you're there to spy on people she considers her friends?"

"That's exactly what I'm *not* going to do, in case you've forgotten, Aaron," Flint said acidly. "I know I said I'd keep an eye on the casino for a while, but that's all I intend to do. Regardless, I intend to let her know my connection with her employer, and I expect to let her know what I'm doing at the Goldorado. How do you think I'll be able to explain it when she sees me hanging around the casino every day? She's much too smart not to put two and two together and decide I'm a hard-core gambler."

"Would it matter to you if she did?"

Flint studied his coffee in silence for a moment. His sister, Rozlyn, who was at the far end of the kitchen taking care of the clutter left over from breakfast, was suddenly still. She raised her head and turned her attention to the men at the table.

Flint looked up. Catching both pairs of eyes on him he said on a faintly truculent note, "Look, you two...." Then with a sigh of resignation, he conceded reluctantly, "Okay. Okay. I guess there's no valid reason to hide it. Yes. As a matter of fact, I'm beginning to believe it would matter a great deal to me if she did."

His sister, a tall, cheerful-looking young woman with ash-blond hair and gray eyes not unlike Flint's, gave up all pretense of loading the dishwasher and crossed the room to take a place at the table beside her brother. She craned her neck to look up at him, her eyes bright with curiosity.

"No kidding?" she said, her voice registering both interest and candid approval. "You mean to say some beautiful female dealer has actually eased her way into that cynical heart of yours? Tell me about her."

"I'll do better than that, dear Roz. If you'll invite us, I'll bring her to dinner tonight."

Rozlyn sighed. "Make a simple request, and he expects a handout!" Wrinkling her nose at him, she reached over and rumpled her brother's hair.

"Cut it out, Roz," Flint said, clearly in no mood for games. With an impatient gesture he pushed her hand aside. His hair stayed in disarray.

She gave an injured sniff. "You don't have to be difficult to your underprivileged sister!"

Flint grinned. "If you're underprivileged, dear sister, Jackie Onassis is on welfare!"

"Oh, I don't mean like that. A woman has a God-given right to run her fingers through a man's hair once in a while. Just take a good look at Aaron, then tell me I'm not underprivileged!"

She unfolded herself from the chair to bend down over her husband and plant an affectionate kiss in the middle of his head—a head quite bald but for a small hula fringe of hair above the neck and over the ears. Burney's response was an indulgent laugh and a fatuous smile.

Rozlyn turned her attention back to her brother. "Then it's all settled. You'll bring her to dinner tonight. I can't wait! I've been dying to

meet a dealer ever since Aaron bought the Goldorado. I'm thinking of going over and taking the
dealers' training course they give. I might even
talk Les Mansfield into using me as a kind of
substitute dealer when he needs one.''

Aaron and Flint glanced at each other. It was
plain Roz knew very little about casinos, Flint
thought, but at the same time her words roused in
him a certain uneasiness. Yesterday he would have
been willing to bet the last thing in the world his
sister would ever want to do was deal cards in a
casino, but the odds had just changed. It was only
one of several things he'd thought he was sure of
forty-eight hours ago, but wasn't so sure of now.
Perhaps an unbroken string of business successes
had given him overconfidence in the rightness of
his own judgments. Now that clear sense of his
own rightness was becoming blurred.

With a rueful shrug, Aaron said dryly, ''Well,
now that Roz has settled the question of dinner,
the matter of advising Ms Andrews of the Tancer-
Burney relationship has become purely academic,
it would seem. While I'll be delighted, of course,
to meet this young lady, I can't say I go along with
having an employee of the casino privy to the precarious state of its affairs.''

''That's not very nice of you, Aaron,'' his wife
chimed in indignantly from the neighborhood of
the sink where she'd returned. ''Mind stating your
reason?''

''I don't have to state it to Flint, since it's in line

with one of his own axioms," said Burney. "The quickest way to send a business down the tube is to let the employees get the idea all is not well. What makes you think the young lady can be trusted not to broadcast to the other dealers the fact I asked you up here to help salvage a shaky investment you'd advised me against in the first place?"

"You can trust her, Aaron, believe me. I'm sure of it. Don't ask me for reasons. If you trust me, then believe that you can trust her," Flint said seriously. "And I don't mind telling you, you're making a big deal out of something that doesn't matter that much. There's nothing dire to broadcast. I keep telling you, Aaron, there's nothing shaky about the Goldorado, for all you say. With a few changes the business will come out of the doldrums fine."

"Except that Mansfield's sure we haven't finished with the trouble in the casino. If you tell this young lady about that you put her in a very uncomfortable position and don't do yourself any good," said Burney. "On the other hand, if you say only that you're up here to look over the operation for me and make recommendations to develop a sound economic policy for the company, she'll think you're just doing your thing."

"I've heard you say that so often you've almost got me believing it. I must say, Aaron, you've got a way with words. You manage to make what I do sound a hell of a lot more impressive than it really is," said Flint with a kind of grudging admiration.

Burney was unflappable. "You've got to admit it pretty much covers everything, but you might suggest to the young lady—"

"Stop calling her the young lady, Aaron," Flint said sharply. "You know her name. It's Lia Andrews. Do me a favor and call her that."

"You might ask Ms Andrews," continued Burney, hardly missing a beat, "as a favor to me, not to mention our connection and the reason you're here to anyone. You can say I think it's bad for the morale of the employees, which, as you know, is true. They get to speculating about why an expert has been brought in. Then they begin to worry about their jobs, and next thing we're short of help."

"You understand, I expect to tell her about this watch I said I'd keep over the casino."

"Flint, I can't see any reason you have to go into all that. As far as I can see all it does is put Ms Andrews on the spot."

"In a way you may be right, but it goes against the grain with me not to. I think she has a right to be told," said Flint. "You hold back one thing and that leads to something else. First thing you know you've got a solid wall between you. Not exactly the open relationship I'd had in mind."

"Suit yourself, Flint," said Burney mildly. "It just looks to me like you'd be saving both yourself and Ms Andrews a lot of trouble if you'd let her think *she's* the only reason you'll be spending a lot of your working time on the casino floor."

"I'll give it some thought. We'll see."

Through the sliding glass doors that opened on to the deck, Flint spotted his six-year-old nephew, Chap, racing the family's huge nondescript dog up the sloping pathway from the beach to the deck, where he threw himself panting on top of the shaggy mongrel. Trudging along a short distance behind came Missy, three, crying with every ounce of energy in her small body.

"Don't panic, Flint. That's not a hurt sound," said Roz calmly as her brother sprang to his feet in alarm. "She's just mad that Chap and Sooperdog ran off and left her."

"Isn't she pretty little to be down there on the beach by herself?"

"She's not alone. Several families use the beach and most of us have kids, so we've hired a college student to ride herd for the summer. He lifeguards and keeps them from doing bodily harm to each other and themselves. Believe me, he's a mother saver!"

Halfway down the slope, Flint saw Missy come to a complete stop, execute a calculated tumble and land in a heap in the middle of the path, where she settled into a lusty wail.

"For heaven's sake, Chap, go back and get your sister," Roz called out crossly to the youngster on the deck.

"Never mind, Roz, I'll go," said Flint, heading out the door. His nephew, all arms and legs, came scrambling up from where he had pillowed himself on the dog's back.

"Hi, Uncle Flint!" he yelled delightedly, coming on Flint in a wild diving tackle and clutching him around the middle with a pair of wiry young arms that had the grip of a vise.

"Come on, Chap. Looks like Missy isn't going to make it without some help. Let's give her the old fireman's carry."

"Yeah! Let's give her the old fireman's carry," the boy repeated, his voice loud with excitement. He repeated the words over and over in a kind of singsong refrain as they jogged down the path together, the boy stretching himself to match the stride of the man, and the big unkempt dog running exuberant circles around them both.

"Hey, Missy, we're going to give you the old fireman's carry," Chap announced triumphantly as they neared the wailing child, whose howls had lost much of their steam. Missy sat up, her green eyes surveying the approaching man and boy woefully from a face smudged with dirt and tears.

"Uncle Flint!" she cried, and was in his arms, sniffing damply into his shirt. "Chappie and Sooper ran off."

"Yeah, but we came back. We're going to give you the old fireman's carry," Chap sang out for a last time. He turned his face up to Flint and asked plaintively, "Hey, Uncle Flint, *what's* a fireman's carry?"

Setting his little niece on her feet, Flint bent down and crossed Chap's arms, then crossed his own and took the boy's hands in his to make a seat—a very unbalanced seat, albeit. Missy, sensible child that she was, balked when her brother ordered her to climb into it and put her arms around their necks.

"I want to ride on Uncle's neck," she announced flatly.

"No you don't. We're going to carry you the way the firemen take people out of a burning building," Chap insisted angrily. "Don't be such a baby."

"I'm not a baby," declared Missy.

The impracticality of a makeshift chair formed by two such disparate bodies as his and Chap's had become apparent to Flint the moment the words caught his nephew's fancy. Only the appearance of two youngsters about Chap's age and size averted a donnybrook.

Promptly losing all interest in his sister, Chap called out, "Hey, you guys, I bet you don't know how to do a fireman's carry." Letting go of his uncle's hands, he tore off to join his friends.

Flint hoisted his niece onto his shoulders and started up the pathway to the house at a dogtrot. Missy bounced and giggled joyfully, hanging on for dear life by clutching his hair with both hands.

At the deck, Flint looked back over his shoulder to see that Chap and one of the boys had succeeded in getting the other boy seated uncertainly on their crossed arms with a stranglehold around their necks, and the three were making a kind of crablike progress down the pathway to the beach.

A short time later as he was taking a late-morning run along a meandering mountain path within easy access of the casino, Flint again considered Burney's suggestion about what he should and should not tell Lia in regard to his functions at the Goldorado. Under the circumstances, perhaps Burney's advice made a certain amount of sense, he decided at last.

It did seem unnecessary, somehow, to try Lia's loyalties over something that was unlikely ever to come about, especially since Flint did not share Mansfield's opinion that trouble would soon show up again at the casino. Having disposed of a suspicious player and a suspicious dealer, it seemed reasonable to assume the problem had already been solved.

In any case, he'd promised Aaron no more than to keep an eye on the casino for a time. He'd never agreed to spy on the gambling pits, and he was even less inclined to do so now. If something did turn up while he was there, it would be time enough then for Aaron to hire a real casino detective to track down the offenders, and Flint would bow out. Time enough to tell Lia about it then. There was too much else that mattered tonight.

LIA WONDERED if he would be there that morning. She'd found herself hurrying to get to the casino early, declining Carrie's invitation to come in for a cup of coffee when she stopped at the gate house to return the soup kettle her friend had brought after Flint had fished her out of the lake. She went through the playful routine with Reilly, the doorman, bought the city newspaper, wandered up the slot machine alleys and put her change in the machine she'd visited the day before. In one quick pull of the handle her three quarters disappeared. Flint was nowhere to be seen.

Nothing was working today, but she hadn't really expected it to. The only part that mattered was the unexpected appearance of Flint, and something told her that if he didn't come now, sooner or later she was bound to see him. Meanwhile she felt a certain contentment in turning the previous day's steps into a kind of ritual.

It was late morning before she saw him. He was moving in the direction of her table from across the casino. Even at that distance, his head rising a bit above the level of the milling crowd, the features of his face were strongly defined.

She was in the act of shuffling the deck when her eyes first found him, and for a single panicky instant she imagined she was going to lose control of the cards and send them splaying across the table.

The casino was alive with weekenders. Blackjack tables out of service during the off-hours were all running full tilt. Up and down the alleys of slot machines regulars jockeyed elbow-to-elbow for positions at favorite machines. In a few minutes it would be Lia's turn to put her table in the hands of the break dealer and take her allotted time off.

I might have missed him, she thought when her facile hands had recovered from their momentary awkwardness. She finished mixing the cards and began to deal, keeping her eyes turned down to the table by an act of sheer willpower.

She didn't look up again, yet she knew the exact moment when he reached her table, knew it was his lean hard-muscled body that slipped into the last vacant chair, though she refused to raise her eyes enough to see his face. He put money on the table, and she pushed forward chips in return, but still she dared not risk the distraction of meeting the gray-green eyes she could feel willing her to look at him. She went through the motions of dealing, collecting, paying, until the relief dealer came. Then she stepped down, still not looking his way, knowing somehow that in a few steps after she left the table, Flint would be at her side.

When the moment arrived, Lia took a deep breath and looked him full in the face for the first time since he'd come on the scene. Their eyes met and held, and she smiled.

"Whew!" she exclaimed. "You don't know how near you came to putting a quick end to my casino career just now. I...I wasn't expecting you to suddenly pop up. It was unnerving. I almost dumped the cards."

"You looked all right to me. Matter of fact, you looked so cool and collected you had me worried. I thought I'd slipped your mind."

A newly arrived bus brought an influx of people

into the already busy passageway, separating them for a moment. Flint pushed his way through to her and grabbed her elbow. He steered her toward the coffee shop, where they found a quiet corner at the far end.

Flint's eyes told her he was glad to be with her. She hoped her own deep pleasure was reflected in hers. Until the waitress had taken their order for coffee there were no words between them. When she was gone, Flint leaned across the small table that separated them and brushed the back of his hand lightly across her lips.

"Long time no see," he said with such wishful ardor the foolish old cliché became suddenly fraught with sexual overtones. A prickle of pure excitement raced through her, and she caught his hand between hers and laid it against her cheek for a moment before letting it go, not without a bemused smile at her own behavior in a manner she would never have dreamed of.

"Can you have dinner with me tonight? There are some people I'd like you to meet," he said abruptly. Lia looked at him in surprise.

"I'd love to, of course. Who are the people?

"Someone I want you to know."

She gave him an answering smile, and though her voice was teasing there was a slight note of impatience in it, too, when she said, "Don't be so darned inscrutable! Tell me about them, Flint. It's a lot easier to meet strangers if you have some idea who they are and what they're apt to be like.

"Don't worry, you will have, but you have to go back to work in a few minutes. It could take a while. I'll tell you about them tonight when I pick you up."

Lia, who carried her watch in her handbag in line with the casino's no-clock rule, reached again for Flint's hand and looked at the watch on his wrist. With a shrug she gave in, but not without wondering what there was about these mysterious friends of Flint's that would take so much time to explain.

That evening Lia couldn't believe the trouble she was taking in choosing what to wear. Her dress wardrobe was limited, numbering four at the moment, and her usual practice was simply to reach in and put on the first thing she pulled out. Since she never gave closet space to a garment she wasn't crazy about or one that couldn't be dressed up or down to suit almost any occasion, it was not the haphazard action it might seem. Whatever dress she drew out was in there only because it pleased her, and it remained there until it began to look tired and she regretfully cast it out.

Even then she didn't shop for a replacement. She hated shopping, per se. She waited until she came upon something in a store or window, something a little special that she liked as much as the one she was replacing. The new dress was usually priced so outrageously she couldn't afford it except by prorating its cost over the number of years she could expect to wear it. If she paid two hundred dollars for a dress she could wear as long as four years, it was as affordable, by Lia's system, as four fifty dollar dresses that pleased her less, even if she bought a new one each year. By such rationale, Lia maintained a wardrobe that was simple, elegant, extravagant and small—and saved herself the bother of having to shop to keep it up.

Tonight she couldn't decide whether to wear the blue again, which had already won Flint's seal of approval. In the end she chose at random as usual, reaching in her closet to bring out the first thing her hand fell upon—a simple though intricately fashioned dress of silk crepe de chine woven in pale abstract splashes of bisque, sea-green, muted apricots and pinks and a smoky hyacinth blue. The price she'd paid for it had made even Lia blanch, but it was still as beautiful as the day she first wore it five years earlier. It made her feel as if she were wearing a bit of a Monet landscape.

You'll do! she told herself, giving one last backward glance at the mirror as the door knocker signaled Flint's arrival. A moment later she opened the door and saw her own approval magnified a thousand times in Flint's eyes.

Then, as if he'd heard or read her mind, his whole face rewarded her with a smile that tindered a flame deep within her and he said, "You'll do!"

By the time the car passed the Sapphire Point gate Flint had shown no sign of disclosing the identity of his friends. Lia began to wonder uneasily if he had decided to let her wing it. She would appreciate a little briefing, but she'd be damned if she'd beg for it. It wasn't the first time she'd gone into a group where she was the only stranger, but she usually knew how large a group it was going to be.

Some people... was all he'd said, meaning more than one. It could mean any number from two to a dozen or more. She wasn't able to beg, but neither was she going to sit still for any cavalier treatment at his hands.

"Is it bigger than a bread box?" she asked on a caustic note.

"Bread box?"

"Never mind. It's a line from an old TV quiz show," she explained with a fine show of patience. "I was just wondering how big a group of people I'm about to meet."

Flint flashed her a grin. " 'What's My Line?' I was watching a lot of TV in hotel rooms when that show was going strong. I'd almost forgotten."

He was stalling for time, Lia realized. She wondered what it was he wanted to tell her that he was finding hard to say.

She reached for a nice safe subject. "Where are we going to have dinner?" she asked. It was a roundabout approach to the question she really wanted to ask: "Where are we meeting your friends?"

"I was just about to get to that," said Flint. "We're having dinner at my sister's house. My sister and brother-in-law's."

For a moment Lia could find no words. Flint had told her he had a sister whom an aunt had raised, but Lia had imagined her as someone far away and involved with Flint in only the most peripheral way.

"I had no idea, Flint. Somehow I thought your sister was someone in your past. I never dreamed she lived around here."

"She doesn't, really, except during the summer. The rest of the year they live in Woodside, south of San Francisco. The house where we're headed, is about fifteen miles away on the California side of Tahoe."

"Are they both here now? Your sister and brother-in-law?"

"They're here, all of them. My brother-in-law and my nephew, Chap, and my niece, Missy, and of course my sister, Roz. You'll meet them all... my entire allotment of living relatives. I... well, I thought it was time you got to know each other. I hope you don't mind."

"Mind? I'm delighted, Flint, but almost too surprised to say so. Somehow, the way you've spoken of her, I had the idea your sister was still very young. I never imagined she was married with children."

"For something like ten years. She married my business partner and best friend—as good a friend as a man could have."

Flint's serious tone brought a moment of silence between them. Then he said, "You'll probably recognize him when you see him."

"I will?"

"You've seen him around the casino."

"He's a gambler?" asked Lia cautiously.

Flint's laugh broke the tension. "He'd like to be, but he's terrible at cards. He was so lousy he had to quit. He bought a casino instead."

"A casino?" An uneasy suspicion was taking shape in Lia's mind. "Flint...what's your brother-in-law's name?"

"Aaron Burney."

"Aaron...Burney?" she repeated. "Not the Aaron Burney who owns the Goldorado? Not the Aaron Burney I work for, Flint!"

"The same."

CHAPTER THIRTEEN

IN THE FIRST STUNNED SECOND after she learned that Flint's brother-in-law was Aaron Burney, her employer, Lia had only one thought: she was glad she hadn't told Flint the entire reason she'd taken a dealer's job at the casino. During the short time since the rescue in the lake she'd learned that Flint had a fine-honed sense of honor. She guessed now that he might feel obliged to tell Burney there was a dealer on the Goldorado payroll who was using his blackjack tables as a research field for her psychology master's study on compulsive gambling. Lia had observed an almost paranoid sensitivity among people of the casino establishment when the subject of problem gambling came up, and she was sure her employer's reaction would be negative. If Burney found out it could cost her her job.

"I really have Burney to thank for meeting you," Flint told her. "I wouldn't be here if he hadn't asked me to come up and look over the hotel and casino."

"You mean you're not here for the gambling?" Lia asked. She was stunned at the force of the relief that rushed through her. She certainly hadn't been happy believing Flint was a high-rolling gambler, but she hadn't realized it had troubled her so much.

"You thought I was one of the gambling crowd?" he asked in a surprised voice, and hastened to explain that when his brother-in-law bought the Goldorado, there had to be changes made in order for the business to move ahead. Flint's purpose in being there was, in his own words, merely "to give Burney moral support."

"Aaron and I have bought and salvaged so many businesses together over the past ten years that he thinks whatever he goes into has to be done in tandem. It's become almost a superstition with him."

"Don't tell me you're a silent partner in the Goldorado?" asked Lia, alarmed. It was bad enough to have Flint's brother-in-law as her employer, let alone Flint himself.

"Hardly!" exclaimed Flint dryly. "Not that Aaron didn't try to talk me into it. He wanted our firm, Tancer and Burney, to buy it, but I wouldn't go along. To get him off my back as much as anything I agreed to come up here as a consultant. It's beginning to look like the best move of my life— only one of many debts I owe my brother-in-law."

"Owe him? It looks to me like the benefits are on his side."

"Not the only one I care about, which is you."

Her head turned to look at him. His eyes left the road and met hers with a glance that embraced her and sent her heart into orbit before he gave his attention back to his driving.

They had left the main stream of traffic, and the car was snaking its way upward around a boulder-studded cliff with a rocky drop on the lakeside. Flint gave his full attention to the narrow two-lane highway as the car approached and moved along a high narrow rib of land like the backbone of some gargantuan beast.

Below them on one side lay a loop of brilliant green water. Except for a channel connecting it with the main body of the lake at the far end, it was surrounded by steep forested slopes that dropped to a scalloped shoreline with a thread of beach. On the other side, hundreds of feet below, lay a small blue lake like a glistening jewel in the bottom of a dark green cup. Lia drew in her breath at the sheer beauty of the scene.

"It's awesome," she said softly. "What's the small lake to our left?"

"It's called Fallen Leaf," Flint told her. "To our right is Emerald Bay."

"So that's the celebrated Emerald Bay! If I'd had any idea how beautiful it is I'd have made a point of getting around here before."

"You mean this is the first time you've seen it? Well, that won't do. It's my favorite part of the lake. We'll stop at the vista point up the way where you can get a much better look at it."

With a mix of skill and caution, Flint piloted the car along the narrow road that wound around the landlocked end of the lake. Fallen Leaf Lake was lost from view and Lia turned her full attention to the sparkling bay until the click of the signal light told her they were approaching the vista point.

Flint slowed and pulled across the highway into a small parking area beyond which mammoth outcroppings of granite marked the cliff's edge. There was not another car in sight.

"We're in luck," he said. "It's late enough for us to have the place to ourselves. During the day it's mobbed."

He turned off the motor and got out of the small car, coming around to her side to open her door. Taking her hand he led her across the sand-dusted lot and down a path of hard-packed earth until they stood alone in a niche between two great rocks that overlooked the bay and a small portion of the lake beyond.

In the afterglow of the sun, now hidden by the great wall of the Sierras, motorboats cut ribbons of wake through the pristine water, and an occasional sailboat dipped white canvas in the early-evening breeze.

Lia drew a deep breath, filling her lungs with alpine air, her attention fixed on a small, rocky, timbered island that rose up out of the lake like an Arthurian castle a few hundred yards offshore on the near side of the bay.

"Fannette Island," Flint told her. "On the shore of the mainland is an impressive Nordic château some early lumber baron built for his wife. There is a teahouse on the island where the visiting honchos boated in to take tea with his baroness around the turn of the century, I understand. It's now a government-run museum, open to anyone who's willing to hike a mile or so down to it and pay a small fee. Vikingsholm Castle, it's called.''

As he talked, Flint eased his body back lazily to lean against the giant rock behind him, his legs spread-eagled to fit its curve. His arms reached out to encircle her waist and carry her with him.

He was more upright than reclining, his feet wide apart and planted solidly on the ground. His movement lifted Lia off her feet so the full weight of her body was upon his. His hands moved from her waist to fit around her buttocks and press her to him until, in the rapture of the moment, they seemed almost as one. Her body thrilled to the rise of his pleasure and to the soft sound of yearning from deep in his throat. She knew they must stop and wondered how they possibly could.

"Flint..." she managed to whisper, but the words were silenced as his mouth captured hers. In the next instant they were locked in a deep ravening kiss that seemed to plunder the depths of her being. When the pleasure of the kiss grew into the exquisite pain of desire they drew apart, only to return and kiss again.

Motionless, as if suspended in time, they finally drew back and looked into each other's eyes, promising, asking questions, seeking answers.

"Shouldn't we go?" Lia asked reluctantly, knowing they should, knowing that if they were to find fulfillment it would not be on a ledge of rock ten feet off a public road with a sheer drop of hundreds of feet on its open side.

"No," he said, his voice rough with feeling. He bent forward to the neckline of the low-cut dress, his hair brushing her throat as his lips touched the small valley between her breasts. With a spasm of delight she felt the soft flick of his tongue tasting her flesh.

Her body swayed off-balance for a moment, and a sudden shiver of fear raced through her as her eyes caught a glimpse of the blue water far below them, just beyond the ledge a few feet away from where they stood.

"Flint. It's a long way down."

He caught her to him and they swayed together as he took her lips in a last deliberate kiss before letting her go. She turned and ran ahead of him up the well-worn earthen steps, not daring to look back until she reached the car. There she turned to watch the tall athletic body move toward her with easy grace, an unruly lock of hair across his forehead rising and falling with a kind of devilish insouciance in the mountain breeze. She felt a rebirth of the sensual excitement of the moment before.

When he reached her side, he tipped up her face and kissed her with a sweet light touch, quite unlike his previous kisses.

"Nice parting shot," she murmured.

"That's where you're wrong, my sweet. That's a reminder we still have unfinished business on the agenda tonight."

And of course they did have, thought Lia, back in the car again. The situation between them was fast becoming untenable. Since Flint had never left any doubt about his own course of action, she knew the future direction of the affair was entirely hers.

"Just what do your sister and brother-in-law know about me, Flint?" she asked. She had regained her composure, and the car was moving again.

"They know you're a dealer at the casino, and that I've never brought a woman around to meet them before. You wouldn't believe how much my sister can read into such a simple fact as that," said Flint, turning his eyes briefly from the hairpin road to give her the teasing, side-slanted smile that did unreasonable things to her pulse. "And well she should!" The emotional undertone of the remark told her far more than the words alone. "You'll have to forgive her if she seems a little presumptuous. She's a very direct person, my sister, Roz."

"How does...Mr. Burney feel about having a psychologist working as a dealer, Flint?"

"I didn't tell him, or my sister. I also didn't tell them that you are incredibly beautiful, or that I nearly drowned you, or that I've hardly thought of anything else since I fished you out of the lake."

"Come on, Flint. You told them something!"

"I haven't the words in my vocabulary to say what I want to say about you, Lia...about the woman I've waited for most of my adult life. They'll have to see for themselves."

Bathed in the warmth of his words, Lia looked at him, only half believing. "You mean all you've told your sister and brother-in-law about me is that I'm a dealer at the casino your brother-in-law owns?"

"The only thing that matters to Roz and Aaron is that you are someone special to me. The rest is all yours, Lia. Tell them whatever you like." The trust implicit in the words and voice brought an unexpected tightening to her throat.

WHATEVER UNEASE she might have anticipated in her first meeting with Roz and Aaron Burney never materialized. Flint's sister, whom Lia liked at once, gave her a candid appraisal with eyes so like her brother's Lia might have found the shrewd scrutiny somewhat unnerving had the eyes not immediately registered warm approval of what they saw. It soon became apparent, too, that Burney was prepared to look kindly on anyone Rozlyn liked. It was as if he hardly saw Lia except through his wife's eyes.

Though she and Flint's sister were "Lia" and "Roz" at once, Lia felt constrained to address Flint's brother-in-law as Mr. Burney. She was relieved when he erased that stricture of their employer-employee relationship by immediately insisting she call him Aaron. Introductions over, Aaron took cocktail orders and repaired to a built-in bar at the far end of the kitchen-family room to mix them.

"Come on, Flint. You can help me tend bar and give Lia a chance to watch the best cook in the world in action," he said as he turned away. As he moved to join his brother-in-law, Flint laid a hand on Lia's shoulders in a passing caress. His fingers stroked up from the base of her neck and gently ruffled her hair, sending a tingle along her spine.

Momentarily undone by the passing endearment, Lia turned away to post herself near the butcher-block island where Rozlyn worked, hoping her sudden inner response didn't show on her face. It took but an instant to see that Roz was much too preoccupied with her chores to take notice of her brother's surreptitious caress.

Refusing to let her senses linger in the afterglow of Flint's touch, Lia absorbed herself in watching the elaborate preparations that were going into the cocktail food. Clearly this wasn't the sort of raw vegetables, chips and cheese and dry-roasted nuts affair she presided over herself, Lia thought ruefully.

She watched curiously as Roz popped a cookie sheet filled with assorted hors d'oeuvres into an oven, then filled hollowed-out ice cubes with caviar and arranged them on a bed of crushed ice, surrounding them with thin slices of black bread, small bowls of lemon wedges, sieved eggs and finely chopped parsley. A second small tray was decked out with bite-size puff shells stuffed with deviled crab. It was all done with a kind of loving care. Lia, whose culinary efforts tended toward steamed vegetables, broiled meat and fish and simple dishes that could be cooked in a wok, was spellbound by such rites of preparation.

A short time later as she watched Aaron Burney wolf down crab puffs and sausage-stuffed mushrooms and an incredibly rich pâté jeweled with pistachio nuts, all created from scratch by Roz, she had a clue to the origins of his extended waistline and the somewhat Churchillian curves of his face.

"It's simply superb, Roz, but don't you have to spend half of your life in the kitchen if you're in the habit of coming up with miracles like these?" she asked as she bit into a generous dab of the fine beluga caviar on a sliver of black bread and followed it with a sip of white wine.

Rozlyn shrugged. "I suppose I do, but Aaron does love good food, and I've puttered around kitchens most of my life until I've gotten to be a pretty good cook. I'd have to be really stupid not to be. I've probably taken every cooking course that's offered in the Bay Area."

Lia hesitated before she said with a touch of awe, "But you must really like doing it."

Roz's brow furrowed. Lia realized the woman was facing the concepts of like or dislike in relation to one of her basic functions for the first time, and she wondered what she would choose to say.

"A moment ago I said I was pretty good at it, which is not true. I was just being modest," Roz said slowly, as if examining herself for an accurate answer. "The truth is, I'm *very* good at it, and yes, I guess I really do like to cook, though I'm not exactly sure why. It's a lot of work. Maybe I enjoy it because I am so good, and I do like to please Aaron. Don't people usually like to do what they're good at? I suppose the reason I like to cook is that it's the only thing I really do well."

Besides pleasing Aaron, thought Lia with an inner smile and a rising respect and affection for the other woman.

A banshee wail from far down the path to the beach heralded the impending arrival of a sturdy boy Lia took to be Flint's nephew, Chap. He came scrambling up the steps to the deck a few moments later with a huge, incredibly shaggy dog hard on his heels. Flint tackled the animal inches before his black nose hit the caviar.

"You ran off and left Missy again!" accused Roz. "Go back and get her, Chap."

But Flint, turning the dog over to the boy's keeping, intervened. "I'll go after Missy. Chap, you take this beast around to the back and feed him before he gobbles up the caviar."

After that, it was an evening of ups and downs.

Upon her arrival atop Flint's shoulders, Missy

would not be put down. She buried her face in his hair and refused to look up until forcibly removed by Flint. He set her gently onto her feet, whereupon she seized him around his legs and clung like a determined barnacle.

"Uncle Flint brought a friend of his to see you, Missy," her mother said coaxingly. "Aren't you going to say hi to her?"

Flint's grin in Lia's direction was apologetic. He bent over to release the child's grip on his legs, and the chubby arms flew around his neck. They made an appealing picture—the splendidly stalwart man balanced on the balls of his feet holding the pretty curly-haired little girl in the circle of his arms. Then Flint said something quietly in her ear, and the child responded in a sulky mumble that translated uncomfortably in Lia's ears.

"No. I don't like her."

Missy was promptly shipped off to another part of the house, where the family's part-time sitter, Bessie, waited to feed the children and put them to bed.

As the little girl was whisked away by her mother, she turned her rosebud face to Lia for the first time. To Lia's discomfiture the child sported as baleful a look as she had ever seen. It was all too clear whom Missy blamed for her immediate woes. Disappearing from view, she stuck her tongue out at Lia, a malevolent gesture unseen by her father and uncle, who, in the sudden quiet of the child's departure, had picked up their conversation where it had been dropped.

Unnerved, Lia rummaged frantically in her mind for remnants of a child-psychology course she'd taken four years earlier. The child felt threatened. She felt threatened because one, Lia was a stranger, and she was afraid of strangers or two, she feared Lia would replace her in her Uncle Flint's affections. Or she *didn't* feel threatened, and her actions were a bid for attention. Or none of the above, Lia finished wryly.

The fact was, Lia had had very little to do with children since she was a child herself—an only child, at that. As a psychologist her interests had been focused on those who had reached the age of discretion. Even so, she'd taken copious class notes and put together a sizable store of reference material to earn her usual A in the child-psychology course, and she was shocked now to find how little she'd retained.

As a psychologist she was at a loss. As an outsider in the Burney home she entertained the traitorous thought that Missy was nothing more complex than a spoiled brat.

"I hope you'll excuse Missy's little tantrum," Burney's voice broke in upon her thoughts. "I keep telling Roz she's got to get tough with her."

Though mildly stated, the comment raised Lia's hackles. *She's* got to get tough with her! she repeated silently with growing indignation. Just where did Aaron Burney get off dumping the responsibility all on Roz!

"Maybe you're right. She was pretty obnoxious just now," Flint agreed absently to Lia's further dismay. She was framing a rejoinder to Flint that wouldn't reflect too harshly on her host and employer when the matter was lost in the rambunctious return of Chap and Sooperdog.

To her chagrin Lia found her exuberant acceptance by Chap almost as upsetting as his sister's open hostility.

"Hey, wanna see me stand on my head?" he called out, and did a wobbly headstand to the noisy accompaniment of the dog's barking without waiting for an answer. Seven headstands later, after Lia had run out of ways to tell him how good he was, Chap lost interest in the stunt. He also lost interest in Lia.

"Hey, Uncle Flint, come see the neat fort us guys built," he cried out, jumping to his feet and tugging insistently at Flint's hand.

"Don't be long about it," Roz called from the kitchen. "Bessie says she wants you in for dinner in ten minutes."

As he allowed himself to be pulled from his chair, Flint turned to Lia, reaching down to take her hand. "You don't want to miss seeing a neat fort, do you?"

"In these shoes? No thanks. Tell me about it."

"Will you mind?" Flint asked, looking down at her, loving her with his eyes. "Headstands are but

a small part of this guy's gymnastic repertoire.
Who knows what I may be saving you from?''

Watching the man and boy move off down the
path to the beach side by side, Chap's face turned
up to Flint's in rapt attention, Lia felt again the
swell of emotion that she'd felt as she watched
Flint shelter an unhappy Missy in his arms a short
time ago. She wondered what he and his nephew
were talking about. What did one say to a child?
she asked herself helplessly, and realized that tonight was the first time she'd had anything to do
with one since she'd worked as a flight attendant.
Even then, she'd usually managed to trade off
with one of her co-workers when an unaccom-
panied child was put on the plane in the care of the
flight attendants.

Though she was not at first aware she was doing
it, Lia marked time as she made small talk with
Aaron Burney and waited for the man and boy to
reappear at the spot on the down slope to the
beach where they had dropped from sight.

Though critical at his abdication from the disci-
plinary responsibilities of fatherhood, Lia found
she liked Burney nonetheless. He was a delight-
fully shrewd and entertaining man who frankly
adored his wife, took a rather detached and
fatuous pride in his children and considered Flint
Tancer a true genius. Under the soothing effect of
Burney's social grace, Lia ventured to tell him, in
effect, what she'd already told Flint of her background. He accepted the fact that she was a psy-

chologist without a blink. She wondered if he would take it so coolly if she was to tell him she was using his casino as the research field for an academic treatise on the pathology of gambling that might eventually reach the press. It wasn't something she cared to test.

Flint and Chap were gone but a short time when they reappeared on the path. Flint's head was turned down to the boy, who kept up with his uncle's long easy stride by taking a step and a skip to every step of Flint's. It was Flint who was talking, she knew, though she couldn't make out his words. What she heard was the music of his deep baritone, punctuated occasionally by a burst of Chap's high-pitched laugher. *What* did they find to talk about—an adult and a child? she wondered again with a kind of envy.

"He really likes kids," remarked Burney admiringly, as he watched the two approach.

This was a new side to Flint, and Lia found it strangely endearing and at the same time disturbing. It was a side she wasn't altogether sure she was prepared to think about.

But it was there, hiding in some discreet cell of her psyche, all through Roz's tenderloin of beef bordelaise with broiled tomatoes and mushrooms and fresh new green peas, through her tangy lemon mousse; all through Flint's zany, self-deprecating account of his own heroics in the drowning-rescue of Lia from the lake; all through the warm goodbyes at the end of the evening when

Roz begged Lia to come for lunch on her next day off "when the kids are at the beach, and the men are gone, and we can really talk."

Then, as they started off in the car alone together for the first time all evening, Burney's words came back to her: *He really likes kids!* The thought she'd tucked away, held as tenuously as a jack-in-the-box, sprang out: Flint liked children. She wished she was as sure of herself.

Did it matter? she asked herself. Did they have to like the same things to like each other? It would only matter if she and Flint were thinking of marriage. It would only matter if she was in love with Flint.

But she knew, suddenly, that it did matter, and she was afraid.

They drove back through the long dark corridors of trees and over the treacherously winding road on through the glittering lights of the south-shore gambling community and the gates of Sapphire Point, hardly talking, alone in their own thoughts.

In front of the house Flint turned off the car motor and reached over to cup her face in the palms of his hands, tipping it up in order to look directly into her eyes.

"You're wrong. You are dead wrong," he said softly. "I don't know if you learned it in some cockamamy psychology course or it's your own idea, but you're wrong, wrong, wrong."

"Wrong?" echoed Lia, mystified.

"You told me there is no such thing as love at first sight, and I'm telling you, you are wrong. I know the exact moment I fell in love with you. I saw that lovely body streak off the end of the dock and cut the surface of the water like a sleek sea otter, and I was in love. Tonight when I realized I loved you, I knew it happened then."

She wasn't ready for it. A shiver of fear coursed through her. It was too soon. She was only now getting her life back on track after the debacle with Toby. This time there could be no mistakes. Yet to reject Flint was unthinkable.

He held her face in his hands, eyes questioning, mouth slanted in the wry suggestion of a smile. When she said nothing, he leaned forward and kissed her gently upon the lips.

"I'm rushing you. Forgive me. I'm in a terrible hurry. Tonight all at once I knew beyond a doubt that I love you, Lia...with all the love I've been storing up through all these years. I want to give it to you. Now. I don't want to wait," he said quietly.

Without willing it, not even knowing she was going to, Lia said, "Oh, Flint, I love you, too."

"Oh God!" he whispered hoarsely, his voice constricted with emotion. His hands dropped from her face. "I never expected...Oh, my sweet Lia. Let's get married."

"Now?"

"Now? Of course *now*! That's the thing about this crazy, wonderful state of Nevada. We can drive out the gate and go a mile in either direction and get ourselves married to each other in less than twenty minutes from portal to portal,'' Flint crowed exuberantly.

"Flint, I love you, but I can't get married like that."

"Why not, if you love me?"

"Of course I love you, but that doesn't mean I'm ready to marry you in the next thirty seconds. There are too many things we should know about each other before we can even think about getting married."

"I know all I need to know to love you, sweetheart. Everything else I'll take on trust."

"It's not a matter of trust, Flint. I *do* trust you. I trust you with all my heart."

Flint sighed. "But you won't marry me."

"I didn't say I won't marry you. What I meant is, not yet." She opened the car door and slipped out, knowing that in this there was no compromise, yet with a heart so full of her own love for Flint and his love for her she didn't dare stay longer.

Flint caught her at the front door as she turned the key to unlock it. She didn't resist, and let him enfold her in his arms as she stood with her back to the door. They clung together for a long hungry moment as if to draw sustenance from the embrace.

"Lia, Lia, I've waited so long for you."

He was speaking, she knew, of his ideal woman,

but in these few short days how could he be so certain she was the one? Would she still be the right one if he guessed this newly discovered uneasiness she had when it came to children? She slipped her arms around his neck and hugged herself to him, almost afraid to let him go.

"I love you, Flint. I really do love you." It was the best she could do. They'd each made a declaration of love and trust to each other. It would have to do until they found the answers to the other questions.

"Are we going to make love?" he asked bluntly, letting her go.

But he didn't wait for words. As if to find the answer in her body he drew her closer and covered her mouth with his lips. Whatever she might have said was forgotten in the urgency of his kiss, and her own lips softened and clung, hungering for his seeking tongue.

Oh yes, Flint! Oh yes. Yes! In an ecstasy of longing, her body molded itself to his, leaving no need for words to give testimony to the depth of her desire or to confirm the urgency of his.

Poised there in delicate balance, Lia's weight pressed tightly against the unlocked door she'd left ajar when she turned the key, they were obliged to pull apart or lose their equilibrium as the door gave inward. The moment of imbalance was suddenly a metaphor for the uncertainty in Lia's mind.

If he only hadn't brought up the question of marriage!

She could see the hurt in his eyes as she drew away from him, and she felt a stab of pain.

"I thought the missing ingredient until now was love," he said.

"Not a missing ingredient," she said softly. "I do love you, Flint. I do. I do. I want to make love with you, but I... I'm just not ready yet. I love you too much to take a chance on any mistakes this time. I... I don't think I could handle it."

A look of anger and frustration clouded his eyes, and she felt a moment of terrible doubt.

"Flint..." she whispered, reaching up to touch his face, but he caught her hand and put it aside.

"If you love me, don't keep me waiting forever, Lia," he said gruffly. "I'm not a patient man."

He turned on his heel and left.

CHAPTER FOURTEEN

SHE WATCHED HIM walk out into the darkness, poignantly aware of the crisp anger in his step, wanting desperately to call him back. Alone in bed the bright jewel of her love for him, made brighter by the love he'd just declared, was wonderful to think about, but it lacked the passionate affirmation of their bodies to make it come to life.

She'd been wrong to let him go, she'd told herself in those first hours of solitary sleeplessness. The moment he'd told her he loved her, her own love had come bubbling forth as if waiting only for his words to set it free. Her first thought had been a powerful desire to reveal to this man she loved the most intimate secrets of Lia Andrews—the inner private person. Her whole being overflowed with welcome. She wanted nothing so much as to share their love on every level.

Until Flint walked into her life she'd never believed in love at first sight. Her infatuation with Toby had destroyed any such notion. Infatuation was easy. True love took time. These were axioms with her, reminding her constantly to go slowly, telling her she could not be sure so soon that what she felt for this man was love. She and Flint hardly knew each other.

Then, in a dazzling moment tonight, she knew she loved him. She was as sure as she'd ever been of anything in her life. If they'd seized the moment, which had been her passionate intention. . . if they had gone together into the house, into her bedroom, into her bed. . . .

But then he'd said, "Let's get married," and instantly there was a new dimension to be considered. No longer was he simply the man she loved, the man she wanted to take as her lover. He was the man she loved, and he wanted her to marry him. The unexpected new element changed the rules. Love wasn't enough. Now there were irreconcilable differences to think about.

Irreconcilable differences. The catch-all term of the divorce courts. She'd seen too much of it as a psychologist in her family-counseling service. Differences, for instance, such as the matter of having or not having children. Differences nobody thought to mention until after the vows were said.

In silent reproach she cried out against the impatience of the man: *Darn you, Flint, why did you have to rush it? Couldn't you just let things take their course?* Love at first sight was one thing. Marriage at first sight was something else. Somehow she must make Flint see that all she could give him for the time being was her love. She had to make him understand that marriage necessarily would take longer. Lovers, yes. Marriage, no.

On this nebulous note she fell into an exhausted sleep long after midnight and dreamed of gremlin-like children who bobbed around her in gymnastic contortions and stuck out their tongues at her.

Shortly before 10:00 A.M. she awoke to peer out at her clock with heavy-lidded eyes.

"Oh, no!" she cried, scrambling out of bed in a mad dash for the shower. Groaning at the prospect of putting in an appearance an hour late for her shift with no better excuse than having slept through her alarm she turned the shower to Cool and let the full force of the chilly water splash over her head.

She was out of the shower, half-dressed and fully awake when she remembered that today her shift was scheduled to start at eleven instead of ten as it had on the day before. Though she didn't slow down she breathed a sigh of relief, glad for the casino practice of staggering shifts in order to have an almost continuous change of dealers every hour throughout the day. Even so, it would take some doing to get her to work on time.

Beyond a smile and a wave of her hand in passing she had no time for pleasantries with Reilly that morning as she hurried past him across the casino and up the stairs to check in with the pencil man. She was at her table ready to take over with exactly two minutes to spare.

She was not surprised to see Flint in the casino that morning, watching at a table in one of the other gambling pits. He had told her that he had finished looking into the operations of the Gold-orado hotel and its restaurants and bars and would be turning his attention to the casino.

She remembered her brief conversation the night before with Aaron Burney while Flint was off with his son. He'd made it clear that he pre-ferred she didn't mention to other employees that Flint had a connection with the casino or what it was he was doing there. The last would be easy, she thought wryly, since she wasn't very sure her-self. As for the other, she wondered if the two of them were expected to pretend they'd never met when their paths crossed in the casino, as they were about to now.

If that was what Burney expected he was to be disappointed, she saw with amusement. Flint looked her way and smiled at her, that wonderful rakish smile she found so unsettling, and raised a hand in a casual salute. She might have known that Flint Tancer was his own man, not one to let Aaron Burney or anyone else maneuver him in a direction he didn't want to go.

He took a place at her table a short time later, bought chips and began to play. Though he was only one of the four players she had to deal to, she found her attention focused again and again upon him to the exclusion of the others. In spite of her-self her eyes kept following the long, square-fingered hands as they played the cards so adroit-ly, yet with a kind of lazy indifferent grace. She tried to ignore the tingle that raced through her body when the memory of his smooth hard palms lifting her face to his slipped unbidden into her mind.

He gambled with the expertise of an old pro, Lia observed uneasily. He watched the fall of the cards, knew when the odds were with him, and bet accordingly. The cards were against him today. In spite of his skill, he was obliged twice to buy more chips to stay in the game.

Until now Lia had had no problem maintaining dealer detachment. She'd never cared much how the cards fell. But suddenly all that changed. Lia's objectivity mysteriously vanished. She was partisan. When Flint tipped up his down cards to take a look at what he'd been dealt she found herself holding her breath, unreasonably hoping she'd given him an ace and a face card for a sure-winning blackjack, or at the very least two face cards or a pair of tens. When he flicked the corner of his cards along the table in the universal hit gesture to ask for another card, she willed herself to deal one that would fit with the two she'd dealt him facedown, the right card to make him a winner.

Sheer nonsense, she knew, but she loved the man. Of course she wanted him to win. She also knew that she'd better get a hold on herself before she made some fool mistake at the expense of one of the other players and was reported to the pit boss, Ed Shields.

She welcomed the relief dealer gladly when time came for her hourly break and hurried away from

her slot almost in flight. A few steps away from
the table Flint fell in step beside her, as Lia had
hoped he would, and she turned to smile at him.

"You're going to get me fired, Flint Tancer!
When you're playing at my table I keep forgetting
you're not the only one there," she informed him,
at the same time telling him with her eyes that she
loved him, letting him know without saying the
words that she was sorry the way last night had
ended, that she hadn't wanted it so.

"Oh?" The monosyllable carried a sardonic
query that brought a swift questioning glance
from Lia, and she saw in the crooked half smile
that for all she'd put into her eyes, she had told
him nothing. Nor was there a message in the un-
fathomable eyes that met hers. Neither anger nor
love. She could not call them hostile or even cold.
What she saw was a kind of impersonal friendli-
ness that simply did not acknowledge that anything special had gone between them. It told her
nothing. It was as if a curtain had been drawn between the Flint who had offered himself to her
with passionate fervor the night before and the
Flint he was willing to present to her today.

IT WAS THE FIRST of several visits Flint paid Lia's
table during the next few days, and though she
grew used to his presence as a player and was soon
able to carry on as if he meant no more to her than
any of the other players, the change in his manner
toward her became more and more disconcerting.

He was in the casino every day, betting steadily. For the most part he frequented her pit, making the rounds of all the tables, yet often playing at hers. Occasionally he appeared at her elbow when she walked away from the table for her break and joined her in the crowded cafeteria for a cup of coffee. When he learned she would be dealing the noon-to-eight shift for the rest of the week he suggested they have dinner together at one or another of the casino's restaurants where he normally ate, and he took to dropping by her table to meet her at the end of her working day. Under the prevailing circumstances, as Flint explained them, Lia gave in to his insistence that these dinners be on the house.

"It's in the contract," he assured her with a grin. "I don't charge Aaron for doing his trouble-shooting, and he agrees to give me a penthouse suite and the best food in the house for self and guests."

One early morning after Lia declined his invitation to run on the beach and Flint refused to swim in the lake, they played tennis together. They discovered in the first set that they were evenly matched, and the tenuous compromise became a daily practice.

It was all froth. . and frustration. There was no further mention of marriage and, except at tennis, no word of love. Flint was witty, urbane, entertaining, considerate. He was also maddeningly impersonal.

I might as well be his maiden aunt! Lia wailed in silent dismay each night as he walked her from the Monte Carlo Room, the casino's top-of-the-line dining spot, to her car in the employees' parking lot. There he would give her a light kiss on the lips and walk back alone across the floodlit lot toward the casino as she drove away.

That dispassionate kiss was the index to their present relationship. She didn't need his careful evasion whenever she lifted her arms to embrace him to remind her that she was the one who had set the pattern for the present state of affairs by sending him away after he'd paid her the highest tribute a man can pay a woman.

He'd asked her to share his life. The question she hadn't expected—hadn't even considered before the moment it was asked—knocked her completely off keel. Stumbling, inarticulate, she'd rejected him, and then compounded the injury with ambivalence an instant later by putting him off when he asked for her love.

Looking back on those few minutes she couldn't believe she had sent him away as she had without talking it out, without making sure he understood how she felt.

Yet how could she have made him understand something it had taken her most of the night just to begin to understand herself?

She had hurt him, she realized bleakly, and it seemed the canny Flint Tancer wasn't eager to risk taking any lumps from her again. He made no new overtures, and twice when she'd suggested he follow her home to Sapphire Point in his car after dinner he found reasons not to. He was clearly of a mind to see her only in public places until.... Until what? And when?

How could the problems between them ever be resolved if the only times they were together were at public places such as the Goldorado and the tennis courts? Even in the candlelit quiet of the Monte Carlo Room they never seemed to be alone. The fact that Flint signed the dinner checks with the number of the penthouse suite had not gone unnoticed by the dining-room staff. Lia never had to look to know that a waiter hovered over them, alert for small services to perform.

Oh, Flint, what have I done? she thought desperately, about to drive off to the Sapphire Point house alone again at the end of another day in which they'd been with each other but seemed miles apart. They'd had dinner together at the casino. At the car Flint had given her another of those sterile good-night kisses under the bright lights of the employees' parking lot and seen her safely behind the wheel. He stood by, waiting for her to start the car and be on her way. As the car began to move he raised his hand to detain her. She braked, and he stepped nearer and leaned down to the window.

"By the way," he said, "I won't be seeing you tomorrow. I have to drive into San Francisco on business. I'll look for you at the casino when I get back the following day.''

She felt herself sag with disappointment.

''You won't find me at the casino. Tomorrow and the next are my days off.'' Then, as an afterthought she said, ''Your sister has invited me to lunch at their house tomorrow.''

''Enjoy yourself. Rozlyn's a great cook.''

With talk like that they might as well be nothing more than casual acquaintances, thought Lia with a flare of annoyance at them both.

In a stubborn now-or-never desperation she said, ''When you get back, Flint, will you have dinner with me?''

''Why, yes. I'd expected we'd go on as before,'' he stated matter-of-factly. ''Since it's your day off, if you'd rather, we don't have to eat at the casino.''

''You're darned right we don't,'' interrupted Lia snappishly, stung by his flat-out acceptance of the situation as it stood. She glared at him, daring him to refuse her now. ''We're going to sit on the deck at Sapphire Point and watch the sun set, and I'm going to cook dinner. I'll look for you around seven.''

Easing up on the brake, she let the car begin to move. Flint took a quick step back.

''Lia, wait,'' he called out, but she touched the accelerator lightly and kept going. Looking into the rearview mirror she saw him standing in the bright floodlight of the parking lot, a tall, well-built man, hand raised to his head in a gesture of puzzlement as he watched her go. For a moment she was of half a mind to turn back, but a sudden perversity would not let her. She'd waited four days for him to say something. Now he could jolly well wait for her.

FROM WHERE THEY SAT on the Burney deck in the early afternoon the following day, Lia could look over the manzanita-covered slope through which a footpath meandered to the beach a short distance below. With only the sounds of the children playing down by the water and the rise and fall of Rozlyn's voice as she talked to break the quiet, it was a scene of genteel domestic tranquillity.

Lunch, from the chilled cream-of-artichoke soup to the freshly baked, warm-from-the-oven cherry pie, had been another of Rozlyn's culinary triumphs. Now the two women sat in the shade of the table umbrella with their pie and coffee, and Roz met Lia's circumspect curiosity with a ready account of her own sheltered life under the loving protection of a maiden aunt during years when Flint was junketed around from one gambling spa to another in the free-wheeling care of their father.

"For a long time after they split us up we missed each other a lot. Mama was gone, and I missed her. I missed Flint," Roz confided on a wistful note, and Lia felt compassion for the motherless little girl torn from her brother. At the same time she felt a keen tenderness for the young Flint, who'd spent the sensitive years of his adolescence on the periphery of a gambling world that was callously indifferent to the needs of a lonely boy.

"I missed Papa, too," Roz confessed defensively after a moment. "In spite of the way it may look, he really loved us. The only thing wrong with Papa was that he couldn't stop gambling."

"I guess it's not surprising Flint plays blackjack like an old pro," Lia said regretfully.

Roz darted a surprised glance at her. "Have you seen him play?"

Sensing anxiety in the other's question, Lia was anxious, too. She skittered away from telling Rozlyn that her brother had been gambling heavily every day. She'd sold herself on the idea that Flint's gambling was a necessary part of whatever it was he was doing at the casino for Burney, but she wasn't sure enough of her ground to sell the idea to his sister.

As she answered Rozlyn she modified the truth to make it more reassuring than the case might be.

"Oh, I've seen him play at my table," she said in her best offhand manner. "We've been having dinner together at the casino, and sometimes when he gets there a few minutes early he'll play a few hands until the dealer for the next shift takes over."

Rozlyn sniffed. "Well, don't encourage him. When my aunt was alive she worried all the time that Flint was going the way of Papa, and of course I did, too. You know, he put himself through college with his winnings from blackjack and stud poker—a lot of which came from Aaron. That's where they met, so I can't knock it. If it hadn't been for the gambling, he and Aaron would never have become partners, and I would never have known Aaron.''

''You don't worry about Flint's gambling now?''

Roz shook her head. ''Heavens, there's no cause! He graduated from college and quit gambling the same day. I really don't think he ever cared much about it anyhow. It just happened to be the easiest, quickest way to make enough money to get himself through college. I heard him tell Aaron one time that he didn't give a damn if he never set foot in a gambling casino or saw another deck of cards for the rest of his life. I'm sure he meant it.''

''It's a little ironic, isn't it, that he's back in the casino again.''

''He wouldn't be there if Aaron hadn't needed him on the business end,'' Roz assured her. ''Aaron says Flint's just plain old bored with the gambling scene. Since he doesn't have to do it, he doesn't. Aaron just shakes his head. He says Flint has always looked on gambling as hard work. Flint gambled the way he runs a business. At least that's what Aaron says.''

''What do you think?''

"Me?" Rozlyn looked at her in astonishment. "Why. . .Aaron's right, of course. He says that if gambling ever did have any fizz for Flint it all went flat when Flint discovered the challenge of real business, which produces something—you know, like goods or services. That's what Aaron says."

Lia sat for a moment watching the whitecaps flirting across the lake. She wished she had Roz's absolute trust in the infallibility of Aaron's judgments. She shrugged it aside and turned her attention back to her pie.

"This pie never saw the inside of a grocery store frozen-food dispenser, which is where all my pies come from," she said. "It's almost wicked, it's so good."

Rozlyn's cheerful face beamed with pleasure. "Thanks. Cherry pie is what got me started cooking. I was. . .oh, maybe eleven, and Papa and Flint were coming for a visit, and I wanted to do something special to impress them. Aunty spent two weeks teaching me how to bake a cherry pie. *Voilà!* A smash hit. I've spent the rest of my life working at things to keep people telling me what a good cook I am."

"You're a hard act to follow," Lia told her. In answer to the other's questioning look she explained a bit ruefully, "I had a momentary lapse and volunteered to cook dinner for your brother tomorrow night when he gets back from the city."

Roz's eyes widened with interest. "Oh, that's

great!'' she said delightedly. "I can tell you all the things that are his favorites. I'll give you recipes and I can show...."

Lia shook her head, laughing. "Not that I don't appreciate the offer, but they'd never come out for me. Just the thought of trying to follow in your footsteps overwhelms me."

"I've got an even better idea," Rozlyn insisted. "I'll cook the dinner and bring it over in the afternoon. You can put everything in the microwave at the last minute, and Flint will never know...."

Lia's eyebrows shot up. "You're a devious little sister!" she exclaimed with amusement. "I could even consider taking you up on it if I wasn't afraid it might establish a standard I'd be expected to live up to at another time."

"Oh, Lia, let me! I'd love to do it. Flint—"

"Don't worry about your brother," Lia said dryly. "I'm no Julia Child, but I'm a reasonably good short-order cook. I don't ever expect to turn out the culinary extravaganzas you do, so it's only fair that he be forewarned."

She thought that had put an end to the matter until Rozlyn walked with her to her car a short time later and thrust a flat round foil-wrapped parcel in her hand.

"It's the rest of the cherry pie, Lia. Please take it," she begged. "It'll save you having to make a dessert and Flint loves it. If you don't tell him...."

She was right, of course. It would save having

to think about dessert, which otherwise would probably be no more than fruit and cheese. Besides, Lia didn't have the heart to refuse a gift offered with such good heart.

"Thanks, Roz. You are really a darling."

CHAPTER FIFTEEN

LIA FOUND HERSELF CAUGHT UP in a kind of frenzy
the following morning as she pored over a gour-
met cookbook her mother had once given her and
planned a dinner for Flint that would merit a cor-
don bleu. She'd had in mind Beef Wellington, but
a second reading of the recipe cured that particular foolishness. She'd be at it all day, she
thought in dismay, and decided Beef Wellington
was a highly overrated way to gild a lily. Come to
think of it, she'd never much liked it anyway.
Upon this revelation she cut two thick steaks off
the filet strip she'd bought for the Wellington and
put the rest in the freezer. She scrubbed two
potatoes for baking and rinsed salad greens and
put them away to crisp.

It took all of ten minutes. In the time she'd
saved, she treated herself to a visit with her friend
Carrie. She climbed the slope to the Sapphire
Point gate, where she spent a half hour over coffee
with her friend. She was pleased to find Carrie in
better spirits than she'd been the last time they had
visited. It seemed Rick had begun to put his bitterness over his problems at the Goldorado behind

him and was turning his energies toward looking for ways to finance his return to engineering school.

Back at her own house before eleven, Lia retired to her desk in her work cubbyhole behind the screen at the far end of the living room. She spent the rest of the day at her typewriter, sketching out the first phase of her master's thesis.

Shortly before six she stowed the telltale material away in a file drawer, covered her typewriter and headed for her bedroom. She had concentrated all day on her work to the exclusion of everything else, but now her thoughts raced ahead to the moment when Flint would come. Her heart quickened and her body warmed to the thought of his impending embrace.

Showered and shampooed, she towel dried her short hair into a cap of loose curls and smoothed a body lotion scented with the faintly citrus fragrance of daphne over her arms and legs. And all the time her mind, freed from the academic strictures she'd imposed on herself all day, sang in ever-recurring refrain, *Hurry, Flint. Hurry, hurry, hurry.*

She looked at herself through the eyes of the man she waited for in a kind of breathless anticipation unlike anything she'd ever felt before. Her mind overflowed with a fullness of him. Her heart swelled with the awesome realization that until Flint came into her life she'd never known love. With it came an understanding that should they become lost to each other, no other man could ever fill the void.

Naked and dewy from her shower, she took out a white flowing gown of soft opaque cotton, intricately embroidered around the neck, and opened a drawer to get a bra and bikini pants to wear under it. For a long moment she looked down on the folds of soft-colored silk and lace neatly stacked inside. With a defensive lift of her shoulders she closed the drawer. There would be no barriers tonight. From the moment she circled his neck with her arms in welcome and came into the warmth of his embrace, she wanted him to know that she had been waiting for him, that she wanted him...needed him...that she was ready for his love.

No need for words tonight, love, she told the absent Flint silently. She wanted him to know the moment his hands touched her unfettered body beneath the folds of soft cotton that before the night was done they were to make love.

She had no fear he would not come or that he would try to pay her rejection back in kind. She understood the hard stubborn pride that had impelled him to keep her at arms' length since the night she'd said no to his marriage proposal. In a sense he'd been telling her all week that she had created the breach, so it was up to her to mend it. In declining her offer for the hasty reconciliation implied in her invitations to come home with her after work he'd told her, too, that it had better be good.

She didn't buy all of it, but she knew how he felt and wanted with her whole heart to heal the hurt she'd inflicted upon him and reassure him of her love. Somehow she was sure that Flint was ready to be healed—to be reassured.

She was so sure that she had no fears about his coming. The other fears—children and gambling and the possibility that the archetype of Flint's ideal woman was his sister, Roz—she buried in a dark corner of her mind. Along with the aesthetics of her preparations she had not overlooked the need to protect herself against a future cause for anxiety. Having seen to that, she hardly intended to let imagined potentials for future worries mar the wonder of their first coming together. Tonight she had no concerns, she was simply Lia Andrews—woman awaiting her lover.

She touched a drop of daphne-scented perfume to the hollow of her throat and paused, smiling. She was amused at the thought that perhaps there was a bit of the pagan in the almost ritualistic attention she'd lavished on her body, as if the goddess Venus had been looking over her shoulder, telling her what to do.

The rattle of the front-door knocker sent her heart fluttering like a bird startled from its cover. She slipped her bare feet into a pair of waiting sandals and gave a last flurried glance at herself in the mirror. The folds of soft white cloth fell away at the swell of her breasts, leaving them covered with a single thickness that failed to hide the darker areolae. The taut nipples thrust out against the layer of fabric, making no secret of her arousal

She hesitated, not daring to take time to put on the bra she'd rejected only a minute before. She rearranged the loose folds of the material across her breasts and saw that the slightest movement left them again exposed.

Fool! It's your lover Flint out there!

A laugh rippled up from deep in her throat. Lifting her shoulders she walked proudly down the hall to the door to welcome the one man she'd ever loved.

And yet for all her bravado, she was caught in a moment of unaccustomed shyness when she opened the door and saw him there, as tall and splendid as she had visualized him during the short time they'd been apart. Far from circling his neck with her arms, as she'd expected to do, she stood in a kind of motionless celebration of his return.

"This *is* the night?" he asked, and she was astonished that the urbane Flint Tancer sounded almost shy himself. He carried packages, she observed distractedly. How could you throw yourself into the arms of a man whose arms were already full? She laughed. It broke the spell.

"Of course it's the night," she said. "Come in. I've been waiting for you. Where do you want to put all of this?" She motioned to the packages.

"In the kitchen. It's a loaf of bread and a jug of wine."

"And thou?"

He smiled and his eyes caressed her, and she knew then that everything would be all right. Maybe she *had* been afraid he wouldn't come, she admitted as she led the way to the kitchen.

"San Francisco French bread and champagne... Mumm's!" she exclaimed when he unloaded and unwrapped his two bundles on a drainboard. "Some loaf of bread and jug of wine!"

When he turned to her she knew by the look in his eyes that the moment had come. She crossed the few steps between them and slipped her arms around his neck.

"I missed you," she said softly, and was surprised at the sudden rise of tears to her eyes. "I'm glad you've come back."

"Oh God, what an idiot I was to leave," he said, and she knew when they spoke of his absence neither was talking about his San Francisco trip.

He pulled her hard against him and the wonderful mouth that was her first memory of him came down over hers in a hungry searching kiss, very unlike that other first meeting.

She knew when his hands understood the natural state of her body under the flowing gown. They moved tentatively along the line of her waist and down over her hips and up again, gently feeling for the obligatory scraps of material that might ordinarily confine her breasts and thighs. He held her in the tight circle of his arms, and his hands moved down again to curve around her buttocks and press her hard against him, his body telling her the extent of his desire.

While their lips still clung together, the full implications of her nakedness suddenly became clear to him. From his throat came a hoarse sensual murmur as he tore away from her. Deep within her she felt a hot answering throb. He stood for a moment, not touching her, looking down at her. A kind of wonder was reflected in his face, and then, as if to make sure he'd made no mistake, he trailed his fingers lightly across her full-budded breasts.

"Oh, Flint . . . !"

"Lia . . . my lovely . . . my love!"

Lifting her off her feet he carried her through the living room, still sweetly fragrant from the last of the flowers he'd brought in supplication that other night, and down the hall to her bedroom. There he set her on her feet beside the bed and unbuttoned the single fastening that held the deep front opening of the caftan. He undressed her slowly, lovingly, the sensuous mouth tracing a trail of fire down her body as his hands slipped the soft folds of fabric over her breasts. Now that the time had come it was to be savored to the fullest. His hands discovered the delights of her body with gentle deliberation, lifting and shaping each bared breast to take its roseate point in his mouth. His lips moved lower still, and he explored the dimple of her navel with his tongue.

Gently his hands rolled the fabric down over the rise of her hips to expose her lower belly, and he knelt before her, pressing his face into the tawny triangle of curls, his arms closing around her buttocks to hold her fiercely to him. Her body curved out to meet the seductive pull, and from her lips came a murmur like the coo of a dove. Deep within her rose a swell of longing.

"Flint! Oh, Flint," she cried out softly in sudden wild impatience. She lifted his head away with her hands and knelt before him, hurrying to fumble with the buttons of his shirt.

"Oh, sweet," he whispered, and in clumsy confusion they accomplished his undressing, too.

The time of deliberate savoring was past. Locked in a naked embrace they found their way to the bed and fell upon it. His mouth took hers once more in a fiercely passionate kiss, and her own lips softened and melted into the sensuous fullness of his. Still they touched and fondled and kissed, their bodies in rampant arousal, as if to pay homage to all the intimate shrines they had denied themselves before tonight. She trembled inwardly with joy.

When she could no longer bear the exquisite swell of desire that throbbed deep within her, she cried aloud, "Come, Flint. Oh lover, come!" And he covered her body with his."

At his first passionate thrust she opened herself rapturously and embraced him with all of her being.

FLINT ROSE AT LAST from their bed of love, but when he'd pulled her to her feet in front of him, he sat back down and buried his face in her soft firm belly.

"Lia...Lia...most wonderful creature in all the world," he proclaimed hoarsely, his voice still thick with the echo of spent passion. The foolishness of his words brought a soft throaty giggle from her. Her hands fondled the thick dark hair, her fingers memorizing the contours of the splendid head, her mind toying with a captivating picture of what would happen if she suddenly pressed her full weight against him and toppled him back on the bed with herself on top of him.

"When did you eat last?"

The question was so unexpected it took her completely by surprise. It was as if he'd spoken in a foreign tongue. He pulled away and got to his feet, while she blinked at him like a confused owl. In the darkening room his body stood silhouetted against the faint golden glow of the fading sunset through the western window. She was so bemused by the beauty of what she saw that it took a moment for the question to take hold.

"I forgot to eat lunch," she admitted. "Why?"

"Your gastric juices are complaining," he said with a grin. He reached for her gown, which had been tossed carelessly at the foot of the bed.

"What are you trying to do? Get me into the kitchen?" Lia complained with lazy good humor.

"Maybe." He found the neck opening on the caftan and slipped it over her head. When her face came through the hole he leaned down to touch

her lips with his and help her arms find their way
into sleeves fashioned like butterfly wings.

"You're just saying that because you're dying
to find out if I can cook."

"Right," he agreed coolly and pulled his
cotton-knit sport shirt over his head, tucking it
into the waistband of his pants.

In the kitchen Lia put the potatoes in the microwave oven and took the two steaks from the refrigerator. Flint opened the bottle of champagne.
When it was poured he looked over the tall-
stemmed tulip glass in a toast that harked back to
the early evening and that first sweet moment of
communion.

"To the song in my heart," he said.

"To the man I love," she toasted in return.

The small rite over, Flint said, "You make the
salad, and I'll cook the steaks." Then to her surprise, instead of sticking them under the broiler as
she would have done, he put the small thick steaks
in a skillet with a few drops of olive oil and a bud
of garlic. When they were well browned on either
side he emptied his half-filled champagne glass
into the pan, sprinkled a bit of oregano and
spooned the wine and pan juices over the steaks.
When the red juice inside began to ooze up
through the top of the meat he tossed on a small
handful of finely chopped parsley, let the steaks
simmer a minute and turned them out onto heated
plates. Lia, who was slicing tomatoes and onions
and avocados to toss with lettuce and a simple

vinaigrette dressing, watched the performance, first with skepticism, then with awe. He did it with such economy of motion, such easy grace. It seemed effortless.

Dinner preparations had taken less than twenty minutes, but darkness had already settled in upon them and a sharp wind blew across the deck from the lake. They ate at a small table Lia placed in front of the fireplace, where she'd laid a fire that morning. Even in summer at such high altitudes, the extra heat was often needed.

"Where did you learn to fix a steak like this? From Roz?" asked Lia, savoring the first aromatic morsel with delight.

"Not Roz! It's too easy for her," Flint declared with a laugh. "She turns up her nose at anything that takes less than three hours of preparation."

"You didn't dream this up yourself. If not Roz, there's another woman in your life."

"Not a woman. A guy by the name of Frenchy. He'd once been a big-time chef, but he couldn't keep a job. He kept getting in trouble gambling. When he'd had a run of bad luck sometimes he'd stay with dad and me."

As they loaded their few dishes into the dishwasher a short time later, Lia brought the talk around again to his cooking.

"Do you do anything besides steaks?"

"Surely you jest!" he said wickedly. "I can cook a week of dinners and never repeat myself."

"I am impressed," said Lia weakly, taking a

quick inventory of her own resources and deciding there was no way she could top his boast.

"Don't be. Unlike my sister, if it takes more than twenty minutes to fix I don't want to know about it. Most of it I learned from Frenchy. I was cook by default when I lived with dad, except when Frenchy was with us. I could stand fast food and TV dinners and pork and beans just so long. Then I began to cook. To my surprise, I found I liked to, as long as it was simple and not much work. At my place in the city I cook for myself."

Later they finished the last of the champagne and lay together on a soft blanket spread before the fire. After a while they undressed and in a new ecstasy of discovery made love again. When toward midnight Flint rose to his knees in a first move to leave, Lia reached to detain him.

"Don't go. Sleep with me tonight, Flint."

He hesitated a moment. Then, pulling the blanket from under his knees, he bundled her up in it and carried her to bed. She curled her body into the curve of his and fell asleep almost at once.

She awakened sometime later with an instant of exhilaration and the certainty that something wonderful had happened to her. In the next instant she knew what it was and pressed herself more closely to the sleeping man. Then, drifting off to sleep, she remembered she was scheduled for the early weekend shift at the casino in the morning, and that she'd forgotten to set her alarm.

Quietly, so as not to disturb Flint, she sat up

and set the digital alarm for six. With three more hours of sleep ahead of her, she crawled back under the covers and moved her body to seek out the warmth of the man beside her. When she found he had turned over in her absence she fit herself around the curve of his back, slipped an arm over his body and fell asleep.

The alarm rang at six, and Lia hurried to shut off the sound before it awakened Flint. She sat up in bed, then looked over to find him smiling at her, his eyes filled with the same joyous wonder she felt burgeoning within herself.

"Good morning, love," he said, reaching up to cup her bare breast in his hand. She evaded him. Curling her knees under her, she bowed herself over his head and lowered her shoulders until he could close his mouth around her breast's firm tumescent tip.

There was no time this morning for new discoveries, nor was there a need. Still turgid from the night's fulfillment, their bodies remembered the paths to pleasure and they made swift passionate love. Afterward they soaped each other in the shower and let the hot water splash down over their still-excited bodies.

In the kitchen Lia made coffee and told Flint about her lunch with his sister, laughing with him, though a bit ruefully, over Roz's offer to cater last night's affair.

"You've no need to be intimidated by Roz, love. You're my kind of cook. I'd like to go on record that last night's dinner was one of the finest I ever ate," he assured her, but on behalf of her honor Lia felt bound to point out that she'd had nothing to do with the one thing on their menu that required any skill.

"I like your style, Tancer, but—" She broke off with a gasp, suddenly remembering Roz Burney's gold-medal cherry pie.

"Oh, shoot! I forgot the pie," she groaned, and told Flint of Roz's last-ditch effort to help her out. "Don't tell Roz I forgot all about it, Flint."

"Stick it in the microwave for a minute to heat it up and we'll eat it for breakfast," Flint insisted when he'd stopped laughing.

"For *breakfast*? Pie?"

"Of course for breakfast. Best breakfast you ever had."

"We-ell all right, but I'm warning you, if you ever tell your sister, we're through!"

CHAPTER SIXTEEN

THE DAYS THAT FOLLOWED were a time of almost idyllic contentment and tormenting unrest for Lia. She spent her allotted time at the casino and stole a few hours early each morning while Flint slept to focus her full attention on her master's work, but whenever she was away from Flint something inside her kept marking time until they were together again.

On the mornings Lia went to work early Flint got up at the same time and went out for a run. On the days she was scheduled for a late-morning shift they played tennis and in the evening after work had dinner sent up to Flint's penthouse suite—a Sybaritic palace of pearl-colored velvet carpets and pale gold watered-silk walls. There, high above the glittering pandemonium of the gambling scene, they dined in hedonistic self-indulgence on exotic foodstuffs flown in from distant places all over the world to please the appetites of the Goldorado's high-rolling crowd.

In the bedroom, on a king-size bed beneath a mirrored ceiling, they made love. Before she had seen it, Flint had somewhat apologetically described the chamber as "a madam's boudoir." It gave Lia an uncomfortably decadent feeling to act as voyeur to their own lovemaking. But whenever her eyes caught a glimpse of Flint's long sinewy body spread over hers, and she saw his buttocks firm and lift in the thrust of passion, a deep throbbing started up within her, and when his body shuddered in ultimate ecstasy an explosion of fire eddied through her in wave upon sensual wave.

On the days she finished work early they left the casino environs for the Sapphire Point house. More often than not they would prowl the area shopping marts on the way to pick up supplies for the dinner they would cook together that night. Such meals were made under certain agreed-upon rules that allowed no preprepared or frozen foods and only dishes that took less than twenty minutes and no more than three cooking utensils to fix.

They challenged each other to cook-offs, and Lia was gratified to find that although Flint was perhaps more resourceful and had a greater culinary repertoire to draw upon, she created fewer outright disasters. More important, Flint ate what she served him with at least as much gusto as he gave to the food he prepared himself.

Sometimes after a lazy dinner on the deck they walked along the Sapphire Point beach. At times they talked together avidly, often about themselves, in a kind of catching up for all the years that had passed before they met. Other times they walked in easy companionship, arms entwined, listening to the whisper of waves that licked the shore and to the soft swish of their feet in the sand. One rare warm night when the moon was dark they brought a blanket to the beach and made love in the vast openness under the stars, their bodies leaving a single telltale print in the sand that was still there next morning when Lia went down to swim.

They were with each other every night, yet there was no mention between them of moving in together. For Lia, unless she chose to tell Flint about the master's project she worked at surreptitiously every day, such an arrangement was not feasible.

As for Flint, his thoughts were only of marriage, and Lia was not yet prepared to confront the irreconcilable differences that might mar the fragile perfection of their love.

"Please, Flint, not yet," she would plead at his every effort to steer her to serious talk of marriage. "We haven't known each other long enough."

Finally one day he said angrily, "Damn it, Lia, *I'm* sure!"

And because she couldn't bear the look of puzzled injury she saw in his eyes, she lied.

"Oh, Flint, darling, I'm sure too. But I can't forget that if I'd rushed into marriage that other time it would have been a disaster."

"Not this time, Lia," he said quietly.

"I know you're right, Flint. It's just that I made a pledge to myself I'd never again consider marriage without giving the relationship time. Don't ask me to break it. . .please.''

Voicing his dissatisfaction with a grunt, Flint let it go, and Lia was left deploring her own reluctance to face issues that went unresolved. She knew the day would come when Flint would not let her put him off, and they would be forced to find answers to the issues fermenting in a dark recess of her mind.

So for now she lied and told him she too was sure. But how could she be sure? How dared she be sure he wasn't as much a gambler as Toby Brasford, when every day he moved through the casino betting sizable sums and acting for all the world like a professional blackjack player or a hard-core gambler?

And how could she be sure he could forgive her for using Aaron Burney's casino without the owner's knowledge as a study field on the pathology of gambling? When one came right down to it, Aaron was actually paying for a study unknown to him, unauthorized by him and undertaken on his own turf. As a gambler, Flint could very well resent it. And, though her own conscience told her it was true, she might never be able to convince Flint that in using Burney in this fashion she was not harming him in any way. Suppose he chose to look on her study as a betrayal not just of his brother-in-law but of himself.

Suppose he chose to put an end to the work that had become one of the important goals in her life.

She felt uncomfortable about the situation. She felt guilty because it obliged her to be less than open with Flint, but to be completely candid with him meant risking the whole study, something she refused to do. There was still too much fieldwork left to complete. Now more than ever she wanted to finish it—not because of Toby, who had gotten her started, but because of Flint, for whom she was beginning to feel the first stirrings of fear.

Finish the study she must, but how could she talk of marriage and at the same time hide from Flint the most important endeavor of her life?

Meanwhile, she went out and bought the first consciously provocative garment she'd ever deliberately gone looking for and hung it in a closet at the penthouse suite to change into on the nights she had dinner there.

It was blue—the same blue as the dress that had pleased Flint the first night they went out together. It was not ruffly feminine but blatantly enticing from the deeply plunging neckline to the artful cut, which called subtle attention to each dip and curve of her body. It was a gown made to be admired by a man. In her case the only person who would see it was Flint.

Though the woman in her recognized this precarious world she shared with Flint to be a fool's paradise, it was the psychologist who kept waiting for the serpent to raise its head.

And then Toby Brasford appeared on the scene. Lia arrived for her late shift at twelve o'clock after a morning of tennis with Flint. The casino was already an anthill of activity. She took her place at an almost full table, only to find herself looking right into Toby's face. Except for the glimpse in the restaurant some nights before, it was the first time she'd seen him since the day she'd sent him packing.

He wore an oversize pair of rimless tinted glasses, which lent even more of a Hollywood look to the cinematically handsome face. Except for the glasses he looked much the same as he had when she'd first seen him in the Montgomery Street elevator. There had always been a slick perfection to his features, a self-assured breeziness that caught one's attention. When they had walked down the street together in San Francisco she'd often noticed women turn to give him a second admiring glance as they passed. At the time of their parting, she wondered with a sense of shame if this ersatz celebrity had been one of Toby's attractions for her. If it hadn't been for the exceptionally handsome face she would have quickly squelched his presumptuous approach in the elevator and that would have been the end of it.

She had said as much to him once when anger and frustration lent candor to her tongue. Toby had taken it blandly.

"My looks always work for me," he said smugly. "Being handsome gets me further than a foot in the door."

In the act of taking over the table from Garcia,

who was at the end of his shift, Lia hadn't at once taken stock of the five players already there. As each bet was placed she took a quick glance at the gambler's face. The third face was Toby's. It had been a long time since that too-perfect countenance had been a welcome sight to her.

He grinned at her brashly, his hand absently stacking and restacking a number of poker chips he had before him.

"Welcome to the club!" he greeted with a laugh that was just short of arrogant.

Lia gave him a level look across the table. "Would you please place your bet," she said evenly.

For the next forty minutes, until the relief dealer came to take over for her break, Lia felt as if she was working her way through a nightmare.

Her first thought was one of thanksgiving that Flint had taken the Burney children to Reno that afternoon to see a hot-air balloon festival. It meant he wouldn't get back to the casino until almost time for her to quit. Her next was an uncharitable hope that Toby would follow his normal procedure and quickly run out of money, but then she realized that could take forever. Lia wanted him out *now*. When he ran out of money, the pit boss no doubt would still let him play awhile on credit. How long that would last depended on how far Ed Shields was willing to let him extend himself and how good his credit rating was.

By the time her dealing stint grew to a close Toby was a long way from running out of money, let alone going to Shields for credit. It was a situation so atypical of Toby that Lia decided to watch his play with a more analytical eye if he was still at her table when she returned from her break.

To her consternation Toby left right behind her, delaying only long enough to sweep his winnings off the table. Two steps later he was beside her, his pockets bulging with poker chips

"Hey, slow down old girl. I'll buy you a cup of coffee for old times' sake," he said.

Lia sidestepped into an oncoming group of people to avoid his hand as it reached out to take her elbow, but it was no more than a delaying action In the next second Toby was beside her again. This time he made no further attempt to touch her but continued purposefully at her side as she walked swiftly toward the coffee shop.

Looking straight ahead she said coldly, "Get away from me, Toby. I told you I wouldn't see you again until you quit gambling, which you obviously haven't. Well, here's an amendment to that: I don't want to see you again—ever! The gambling's your problem. No one can help that but you."

"What have you got to be so damn self-righteous about, Lia? You've joined up with the gambling world. We both make our money in the casinos. The only difference is you're small potatoes and I do it big I'd like to point out that in the casino I'm the patron and you're the peon. You're hardly in a position for haughtiness, old dear.''

Without missing a step, Lia turned to look at him in astonishment. *He's serious!* she thought. How could she sustain anger toward such a sad case as Toby. Compulsive gambler, egomaniac, pipe dreamer! He seemed to be sinking ever deeper into a morass of his own making.

While Lia, the psychologist, felt an objective responsibility to focus her professional skills on his problem, Lia, the woman, wanted only for Toby Brasford to take himself away from her table, out of the casino. . .out of her life.

A few steps short of the coffee shop she changed tactics. Maybe if she asked him nicely, Toby would be willing to do his gambling at one of the other casinos. Or if he insisted upon playing at the Goldorado, surely he'd agree to go to one of the other pits, or at least to another table when she was dealing.

She slowed her step and made an effort to be friendly, tacitly letting him know she'd decided to accept his company for the moment.

"By the way, didn't I see you in a restaurant on the other side of the lake one night a while back?" she asked in a purely social tone. "Who was the man with you? I barely got a glimpse of his back, but I swear it's someone I know. You know how a thing like that can plague you.''

To her surprise, her question appeared to unstring Toby. For the first time he seemed to lose his aplomb. The color rose in his face, and for a moment he groped for words.

"Well, it wasn't me you saw, I can tell you that. I don't know where you got the idea it was me. I just started selling real estate here at the lake. I wasn't even here last week, so it couldn't have been me."

It was a blustery declaration delivered with far more emphasis than it deserved. That Toby wasn't simply here for a day or two but intended to be in the area selling real estate was a further disturbing development that must be dealt with. Her best move would be to make her position clear immediately.

They seated themselves in a narrow booth, and Lia waited until their coffee was in front of them before she came to the point.

"Look, Toby, don't play at my table anymore, please."

"Are you crazy? Why?"

"Several reasons, and I won't go into them all, the first being that I meant what I said out there—I don't want to see you. Another reason is you can't handle gambling, and I'll be darned if I care to preside at your undoing."

Brasford gave a snort of laughter. "You must not have heard me. My losing days are over. All I do now is win."

"Then would you mind doing your winning someplace else, please?"

"You don't get the picture. I'm winning, I tell you. I know how to beat the house, and I promise you'll get your share, old darling. When Toby Brasford's winning, he takes care of the dealer, you'd better believe!"

"I'm serious, Toby. I don't want you around."

The attractive face across from her grew sullen. "You said you loved me."

"Well, that was a mistake. Whatever it was, it wasn't love," said Lia truthfully.

"But you said—"

"I was wrong, Toby. Don't you understand? I didn't even know what love was then. I wish you well. I hope you'll try to quit gambling, but whether you do or not you're not a part of my life, and I'd appreciate it if you'd stay away from my table."

"That's where my winning streak started. You're crazy if you think I'm going to run out on it. It's bad luck."

"I mean it, Toby."

"The answer is no."

To prolong the discussion was useless, Lia could plainly see. Without another word she got up and left. She was annoyed but not in the least surprised when Toby appeared at her table shortly after she started dealing again and took one of the empty chairs. He stayed there the rest of the afternoon, winning consistently.

She watched his play carefully without detecting any of the usual ploys of card counters. There seemed to be no particular pattern to Toby's playing. For all his experience he seemed slow and indecisive, not quick and certain like Flint. Each time he was to stand or hit, he halted the play for a moment, studying his cards, but he never made a wrong choice. When he lost, it was not because he'd drawn higher than twenty-one. He seemed to know exactly when he should hit and when he should stand. By the end of Lia's shift he was more than a thousand dollars ahead. Not a bad day's work, she thought sourly.

As time to quit drew near, Lia began to hope the ever-timely Flint would not be there early. When she pictured him standing by, watching her deal to this unwelcome patron from her past, small spasms of dread lay siege upon her stomach. Flint had appeared reasonably unconcerned when she'd told him about Toby, but how he would react at finding her erstwhile fiancé settled in at her table was a question she was in no hurry to have answered.

When Annie, the swing-shift dealer, arrived and there was still no sign of Flint, she gave a grateful passing thought to Missy and Chap, who had kept their uncle overlong. As she turned the table over to Annie, Flint arrived, windblown, apologetic and late, but not late enough to miss Toby's all too audible words as Lia walked away.

"I'll see you tomorrow, Lady Luck."

She saw Flint's eyes turn a curious glance toward Toby and his sizable stack of chips. He grinned down at her teasingly as they moved out of the sphere of the table.

"Looks like you made one customer happy. How come I never win like that at your table?"

"Because you're so lucky in love," she said tartly, in no mood for his teasing. But the next moment she relented and poured all her love into a smile. They walked on a bit, then she placed a detaining hand on Flint's arm.

"There's Ed Shields, my pit boss. Would you mind waiting here for me a minute, Flint? There's something I've got to talk to him about." Not waiting for an answer, she hurried forward to catch up with Shields, who was headed up the stairs to the office.

"Could I ask a favor of you, Ed?" she said. "You know that good-looking fellow with the glasses and dark blond styled hair who's been playing at my table all day?"

Shields had turned impatiently when she caught up with him. His small suspicious eyes gazed at her coldly. "Yeah. I know who you mean. What about him?"

"I'd rather he didn't play at my table."

"The hell you say! Just what are you accusing him of?" the pit boss asked unpleasantly, almost angrily.

"I'm not accusing him of anything. It's just that he...I...." For some reason she found it unexpectedly hard to admit to her former relationship with Toby. "We were engaged. Now we're not. Could you ask him to play at some other table? I understand it's something you can do."

"Ask him yourself, why don't you?" said Shields, and started up the stairs.

"Wait, Ed. I did. He said no. I wish you'd do it for me. It makes me uncomfortable to have him there." The pit boss kept on walking.

"That's your problem, baby," he called over his shoulder nastily.

Flint came to meet her, a look of concern in his eyes.

"Something wrong, Lia?" he asked at once.

Lia shook her head bleakly. What could she say?

"It's just been one bummer of a day!" she said on an explosive sigh. In that instant she knew she couldn't go up to the penthouse suite with Flint just as if all paradise weren't flying apart. She had to get away alone and think things out before the next day, when it seemed inevitable Flint would be elbow to elbow at her table with Toby Brasford. She came to a stop, her hand again on Flint's arm.

"Flint, I don't think I'll go with you tonight. I think I'd better go on back to Sapphire Point. I just don't feel like—"

"Headache?"

She ignored the latent mischief in the question. Come to think of it, she did have a headache. "A real nagger," she said.

"You need to eat. What about dinner?"

"I'm still getting mileage out of that soup Carrie brought me the day you fished me out of the lake. Some of it's in the freezer. I can heat it up. I'm not very hungry.''

When they reached her car, she flung her arms around Flint's neck and hugged him fiercely, oblivious to the glare of the bright pole light under which they stood.

"Oh, Flint, I love you," she cried softly, as a sudden inexplicable wave of panic swept over her. He seemed to know that she wanted only to be held, and he pressed her to him as the seconds ticked by, his face buried in her short silky curls.

Gradually Lia's taut muscles began to ease, and her tense grip on his neck relaxed. He turned her face up and covered her mouth in a deep searching kiss that seemed to have no end until a car shot out of a parking spot an alley away in a squeal of tires and adolescent shouts, and they remembered where they were.

"You wouldn't care to reconsider, would you?" asked Flint quietly.

She looked up at him, her heart swelling with her love.

"Oh. . .Flint!"

Arms locked, they walked back across the parking lot together and took the elevator to the penthouse suite.

CHAPTER SEVENTEEN

LIA WAS NOT SURPRISED in the second hour of her shift the next morning when Toby appeared out of nowhere and took one of the empty places at her table. She acknowledged his banal greeting with a cool nod and counted out chips for the amount of money he slid across the table to her, handing him the chips in stacks of five. She was relieved when he made no attempt to engage her in conversation.

Unlike the day before, his bets were modest. Even so, when the pit boss came by with a new deck of cards for the table, he was already down to his last five-chip stack.

As play resumed with the new deck, Flint eased his long athletic frame into an empty seat at the opposite curve of the table from Toby. Darting a quick remembering smile at Lia he exchanged money for chips and began to play. Bathed in the warm memory of having wakened that morning in his arms, she forgot her apprehensions at the thought of having Flint together with Toby at her table. In the next moment the apprehensions came thundering back. Faced with all that was inherent in the ticklish situation before her, she almost wished she had risked the sweetness of the previous evening and forewarned Flint about Toby.

She'd seen the folly of waiting and had tried to tell him, but in the shelter of Flint's arms she couldn't make herself say, "Toby Brasford, the man I told you about, is here, gambling at my table." The words seemed to stick in her throat.

Finally, giving up the direct approach, she'd said, "There's something I have to tell you, Flint."

He'd noticed she was upset before they came up from the parking lot. Being Flint, he hadn't pressed but had tried instead to lighten her mood. Teasingly he'd said, "But you'd rather not tell it now...so wait. I'll hear it another time."

Knowing she shouldn't, she had let him distract her then with tender words and caresses that carried them to the threshold of desire. It was easy to forget that her ex-fiancé intended to show up at her table in the morning and she would have to explain his presence to Flint.

Well, she couldn't forget it now, she thought grimly, and began to shuffle the deck. Not with the two of them sitting there in front of her, waiting for her to deal. The hands that riffled the cards were steady and sure. Underneath she was as taut as a racket string.

Flint, to her right, played a quick, skillful, relaxed game. Whether he won or lost, he showed no distress or satisfaction. Betting with a kind of lazy indifference, he hardly seemed to notice whether he was ahead or behind.

Toby, to her left, played slowly, his face dour, his hands stacking and restacking chips when not busy with his cards. When it came time for him to hit or stand there was the same scarcely discernible hesitation Lia had noted the day before.

Now, almost as if Flint's arrival was the catalyst, Toby's luck seemed suddenly to change. He was calling them right again, rebuilding his depleted stacks of chips, betting heavily. Throughout the rest of Lia's shift he raked in and counted his chips tight-lipped, as if there was little joy for him in his winning streak.

As the week moved on, Lia found it increasingly hard to bring herself to tell Flint about Toby. The two men appeared scarcely aware of each other's presence, whether separated by other players or playing elbow to elbow, and they paid no special attention to Lia beyond the customary impersonal courtesies between a blackjack player and the dealer. Except for his eyes, which often made no secret of their intimacy, Flint had always avoided outward signs of familiarity in the casino. It soon appeared that Toby had decided not to risk advances that might get him rebuffed again. Under such circumstances it was easy for Lia to let the matter of Toby's identity slide.

But as the postponement was prolonged, it occurred to Lia that when she did level with Flint, he might very well think her failure to tell him hinted at some kind of guilty involvement between her and her ex-fiancé. The very act of delaying ultimately became more of a problem than the fact of Toby's presence, had she cleared it with Flint in the beginning.

After a few days it all paled into insignificance and was almost forgotten in her growing concern over a sudden change in Flint's gambling practices. It was as if the insidious affliction that was destroying Toby Brasford had contaminated Flint.

It had seemed reasonable that Flint might be obliged to do a certain amount of gambling to find out for Aaron Burney how efficiently the blackjack games were being run. Now, to Lia's dismay, Flint had given up all pretense of making a study of the casino. Each day, soon after Toby's arrival, Flint would be there, too. He'd come straight to Lia's table, take a seat, buy a stack of chips and begin to play. They might almost have been engaged in an endurance contest—Flint and Toby— to see who could outlast the other.

The coincidence of Flint's settling in at her table almost on schedule with Toby had led her to wonder guiltily if he'd somehow found out Toby's identity and was there to keep an eye on the two of them, but she quickly dismissed the notion when she thought of the nights she spent with Flint. The man who made love to her could not be a man torn by jealous suspicions, not when his lovemaking held a kind of reverence that made it as much an act of trust as an act of love.

She was left with only the ugly probability that

Flint was as much a hard-core gambler as Toby, despite what his sister, Rozlyn, had told her. Flint had paid his way through college with gambling winnings but then quit gambling because it had always bored him, Roz had said. It seemed far more likely that the threat of addiction had impelled Flint to quit, not boredom, thought Lia, just as the risk of temptation had kept him away from gambling environs until, years later, he had come to the Goldorado to help his brother-in-law.

The cruel irony of his downfall filled her with an aching sorrow that swelled in her throat until at times she feared that if she tried to speak, her words would spill out in a cry of pain.

As she watched him at the table, her heart ached for the tormented man she knew must be hidden behind the insouciant face he showed to the gambling world. No wonder they'd thought he was bored! That mask of indifference was the mask that hid his shame.

If any doubt remained in her mind that she loved him, seeing him there at the table matching bet for bet with Toby Brasford dispelled it. Having accepted the evidence she saw before her, her first feeling was a terrible sorrow for Flint, her first thought a realization that her life would be empty without this warm witty man who had a gambling problem. More important, he was the man she loved.

She was sadly aware of the limitations of psychology in dealing with addictions and felt an agonizing frustration with herself and her profession. There were no easy answers. She knew it wasn't within her scope to help him. She could only love him and trust him to break the renewed grip gambling had on him as he'd done once before.

Meanwhile, though she worried over Flint's addiction, paradoxically she wanted him to win. It bothered her inordinately that he was behind in the game as often as he was ahead, while Toby never left the table without his pockets sagging with chips he'd just won. It was an anomaly that merely annoyed her at first, but as the days moved on it continued to nag at her until she determined to find the reason for Toby's continuing run of luck.

With all this on her mind, Lia forgot about the letter she'd written a short time before inviting her parents to come for a visit to Sapphire Point. Then the reply arrived from her mother.

Dear child, we'd love to come. Your father suggests you give us a call to let us know your next days off, and we'll plan to drive up and spend them with you.

As she read the note, Lia had a sudden panicky feeling that as much as she loved her father she wasn't up to coping with him right now—what with Flint's gambling and Toby and the fact that she hadn't been able to put her mind to her thesis for most of the week. She was almost sorry she hadn't waited to invite them.

"Maybe it wasn't such a good idea after all," she told Flint doubtfully as they shared one of their joint-effort dinners on the deck of the Sapphire Point house.

"It's a great idea, of course," Flint assured her. "It's about time your parents and I met. What does your dad do outside his office?"

"Do? Oh, you mean like fishing and golf. He does both of those, but his favorite hobby is me," she told him ruefully.

Flint looked at her curiously. "Good. You're my favorite hobby, too. We've got a lot in common. I'll take care of your father."

"Thanks. You *are* a nice man, and I love you, but that's really not what I meant. It's me I'm worried about. Dad and me. The first hour he'll be on his good behavior, but keeping his eyes peeled. After that he'll spend the rest of the time he's here telling me everything he sees I'm doing wrong with my life."

"It shows he's interested," said Flint quietly. "Be glad for that."

"I know, and I am, and I love him, Flint. You just don't know my dad. I'm not sure I'm up to him right now." In the face of one whose own father had shown little enough interest in him, Lia felt suddenly ashamed.

But Flint said cheerfully, "It's as good a time as any to get to know your father. One day we'll spend on the golf course, and the other we'll take the boat out on the lake and fish. That doesn't leave you much time to worry about."

"Why, Flint, you darling. You really mean it, don't you?" said Lia. After a moment's hesitation, in a voice bleached of all expression, she asked, "Are you sure you can spare the time?"

There was a question in the brooding eyes that looked across at her, a shadow of indecision. He seemed about to say something. Instead he pushed back his chair and left it to circle the table and lower his arms for her to come into them. For a long moment they held each other in a close embrace, Flint's face buried in her hair, her cheek against his chest, where she could hear the strong steady beat of his heart

"Lia, oh, Lia, how I love you!" His voice came to her from somewhere in her curls, and then he held her away from him until they could look into each other's eyes.

"There's nothing to worry about, sweetheart. Trust me, love. Everything will be all right. I promise it will," he said, and she knew he was not talking about her father.

The strain of the week brought tears to her eyes, and she found little comfort in his words.

"Can you?" she asked, probing stubbornly.

"Can I what?"

"Spare the time away from the casino?"

"To play golf with your father?" he asked

tightly, and when she said nothing in return she saw a muscle in his taut jaw twitch.

"I will spare the time," he said.

LIA STAYED WITH FLINT in the penthouse suite the night before her parents arrived. Flint's enthusiastic approval of their coming had quickly melted her own reluctance. In the spirit that had prompted the invitation in the first place, she looked forward again—though not without some inner qualms—to reshaping her relationship with her father. It seemed as good a time as any to make a play for his admiration and respect. Without these the love between them, unlike the love between her and her mother, would forever be abrasive and incomplete.

In that strange moment of understanding before she lost consciousness the day Flint plunged himself into the lake and into her life, she'd seen in a flash of insight what she should have realized long before. She'd been sabotaging herself with her father all along. In her running battle to make him quit treating her as daddy's little girl she'd been fighting with a kind of childlike petulance, using a child's weapons as often as not. All of which did nothing but fix the little-girl image more firmly in his mind.

So, Lia, it's time for the little girl to grow up, she said to herself as she pressed the door buzzer at the penthouse suite early that evening. She had taken the express elevator up from the casino and was carrying a large yellow plastic tote bag, which she handed over to Flint when he opened the door.

"What's this?" he asked.

Lia grinned up at him sheepishly. "Guess."

Flint fumbled in the bag and brought out his own razor. "You mean I'm being dispossessed?"

"Well, temporarily, yes. I just don't think discovering your razor in my bathroom and your slippers under my bed is the best way in the world for dad to find out the full extent of our relationship."

"What makes you think your father's going to go poking around in your rooms?"

At the genuinely puzzled look on Flint's face, Lia gave a helpless sigh.

"I can't help it, Flint. I know he's not going to, but I will be more comfortable if your stuff's not there."

The tote bag slipped to the floor as Flint enfolded her in his arms and closed her eyes with a pair of small comforting kisses. Her breathing stopped, her lips softened and waited, moist and full, for his. When their invitation went unanswered Lia slowly opened her eyes to find Flint looking down at her, a wry smile deepening the small cleft in his cheek.

"Maybe we'd better give up our plans for the evening and go out and get married," he said.

There was something in his voice that caused Lia to eye him suspiciously. "Please, Flint," she said wearily. "We've been through all that."

"That we have, and I can only say that for someone who feels as guilty as you do over the alternative arrangement, it beats me why you go to such pains to avoid marriage vows." This time there was no mistaking the trace of acid in his voice.

Her heart pounding in sudden apprehension, Lia tightened her arms around his neck and raised her lips to touch his face with kisses. The time was not far ahead when Flint would no longer be put off. The warning was there in his voice. Sometimes she almost convinced herself that to delay the full commitment of marriage any longer was pointless and self-punishing—and then she would remember Toby.

If he'd only quit gambling, she thought. Even if Flint was the kind one issued ultimatums to, she couldn't use her promise to marry him as a bludgeon to make him quit.

"Flint, please understand, darling. I don't feel guilty about us in the least. I love you. I'm proud of our love. I want my parents to know about it, but not in that particular way, if it's all the same to you," she said softly, her face against his cheek. "I thought I'd introduce you to them as the man I'm going to marry. Would you mind?"

There was a moment of silence.

"Well, it's a start," he said shortly, but he sealed it with a lingering pensive kiss that spoke more of frustration than of desire.

He ordered champagne from room service and

toasted their engagement. They ate dinner on their balcony, watching the moon spread a bright path across the lake below, and Lia tried to tell Flint about her father.

"He still treats me the way he did when I was thirteen, Flint. It's up to me to find a way to make him see that the person I really am is not that headstrong, smart-alecky teenager he still thinks of as his daughter."

"You're really uptight about this visit, aren't you, love? Don't sell yourself short. There's nothing to worry about."

"You don't know my father."

Later they made love with a wild passion and lay together until the steady rise and fall of Flint's breathing told her he was asleep, and her arm ached under the weight of his.

Slipping it out carefully so as not to waken him, she propped herself on her elbow and looked down on his sleeping face, taking pleasure in the strong clean-cut line of his cheekbones, the broad sweep of his forehead up from the straight authoritative nose. When her arm tired, she leaned over and kissed him softly and with a sigh let herself down, settling in against his body, her head resting upon his arm.

It was not the same, she thought sadly. Not since Toby appeared on the scene and Flint started gambling. She and Flint did the things together they'd always done. They played tennis and walked and shopped for groceries and watched sunsets and cooked and ate, but it was not the same. They made love, but their lovemaking had lost the joie de vivre that had sparkled between them before. Sometimes it was with a kind of desperation, as if they feared they might never make love again.

They hardly ever teased, and there wasn't much talk. The wonderful wellspring of talk—funny, serious, foolish, meaningful, always revealing—that had bubbled up spontaneously whenever they were together had all but dried up. A shadow lay over them, and though they both knew the shadow was there, they never talked about it. They just went on doing the ordinary things—and making love.

Looking up through the shadowy dark at the outrageous mirror overhead she could see the reflection of their entwined bodies, as pale as alabaster, touched by the light of the full moon through the glass wall.

She wondered wryly if her colleagues in the field of human sexuality were familiar with mirrored ceilings.

CHAPTER EIGHTEEN

THE HEADLINER for the current show at the Goldorado's Comstock dinner theater was an entertainer who had been a crowd pleaser since the days of Chester Andrews's courtship of his wife, Muriel, and was a favorite of them both. The show was a holdover and a sellout. By the simple magic of being the owner's brother-in-law, Flint had secured tickets for the night before Lia's parents were to arrive, so Lia called them and they drove up from the city an afternoon early, in time for the dinner show with Lia and Flint.

It was a favorable beginning for their visit, Lia thought, seeing her father's hand slip under the linen tablecloth in search of her mother's during a particularly sentimental ballad. An engagement announcement would have been ill timed—premature and distracting. Flint's suggestion that they postpone telling her parents until the end of their visit was wise.

"What about giving your folks a chance to know me without prejudice before we spring it on them? If you introduce me to your father as his future son-in-law right off, isn't there a chance he'll look only for flaws? And there are enough to find. He could take a permanent dislike to me even before he gets to know me," Flint had said the night before, and Lia had admitted dolefully that there was a strong possibility it could happen that way.

Seeing her father now, she was glad she'd listened to Flint. Although he watched Flint with a wary eye throughout the evening, he was plainly enjoying himself, and he'd accepted without delay Flint's invitation to go fishing with him the next day.

Though Flint had mentioned the fishing earlier, she'd been half-afraid the lure of the blackjack table would keep him from following through. When he appeared at the door of the Sapphire Point house early the following morning with bait box and tackle, Lia had all she could do to keep from throwing herself in his arms, so great was her relief. Instead she thanked him discreetly with her eyes.

When she and her mother had seen the two men on their way, they took their coffee onto the sun-dappled deck.

"He's a very nice young man, this friend of yours," her mother volunteered after a moment.

Lia laughed and reached over to give an affectionate pat to her mother's blue-tinted hair.

"You'd say that, sweetie, even if he was a punk rocker. You'd never bad-mouth anyone I liked."

"Unpleasant truths have always been your

father's department, dear. I consider it a highly satisfactory arrangement. I've always preferred being left to throw the bouquets.''

Lia's eyebrows shot up. The smile of self-satisfaction on her mother's face brought a grin of astonishment to her own.

''Why you manipulative old darling, you,'' she said with amusement.

''He's very good at it. He certainly needs no re-inforcement from me,'' her mother said defensive-ly. ''I don't agree with him on everything, but I must say where you've been concerned, my dear, it's turned out he's often been right, though you may not care to admit it.''

Lia's instinct was to bristle, but having reached a similar conclusion during her recent soul-searching, she said instead, ''If you thought so, why didn't you say something, too? It would have saved dad and me a lot of battles. I might have lis-tened to you.''

Her mother shook her head and smiled ruefully. ''I hardly think so. Nothing would have changed except you would have had two to battle instead of one. I thought it was better all around for me to stay neutral.''

''Good thinking,'' Lia agreed. She reflected on those growing-up years at home for a moment be-fore she went on. ''Dad's so strong-minded. I guess I was afraid if I gave in without a fight he'd take over, and in the end I'd be no more than a kind of extension of him. I was scared there wouldn't be anything left that was *me*. You were a smart lady to stay out of it.''

"Not smart, dear. I believe the word is empathetic. In my generation most of us just played out the role we were assigned. Having done pretty much what was expected of me—first by my parents and then by Chester—I wanted you to have a chance to learn by your own mistakes. It's funny... I've never worried about you in the way your father has. There's never been a doubt in my mind that you'll work out your life very well, if you're left alone.''

Lia gave her mother a grateful smile, but she couldn't help saying a bit wistfully, "Thanks, sweety. I only wish dad felt the same.''

"Don't be too hard on your father, darling. It's not his fault he thinks it's his mission in life to save us female creatures from our own follies. It's because he cares, and because he's not a woman. No man really understands a woman's need to have control of her own life.''

"*No* man? Some men understand," Lia commented smugly. "Flint—''

But her mother would not hear her out. "Understand, maybe. Deep down inside your father understands, I suppose, but he doesn't know how it feels any more than we can feel what it is to be a man. No one but a woman can know how a woman feels.''

Lia left her chair to brush her mother's cheek with a kiss. "I still say I have a very smart lady for a mother.''

A side of her mother she had never seen before had just been revealed to Lia, and she realized for the first time that in the usual climate of confrontation between her and her father, there hadn't been room for any real intimacy between her and her mother. She'd loved her mother but had taken her for granted. It had been enough to the adolescent Lia that her mother was gentle and funny and rather pretty and chic in her own middle-aged way, and liked by her teenaged friends.

It saddened her now that she'd never made any particular effort to get to know the Muriel Sutton Andrews who'd been in there all along wearing the disguise of Lia's mother and Chester's wife.

She saw yet another side of her mother a short time later at the Burney home around the lake. Rozlyn had invited them both for lunch. In the presence of Lia's mother, the Burney children, whom Lia had thought such a trial the night Flint brought her to dinner, were unexpectedly charming and tractable. Missy's pouting face now wore a wreath of sunshine. Chap was bright and friendly and not at all inclined to make plays for adult attention as he had before.

Did Lia's mother have grandchildren, they wanted to know early in the visit. They murmured their sympathy when she told them no, then later, as Lia and her mother were leaving, the two children sidled up to Mrs. Andrews.

"Missy and me are sorry you don't have any grandchildren. We don't have a grandma. Could

Missy and me adopt you?'' Chap asked in a breathless rush. As she watched her mother bring herself down to the level of the children and pull them to her in a warm accepting hug, Lia could see she was deeply touched.

"They're adorable children," her mother said, looking back to where they stood in the doorway, Missy blowing kisses and Chap waving goodbye as the two women drove away.

"They were today," Lia admitted. "If you'd asked me before I'd have said no. I thought they were pretty bratty when I first met them."

"They wouldn't be normal if they weren't bratty now and then," said her mother in the complacent tone of the voice of experience. "It makes them even more lovable when they're behaving themselves."

"You really love children, don't you, mom?"

Her mother gave her a doesn't-everybody look. "Of course," she said. "But there was a time I couldn't stand them." She fixed a speculative eye on Lia. "I guess it won't traumatize you, at your age, if I tell you that before Chester and I were married I'd made up my mind I didn't want children, but I never had the courage to tell Chester. When I found out I was pregnant, I nearly died. But when you arrived you were such a hundred-percent success it nearly broke my heart when I couldn't have any more children. If your father had agreed, we would have adopted two or three."

Lia almost wished her mother hadn't said anything. She'd always taken it for granted that her mother had awaited her birth with fatuous joy, and she felt ridiculously let down to learn that her arrival had in fact been quite unwelcome.

It was the first time she had seen her mother as a woman, independent of her role as parent. Lia wondered what other surprises lay in store. She was reasonably sure that when she got to know her mother better, something she was resolved to do, they would be good friends.

Lia delighted in her new rapport with her mother but was increasingly troubled that her parents' visit was offering so little chance to redefine her status with her father—the main reason she'd asked them to come. By the end of the first day she'd had only a few minutes alone with him.

With Flint off somewhere on an errand of his own and her mother on a walk to the beach, she was debating how to approach him when her friend Carrie appeared with a basket of rosy-ripe Sutter County peaches from a box that had been brought to her from the valley that day. Her mother came up from the beach just as Carrie was leaving, so that was the end of that.

Carrie's appearance brought to Lia's mind something that had occurred to her the day before. Not caring to stir up her parents' curiosity, she excused herself to walk to her friend's car with her when she left.

"Listen, Carrie, do you suppose I could have a

word with your husband?'' she said when they were outside. ''Something's come up at my black-jack table I'd like to get Rick's thinking on.''

''That bastard isn't giving you trouble, is he?'' her friend asked in alarm.

''How did you know about Tob...oh, you mean Ed Shields. Oh no. It doesn't have anything to do with Shields,'' she said. But all at once, she wondered. ''At least I don't think it does. Anyhow, I'd like to talk to Rick about it, if he wouldn't mind.''

Carrie looked doubtful. ''I don't know, Lia. He's still pretty touchy about all that, but you can try. He's away for a few days looking into a possible scholarship so he can go back to school. He'll be back day after tomorrow.''

''Thanks, Carrie. I may stop by to see him then.''

When Lia came back into the house she found her father regaling her mother with a lively account of his heroic contest with the wily two-and-a-half-pound trout he'd pulled out of the lake while her mother encouraged him with appropriate murmurs of admiration and amazement.

For their dinner Flint barbecued the trout and another slightly smaller one he'd hooked himself, along with fresh foil-wrapped corn on the cob. Lia made the salad, and her mother shelled new peas and sliced Carrie's fragrant peaches for dessert. Then, to Lia's secret astonishment, her father volunteered to set the table.

By nine o'clock the first day's activities in combination with the high altitude caught up with Lia's parents, and they took themselves off to bed.

Left alone together for the first time since her parents' arrival, Lia and Flint went about the cleaning-up chores in uneasy silence. While they'd been involved together with Lia's parents, there'd been no sign of the constraint that had hung over them in recent days, but now it hovered ominously over them once again. Lia felt a knot of fear draw tight in her stomach.

We're losing each other, Flint, she thought in despair.

She could feel their relationship slipping away in the wake of these continued uneasy silences, and she didn't have the slightest idea what she could do to prevent it. From her experience with Toby, reinforced by what she'd since learned from her research, she was reasonably sure it would only make matters worse for her to confront Flint about his gambling.

He had to want to be helped. He had to be the one to bring it up. Forthright by nature, she wondered sometimes how much longer she could make herself hold her tongue about his problem. It was one of the hardest things she'd ever had to do in her life. It was also becoming harder to find anything to talk about at all.

When the silence between them grew oppressive, Lia said at last, "It was wonderful of you to take dad fishing today, Flint. I can't remember ever seeing him more pleased over anything than he is about catching that enormous trout.''

"Don't thank me, it was my pleasure. He's great to fish with,'' Flint said in his most offhand manner, but when he went on he was serious. "I like your father. I like the way he thinks.''

"You do?'' Somehow the idea surprised her.

The silence closed in again. "Your father would like to know when you are going to make an honest man of me,'' Flint said finally, the bite in his voice unmistakable now.

The old familiar feeling of resentment toward her father's high-handed interference in her affairs stirred in Lia, but she refused to let herself give in to it.

Nevertheless, she couldn't restrain the sarcasm that crept into her voice as she said, "I see he's up to his old tricks. Would you mind telling me by what circuitous route my father brought your fishing conversation around to that particular point?''

"Oh, he let me know right off that his little girl wasn't one to play fast and loose with. He didn't leave any doubt that he was asking me what my intentions were.''

"He didn't!''

"Sure he did.'' There wasn't a lot of humor in the slight grin that played at the corner of his mouth.

"Darn it, Flint, my father doesn't have any right to do this to me. I won't have him meddling in my life anymore. I'm sorry he did that to you."

"Don't be. If it was my little girl I'd probably do the same thing."

Not if she was my little girl, too, thought Lia grimly. *Not if she was over twenty-one.*

But Flint wasn't through. "I admire your father. It takes a lot of courage to deliberately involve yourself in your children's lives when you no longer have to. It's a lot more comfortable not to know what the hell they're up to. With the way values change from one generation to another, it must be hard work being a parent. Especially a father who's as sure as yours is that he holds the secret to the good life, if his child would only listen. It takes a brave stubborn man—and a man who cares a lot—to stick to his parenting with the tenacity of your dad."

Seething with indignation over her father's latest intrusion, Lia only half listened to what Flint said.

"So what did you tell him about your intentions?" she asked, her voice heavy with sarcasm.

"I assured him my intentions were honorable," Flint said with a defiant chuckle.

"I suppose you told him mine weren't," she countered, her ire rising again.

"Hardly!" said Flint dryly. "I wouldn't do a thing like that to your father."

How dare her father interfere when he didn't even know the facts! thought Lia furiously. It would serve him right if she told him the truth.

Dad, I'm going to marry Flint Tancer, a compulsive gambler.

She turned on Flint a glare of indignation.

"Men!"

WATCHING CHESTER ANDREWS hit a long drive down the middle of the eighteenth fairway the next morning, Flint thought again of his conversation with Lia about her father. As he recalled the first moments with her father in the boat the day before, he suppressed a smile. Bluntly and forthrightly Flint had been given to understand that as long as Chester Andrews was alive, no man had better try to take advantage of his daughter. But when that issue was out of the way he became a different man—a man who nearly overturned the boat a short time later in the excitement of landing the first fish of the day. Two fish later, he was insisting Flint call him Chester.

Flint felt a growing affection and respect for the man, who in a sense was really two men. He felt something close to pain for the one who was the father, still trying to fit a 1980s daughter into a 1950s mold.

Since this was to be the last day of Lia's parnets' visit, Flint had suggested a leisurely drive around the lake that afternoon. The plan was for the golfers to lunch together at the clubhouse before picking up the two women at the Sapphire Point house, but when they reached the clubhouse after playing the last hole they found the bar and dining

room filled with people assembled for some
private affair.

Flint could see Andrews's impatience at having
to wait to be served, but considering the dim view
Lia's father had taken of the casino scene when
Lia and Flint had shown her parents around the
day before, he hesitated to suggest they have lunch
at one of the restaurants in the Goldorado. Lia's
mother had gotten into the spirit and won a handful of quarters from a slot machine, but her husband had watched with a disapproving eye and
would have no part of it. He'd declined brusquely
when Lia urged him to try his hand at blackjack.

Flint was surprised now to hear Chester say,
"Why don't we eat at the Goldorado if we're going to have to wait here? We're taking the ladies
for a drive this afternoon. I wouldn't like to keep
them waiting."

So it was, a short time later, that Flint and
Chester Andrews entered the lobby of the Goldorado and headed through the casino toward the
Golden Urn. They were moving along the broad
carpeted passageway next to the gambling arena,
and as they passed near the pit where Lia normally
dealt, Flint was aware that the older man's steps
slowed for a moment. Then, with a grunt of
outrage, Andrews quickened his step. Flint turned
his head to see what had offended the other man.

"Something wrong?" he asked.

"That fellow over there in the leather jacket at
that second table. I knew him once. Don't care to

renew the acquaintanceship," said Lia's father, his voice agitated

"You mean Toby Brasford?"

"That's the one. Do you know him?"

"Not much more than his name. Management picked that up. I understand he's a small-time gambler who's been coming here for a year or two. Mind telling me what you know about him?"

"He's a real-estate broker in San Francisco, as far as I know." Andrews hesitated for a moment before going on, though he made no effort to conceal his distaste for what he was about to say. "Lia used to be engaged to him. Thank goodness she came to her senses. I never could understand what she saw in him."

They kept on their way into the lobby, but Flint felt as if the breath had been knocked out of him. The subject of Brasford was dropped and apparently dismissed from Andrews's mind, but for Flint it marked the beginning of a relay of restless speculation and doubts that started and finished always at the same point: *She hadn't told him. Why?... Why?... Why?*

For the rest of the day he moved in a state of numbness, doing what he'd set out to do with an outward semblance of normalcy. It must have passed for real, since he drew no questioning looks from Roz, who had invited Lia and her parents to dinner at the end of the afternoon excursion.

The drive covered some fifty miles of the seventy-two-mile distance around the ink-blue, mountain-locked lake. Flint was a knowledgeable and entertaining tour guide, but he got through the rest of the day only by burying his feelings for Lia under a protective shell of numbness and distancing himself from her.

Not until he was alone in the penthouse some hours later, having said goodbye to Lia's parents at the Sapphire Point house, did the questions surrounding Lia and Toby Brasford break wide open. *Lia and Toby Brasford...oh, God!* That was why she'd steered her parents clear of her own blackjack pit the day before and shown them instead the blackjack tables in another part of the casino. It was no accident that she hadn't told him who Brasford was. It was plain she didn't want him to know...but *why*?

The first and most obvious answer was that she was still in love with the gambling bastard. In which case, what was Flint Tancer doing in her life?

Jealousy licked through him like a hot flame. She was a woman on the rebound, that's what she was, and all he was in her life was an antidote to Brasford, whose life-style she couldn't accept. Even so, she must still be involved in some way with Brasford. Otherwise, what did she care whether or not Flint knew about him?

Through the midnight hours Flint tormented himself with speculations. The crafty, almost too-handsome face he'd come to know from the blackjack table hung sullenly over his thoughts, corrupting the picture of Lia he carried in his mind.

She'd said she loved Flint. She'd said he was the only man she'd ever loved. Yet if that was so, how could she let him sit day after day at the same blackjack table with a man she'd once been engaged to and not tell him? A strange kind of love that was! A strange kind of love...and what was she trying to hide?

Giving up on sleep, he flung himself out of bed and prowled the confines of his penthouse quarters until he found himself at last in a cushioned chair on the rooftop garden terrace. From there he stared across the black velvet distance of the night-mysteried lake, feeding his own poisonous thoughts.

What kind of woman was Lia Andrews? he asked himself cynically. Had she lied when she said she loved him, or was she the kind who could love two men at the same time? Or, out of stubborn loyalty to whatever past they'd had together, had she let herself become an accomplice in the scam to fleece the casino that Flint was sure Brasford was a part of?

With the first hint of dawn, the direction in which his irrational jealousies were carrying him hit Flint like a bolt of lightning. In a sudden shock of revulsion he underwent a kind of catharsis, and his thoughts reached out to embrace the woman he loved. He thought of the commitment between them—a commitment as real and valid as if they had exchanged marriage vows; a commitment that involved trust as well as love.

Had he learned nothing from that first lack of trust, which had almost lost her to him? How could he find fault with Lia's failure to be candid when he had not told her he had become a casino spy. Who was he to define Lia's motives from the tortured speculations of his own jealous mind? He should ask her point-blank why she hadn't told him. The Lia he knew and loved would give the truth, which, for his own peace of mind, he must hear.

SHORTLY AFTER MIDNIGHT, unable to sleep, Lia wrapped the warm fleece robe around her and slipped quietly from her bedroom to her working corner behind the screen in the living room. Turning on her study lamp, she pulled material for her neglected thesis from a desk drawer where she kept it hidden away from Flint's eyes. She had been working for perhaps an hour when the creak of a board told her she was not alone. Rising quietly to look around the corner of the screen she sighted the stout bathrobed figure of her father coming from the hallway into the living room. He peered owlishly in her direction.

"Dad! What are you doing up?"

"I might ask the same of you. I couldn't sleep. A touch of indigestion. I thought maybe I could find some baking soda in the kitchen."

"Let me get you a seltzer," Lia said.

In the kitchen she dropped two of the white wafers into a glass of water and handed him the fizzing potion, which he swallowed in one long breath.

"Too much rich food," he said grumpily, handing the glass back to her. "Flint's sister is a splendid cook, but she's going to kill that husband of hers with all that rich food."

"Now, dad...."

Her father grunted. "I took her aside and told her to talk to you or her brother about the kinds of meals you cook."

Lia stared at him in shocked amusement.

"Dad! You didn't!" she gasped.

"I most certainly did. They're fine people, and I'd hate to see something like that happen, eating all that rich food she cooks. Now the dinner you and Flint fixed for us last night—that's the kind of food mother and I like. When I see how well you two work there together it makes me a little sorry I never went into the kitchen myself."

I'll bet! thought Lia. Aloud she said slyly, "It's still not too late. You and mom still eat, don't you?"

Her father eyed her with suspicion and grunted again. Their eyes met and held, and father and daughter seemed to size each other up for a long moment before Lia's father relented with a small, half-defensive smile.

"Your mother wouldn't stand for it," he muttered and turned away, adding over his shoulder, "We've got a long drive ahead of us tomorrow. I guess I'd better try and get some sleep."

"Dad..." Lia began, wanting to delay him. This was her last chance, the one she'd been waiting for ever since they had come, though she was not sure even now what it was she wanted to say to him.

Her father turned back. "It's been a fine visit. Mother and I were glad you invited us. We're glad we came." She waited. It was plain he wasn't through. "You and Tancer make a pretty good team," he said abruptly, then gave a nod toward her working corner. "Does he know what you're up to back there?"

Lia's brows shot up in alarm. "No. I hope you didn't tell him. It could get me fired."

Her father gave her an injured look. "No, but I certainly think *you* should." He stopped, and again she waited, realizing that whatever her father was about to say, it was to be said with considerable reluctance. The old darling was forcing himself to say something he'd much rather leave unsaid, she thought, and for the first time she understood what Flint had been telling her the night before.

"About Tancer, Lia. He seems to be pretty much at home around here." Again he came to a full stop. She knew now how much he hated to go on—she could see it in his eyes. But he did go on in the familiar angry bluster she'd come to think of over the years as her father's natural voice.

"Are you and Tancer sleeping together?"

He'd asked the question because he saw it as his

duty to ask and because he cared about her. But he didn't want to know. Her heart ached for the beleaguered man.

"Daddy," she said, deliberately using the name she hadn't used since she was a little girl. "Come over here."

She put her hand on his shoulder and steered him toward the sofa, where they sat down together. Looking into his face she smiled. "You know you don't really want me to answer that question, dad, and I'm not going to."

Her father started to break in, but Lia reached over and put a detaining finger on his lips.

"No dad," she said firmly. "I still have something to say." To her surprise, he let her prevail.

"Look at it this way," she went on. "You've already made up your mind about this, so if I say no you'll be afraid to believe me. You'll hate thinking your daughter has lied to you, and I don't much like for you to think it myself. But suppose I say yes. By the standards of your generation I'd be doing wrong, but different generations don't necessarily see things the same. Whether I answer you yes or no we're in a no-win situation.

"I don't mean to hurt you, dad, but I'm the one who has to decide how I live my life from now on, even the mistakes. You don't have a vote. So you see, you don't have to agonize over me anymore. I just set you free."

Her father looked stunned. She waited for him

to say something, but he ran a hand over his bald pate and said nothing, as if struck dumb.

"Trust me, dad," she pleaded gently. "I'm okay. I really am. You've given me everything, and that's something I'll never forget. All I need now is your love and your trust."

He hoisted himself to his feet and headed toward the bedroom wing of the house. Lia watched anxiously, her eyes brimming with tears, as the stout, bald-headed man in the plaid bathrobe who was the father she loved walked heavily away from her.

Not until early next morning when he appeared for breakfast, his face serene and rested, did she begin to feel comfortable about the post-midnight encounter with her father.

"Slept like a log," he said.

A short time later she saw her parents to their car and gave her mother a goodbye kiss while her father stowed their bags in the trunk.

"Thanks," she whispered in her mother's ear. Her mother's blink of surprise was interrupted by her father, who came around from the rear of the car to catch her up in a hearty bear hug that squeezed her breathless.

"You've got a good head on your shoulders, honey," he said gruffly as he let her go.

Knowing they were the last words she was apt to hear from him on the subject, Lia wore them like a crown.

CHAPTER NINETEEN

BACK AT THE CASINO the warm glow Lia felt after seeing her parents off was quickly snuffed out by the appearance of Toby, reminding her that an explanation of Toby to Flint was long overdue.

She should have cleared the whole thing up with Flint the day after Toby appeared. She didn't quite understand why she hadn't, except she'd shunned tarnishing a single shining moment with Flint by bringing into it any thought of Toby. After the first few days, when the two men continued to be oblivious of each other at the table, she'd decided to wait it out. Toby's luck would change. He'd move on to greener pastures.

Only that wasn't what had happened. Toby continued to win and didn't move on. He was, in fact, well on his way to becoming a permanent fixture. The situation was once again beginning to make Lia very anxious. With her parents' visit behind her, telling Flint about Toby became a high-priority item.

She wondered if it would serve any purpose to talk to Toby again. She could try to prevail on him to take his winnings and go somewhere else. It didn't take much perception to see that for all his run of luck, Toby wasn't happy about something. Maybe she could persuade him that a change of scenery was the cure for his woes.

When it was almost time for her break, Flint hadn't yet appeared, and Toby was the only player at her table. As she shuffled the deck, she said quietly, "I want to talk to you, Toby. How about meeting me in the coffee shop when I go on my break?"

She half expected him to refuse, but at that moment, before he had given her more than a questioning look, two more players took places at the table and she became involved again in the game.

She was almost surprised when he appeared a short time later at the entrance to the coffee shop in sight of the booth where she sat. She raised her hand to catch his attention, and a moment later he slipped into the small booth across from her. The handsome face looked puffy. Dark circles lay like smudges of soot beneath his eyes.

"Congratulations on your fabulous run of luck, Toby."

Toby's eyes shifted. "You didn't ask me here for that," he said suspiciously.

"Not really," she admitted. "I can't help noticing that winning isn't making you all that happy. You've been looking pretty mopey."

He laughed nervously. "That's the trouble with psychologists. You're always trying to read something that isn't there into everyone's actions."

"True," she said with a grin. "Leaving the psychology out of it, the person I see out there at the blackjack table isn't the breezy, devil-may-care Toby Brasford I used to know, even when you'd just blown your last cent gambling. And now you're even winning. What's up, Toby?"

The man across from her shifted uneasily in his seat. Avoiding her eyes, he said, "That's a laugh, coming from the one who threw me over." The voice was petulant and lacked conviction, but he had hit on a theme he liked, and when he continued he played it with hearts and flowers.

"How do you think it makes me feel to sit there looking at you hour after hour, knowing I've lost you? Winning can't heal an ache like that, Lia."

She didn't believe a word of it, but she felt a tingle of triumph. Smart Toby had played into her hands.

"I'm sorry to hear that, Toby," she said. "If that's what's making you uptight, why do it anymore, for heaven's sake? Get out before it makes a complete wreck of you. Take your winnings and go someplace exciting. Forget you ever knew me. Have a vacation for yourself."

"Walk out on this run of luck? You've got to be crazy," he said sullenly.

"But the luck could end today, Toby," she reasoned. "And when it ends you'll put everything you've won back in. You know you will. You can't help it. Then where'll you be?"

Toby leaned across the table. Instead of the

brooding dissatisfaction she'd seen in his eyes earlier, there was a kind of feverish excitement. "But it's not going to end this time," he said intensely. "If you'll just hang in there, Lia baby, we'll have that Paris honeymoon, I swear."

Lia's eyes widened in alarm. The conversation had all at once gone mad.

"Toby, listen to me," she said firmly. "You've got to understand. We're through. I wasn't kidding that last time we talked. Since it pains you so to look at me hour after hour, there's only one thing to do. Take your winnings and get out. Go to another casino if you're determined to ruin your life gambling. Just get away from my table and don't come back!"

"No way!"

Defeated, Lia got to her feet. "Do as you like, Toby. If you won't help yourself, just remember that as far as I'm concerned you and I are strangers, and I expect you to treat me as one."

She left him sitting there and walked away. With a few minutes remaining on her break she pushed through the door to the nearest powder room and sat down on a couch, half-sick with disgust over the whole sorry situation. It was foolish to have expected anything positive to come out of a meeting with Toby. He'd made his position clear to her at that earlier meeting. There'd been no reason to suppose he might have changed his mind. If nothing else, she shouldn't have risked being seen with Toby while Flint still didn't know about him.

And in spite of herself, she couldn't help worrying about Toby—poor, despicable Toby, who wasn't vicious, just weak. The fact she no longer had any affection for him didn't leave her without concern. She had a genuine desire to see Toby out of the mess he was making of his life and back on a more solid footing.

She wondered what could be causing all this anxiety right when Lady Luck was smiling on his cards. She saw then that she was still tied in a way to Toby. When she stopped caring for him in a personal way, the psychologist in her had taken over. In the transition Toby Brasford, ex-fiancé, had become Toby Brasford, case study.

When she returned to the table Toby was already there. He didn't look up as she moved in to replace the relief dealer.

A faint hope that Flint had decided to bite the bullet and stay away from the gaming tables was dashed when he showed up a few minutes after she started dealing again. He gave her a wintry smile, slipped into an empty seat and began to play.

He couldn't wait to make up for lost time, she thought sourly as she returned his somewhat less-than-cordial acknowledgment with an equally cool nod.

Lia felt miffed. He was trying to escape his own guilty feelings by acting as if she was the wrong-doer. But even as the thought took shape in her mind, she was obliged to admit a dereliction or two of her own. First there was the matter of her unauthorized gambling study, though it was a deception she considered both harmless and mandatory. And there was the matter of Toby, harmless enough, too, though after such a long silence on her part she feared Flint was unlikely to agree

THE REST OF THE DAY was terrible. A woman at her table slumped down to the floor and passed out before her eyes. Lia, in the dealer's slot, was helpless to reach her before she went down. It was not an uncommon occurrence among newly arrived patrons from the valley, who came up from near sea level to an altitude close to seven thousand feet in little more than two hours. A whiff of oxygen from the first-aid attendants brought the woman quickly around, yet the incident left Lia strangely shaken. The woman was back at the table playing blackjack within the hour, to all appearances no worse for having succumbed to the altitude syndrome, and Lia realized she was more disturbed than she had reason to be

Later, a man who had lost consistently from the first hand she'd dealt him accused Toby of ringing in marked cards and demanded a new deck It was a nasty scene for a moment. Though Toby, a consistent winner all afternoon, stared arrogantly at his accuser, Lia recognized a familiar nervous tic in one of his eyelids that told her he was suffering a high level of tension. She wondered whether the other player was just striking out at the most obvious winner in vengeance for his own losses or if he actually had some solid base for his accusation.

Guiltily she almost hoped he had. That would explain Toby's phenomenal luck. It could also get Toby permanently barred from the casino, which would be worthwhile all around. It didn't take long to realize that her hope was a false one. She watched the pit boss break the seal on a new deck at the table, then waited to see if Toby's fortunes would go sour. In spite of the change of deck, Toby continued to win. After a while the player who had complained left, frustrated and angry. Again the incident disturbed Lia far more than it warranted.

When at last Flint appeared and took a seat at the table he was aloof, watching the play with hooded eyes, betting and playing his cards with a seeming indifference to the outcome, never letting his gaze meet hers. Once she caught his eyes upon her. The look of cool reproach that lay in them was beyond her understanding and touched her like an icy hand.

She saw it all through the cloud of smoke that rolled up from the continuous stream of smokers who played at her table that day. Lia didn't smoke. In her adolescent years she'd taken it up, perhaps as yet another gesture of defiance toward her father, who disapproved. She'd quit at a time when she was short on funds and working hard to stay independent. The satisfactions she found in the indulgence hadn't seem worth the costs. In any case, she'd been indifferent to the cigarette smoke that often drifted around her.

When she started working at the Goldorado she wasn't long in learning that a table full of smokers was the bane of every blackjack dealer's life. In the dealer's standing position at the center of the table's half-circle, Lia's face was enough above the level of the seated players that all smoke moved directly into her eyes, nose and throat. After a full shift of heavy smokers she often went home with her eyes watery and inflamed and her throat feeling as if it had been buffed with a nutmeg grater.

To these common miseries were added other normal dealer complaints—tired feet, an aching back. That day, at the end of her shift, Lia suffered them all plus a rarer affliction for her—a cheerless state of mind.

Like a creature escaped from its cage, she left the casino in the late afternoon, pausing only to fill her lungs with new air as she came into the outside world. Even though it was tainted with exhaust from the steady flow of traffic on the interstate highway that fronted the big hotel-casino, the air outdoors seemed almost fresh compared to the smoky haze she'd just left. Not until she reached Sapphire Point could she breathe in the pure pine fragrance off the lake.

She hurried across the parking lot and was about to unlock her car and start for home when she noticed a fold of paper tucked under the wind-shield wiper.

It was a note from Flint.

Lia, if it will be convenient for you I'll be by to see you at your place around eight tonight. Have the desk let me know if you've other plans.

Flint

There it was—cool, impersonal, scrupulously polite and not one phrase clothed in warmth. The oddest thing was that she didn't know why things were suddenly like this. The aloofness had come so unexpectedly. She'd first felt a breach between them on the trip around the lake the afternoon before and in the evening at the Burneys; even more in the perfunctory good-night he gave her after a warm leave-taking with her parents, and his at-titude to her in the casino that afternoon. And if she had had any hope that this distancing on Flint's part was temporary, the note in her hand put an end to it.

At least she knew he was coming to her house that night. She'd wondered when she would see him again, and there would be no peace for her until she found out what had turned Flint into a cool-eyed stranger overnight.

As she pulled out of the lot she thought she caught a glimpse of the irate gambler who had accused Toby that afternoon. It brought the whole ugly scene back to her. She found it hard to believe that Toby could be doing something crooked, yet as she let her mind work at the problem she found it even harder to believe a single player could have such an unbroken run of good luck.

Not that Toby never lost. He did, but he always lost small. Nor had he made any spectacular hauls that might attract the attention of the casino; just a nice steady income, winning enough to cover his losses and a comfortable surplus each day.

Maybe Toby had devised a card-counting system that worked differently than any she'd ever heard of. When they found him out, the worst that could happen to him was to be barred from playing at the casino. In some ways that might be better for everyone.

Maybe Toby had hit on such a system, but she doubted it. He didn't have the kind of mathematical genius to devise a sure-winning method for keeping tabs on a blackjack deck. She also thought he was too impatient for instant success to master anything but the most rudimentary system, even if it fell into his hands.

Which brought her back to the accusation of a marked deck. That worried her the most. She'd almost welcomed the idea when the man at the table brought it up, but not when she thought it through. If Toby really was mixed up in something crooked it could mean a lot more trouble than simply getting himself kicked out of a casino.

For all her contempt for the man, the last thing in the world she wanted was to case-study him into jail.

Sooner or later the casino was going to take note of his extraordinary string of winnings and start wondering what he was up to. The moment they did, it would be too late for Toby.

If he was involved in something crooked, the only way he could be saved was for her to find out what his game was before the casino began to get wise and confronted him with the evidence. If she threatened to turn him over to the management maybe she could scare him into returning the money he'd won dishonestly. Then she could approach Aaron Burney and ask him to go easy on Toby. Aaron was a fair man. If she talked Toby into giving the money back to the Goldorado and he appealed for leniency, she felt sure Aaron would listen.

When she turned in to Sapphire Point, Carrie Williams was standing in the doorway of the gate house, and Lia pulled over to thank her for her gift of peaches.

"Rick's back, Lia. You still want to talk to him?"

"More than ever. You think he'd mind?"

"He had a good trip. He'll tell you about it. I told him you had a problem. He said he'd be glad to help."

Lia steered her car over to the side and parked. Carrie waited for her at the door, and the women went into the house together.

"Carrie tells me things went well while you were away," Lia said to the stocky young man with the stubborn chin and light brown eyes. He turned off the TV news and stood up to greet her.

"Great!" he said, eyes bright with satisfaction. "The college offered me a graduate assistantship for next semester. It doesn't pay a lot, but I found an apartment house Carrie and I can manage. That'll take care of our rent. We won't have as much money in hand as we had here when I was working, but I'll be in engineering school, and that's what we've been working for."

"Oh, Rick, I can't tell you how happy I am for you both!"

"Funny part of it is, I probably would never have thought of going after it if I hadn't got canned at the Goldorado. One of these days I'll go over and tell Mansfield he did me a favor."

Lia drew a deep breath. "Which brings us to what I stopped by for, Rick. There's something sticky going on over there and I'm not sure what it is. I'm pretty green at this sort of thing, but you've been around casinos longer. Maybe you can tell me a couple of things."

"For instance?"

She told him about the flare-up at her table with the deck that afternoon. "I don't know whether the deck that was retired was marked, but I can swear the new one wasn't. It was a sealed deck. Ed Shields put it on the table for everybody to see, as he's supposed to do, and all of us watched him break the seal. The new deck didn't change anyone's luck. The winner continued to win. Is there any way a lone player can cheat the house with a clean deck?''

"Sure. There are several ways. Most of them involve a certain amount of skill on the gambler's part, even if he has an outside accomplice.''

"I don't think there's an outside accomplice. I happen to know the fellow—Toby Brasford. I used to know him in the city. He's been playing at my table regularly, and he walks out of the place a winner every day. I'm sure I would have noticed anyone who might be working with him.''

"He isn't a sleight-of-hand artist by any chance? If he is and is good at it, he can manage some very effective card switching.''

"That's not Toby. Take it from me, he's a complete right hander with two left hands,'' Lia said with a laugh.

"In that case, let's suppose he's not doing it with his hands, he's doing it with his eyes, which means he probably has an accomplice.''

"But I'm sure he hasn't, Rick. There are times when there's hardly anybody near the table. I use my eyes, too. I'm sure if anyone was hanging around regularly I would remember the face.''

"I'm not talking about an outside accomplice, Lia. I'm saying the guy's getting some in-house help.''

"Like. . .?"

"The usual combination is player and dealer, but since you're the dealer, in this case that hardly applies. There are a number of tricky ways a dealer can tip his hand to a player so the player knows in advance how good a hand he has to beat. A crooked dealer with light fingers can stack the deck in favor of a player or save a good top card by dealing second cards until he comes to his man."

"That's all very interesting, but I don't do second cards, Rick," Lia said wryly.

"So that brings us to the pit boss. Let me tell you about Ed Shields, Lia. Carrie's told you he screwed me over, I think."

"She told me he did. She didn't say how."

"Well, there was this guy winning regularly at my table just like you say Brasford's winning at yours. Mansfield began tightening the screws, and next thing you know Shields goes to Mansfield and tells him I'm in cahoots with the player and am tipping the dealer's hand. They couldn't prove anything, but they kicked the guy out of the casino, and Mansfield took me aside and asked me to go on sick leave until they got to the bottom of it. I told him to hell with his job. Who needs it?"

"Yes, but, Rick, suppose Ed was the man's accomplice. How would a pit boss work with a player?"

"There are different ways, but I'll tell you what Shields was doing then. He was giving the table a marked deck when his man was playing. The cards were marked on the back with an invisible ink that only shows up under a certain kind of glass. The guy wore glasses with lenses made of the stuff. He could read every card in the deck without turning it over.''

"How do you know for sure?''

"I started checking into ways to cheat when this guy kept winning all the time, and I read about it. Then I slipped a couple of cards out of one of the decks one day and tested them, and sure enough. I figure Shields discovered the cards were missing and decided he'd better pin it on me.''

"There's only one thing wrong, Rick. That deck today was a sealed deck. The whole table saw Ed break the seal.''

"Next time Shields brings you a new deck when this guy Brasford is playing, try to get a good look at the seal and see if it hasn't been tampered with. Ten to one, if you can, you'll find it has.''

The whole conversation was staggering to Lia. She wanted to think Rick was mistaken, but so much of it fit she could hardly dismiss it without at least checking the seal on the deck. For one, the very first thing she'd noticed about Toby when she saw him at her table that first day was that he was wearing glasses. She had never seen him in glasses before. Come to think of it, he wasn't wearing them when she'd seen him earlier at the restaurant.

In her mind she saw him again, half turned

away from her in the shadowy passageway of the restaurant. She saw again the back of the man who was with him, and suddenly she knew who it had been. Ed Shields, the pit boss.

Rick was saying something to her, and she turned back to him in a daze.

"How well do you know this guy, Brasford?" he asked curiously.

Lia hesitated uncomfortably and then decided it was only fair to tell him the truth. "Too well, I'm sorry to say. As a matter of fact, we were engaged until I broke it off because of his gambling. The whole thing was a mistake. There's nothing between us now."

Rick gave a short surprised whistle. "A word of advice from an old hand, Lia. Be careful what you do about this. Shields is a real viper. He'll wipe you out to save his own skin, just the way he did me."

Lia's eyes widened in surprise. "I don't see how."

"Management is probably already aware that your table has been losing regularly, so they've got their eyes on you. The minute Shields feels the heat he'll get his man, Brasford, bounced from the casino the way he did his man before, and then he'll point the finger at you. He probably already knows about your connection with Brasford in the city. He may even think you wouldn't turn in the two of them if they got caught. That may be why Shields insists upon keeping the guy playing at your table."

A chill ran down Lia's spine, and she shivered.

"Thanks, Rick," she said. "You've told me a lot." She grinned wryly. "Actually, you've told me more than I really wanted to know, but I appreciate it. I'll remember what you said."

CHAPTER TWENTY

FLINT LEFT HIS NOTE for Lia in the early afternoon before he went back to take up his station at her table. Les Mansfield had been none too happy to have the heavy winner go unwatched for two full days, but Flint had been adamant. Spending time with Lia'a parents was of more importance to him. Besides, as he'd pointed out to Les, whatever the guy was doing to make him a winner he'd still be doing when Flint resumed his vigil.

Well, he was back, he thought gloomily. Ironically, for the first time Flint brought with him real motivation to find out what the SOB was up to. He'd been watching the table more to humor Les and Aaron than because he thought anyone was ripping off the casino; and he'd been minding it far less than he'd expected, except for an ingrown distaste for acting as company spy. He had only to raise his eyes from the table to Lia's piquant face to escape the deadly boredom that crept over him when faced with a deck of cards, a boredom that had kept him away from casinos until now.

Even the sweaty-palmed anxiety of his collegiate gambling years, when winning spelled the difference between tuition money or not, had been better than the ennui he felt now with the whole betting scene. Nor was the fact that he was playing with house money and had no personal stake in the play the reason he was bored. He would have felt the same if the money he laid on the line had been his own. Sometimes he had to remind himself to give his cards a look before he went through the motions of playing them.

It was far too easy to be distracted by the enchanting ballet Lia's hands and fingers performed with the cards, or captivated by the two small lines between her eyes, which furrowed her brows whenever he lost all his chips and was obliged to buy. Indifferent himself, he was pleased immeasurably that she should care whether he won or lost.

It reminded him how incredibly much he loved her and how maddening it was to have her say to him in one breath that she loved him and in the next to wait awhile. He'd waited too long already for the right woman. Now that he'd found her, she couldn't blame him if he chafed when she asked him to wait a little longer. He was puzzled and hurt that she kept putting him off when she gave every sign of being as committed to him as he to her. At least until yesterday he'd been puzzled. Now he had a clue, and he hadn't the slightest idea what to make of it. He wouldn't have had even that much to go on if he and her father hadn't come into the casino after their golf game the day before to have lunch.

As he slipped into an empty chair at her table next to Brasford, Flint was more than a little annoyed with himself for having devoted too much attention to the pleasant distractions of Lia's presence and not enough to watching his quarry. Reminding himself that he intended to see her tonight, he blocked Lia out of his mind. Focused on Brasford alone, he noted the characteristics of his play, his face, his hands, his evident state of mind. He paid particular attention to the gambler's reactions when another player accused him of bringing in marked cards and demanded a new deck.

Shortly before the end of Lia's shift the bell captain from the hotel brought a note into the casino from Mansfield asking Flint to come to his office as soon as he could get away, which meant whenever Brasford quit playing. Flint knew the gambler's hours usually coincided roughly with Lia's shift, though he sometimes stayed on longer and sometimes left before she was through. Mansfield had seen to it that the security people notified Flint each day when Brasford sat down at the table, so Flint was never far behind in his own arrival. Sometimes Flint would leave for brief intervals and then come back. Often he left immediately after Lia did. For the most part Flint had stayed on the job, but until now there had been periods when the gambler had gone unwatched.

With new dedication to his job, Flint followed

through to the bitter end of one of Brasford's longer sessions. It was nearly seven o'clock before he was finally able to leave the table and climb the stairs to Mansfield's office.

Mansfield was waiting for him there. Flint could see by the look on his face that the session would not be an easy one.

"Aaron tells me you've been seeing one of our dealers, Flint."

Flint looked at his old friend and business associate in surprise. It was hardly the sort of question he expected from Les, and he was not sure he liked it. He eyed the Goldorado manager warily.

"*Seeing* her is not the way it should be phrased, Les, and if by one of our dealers you mean Lia Andrews, there's another bad choice of words," Flint responded in a level voice. "It's only fair to tell you, Lia is the woman I intend to marry. You are obviously not very well acquainted with her or you would know how inappropriate a choice that word combination, 'our dealer,' is. Lia is not 'our' anything. She is very much her own woman."

Taken aback by the rebuff, Mansfield waited a moment before he attempted to make amends.

"Sorry, Flint. If I offended you or Ms Andrews, I certainly didn't intend to, I assure you," he apologized, his own voice a little prickly. "I wish Aaron had been a little more specific about your relationship with the young lady. We might have gotten off to a better start."

Flint relented. "It's all right, as long as you understand. There's been no announcement. Aaron may not have guessed, but I'd be willing to bet Roz has."

"Under the circumstances, I doubt if there's any way to say what I've got to say that isn't going to make you madder than hell, so it doesn't matter, I suppose," said Mansfield reluctantly.

"Let's have it."

Mansfield drew a heavy breath and plunged in. "We've got a problem at that table, Flint. This Toby Brasford you've been watching is out to put the casino in the red, and it's got to be stopped. You say he's definitely not manipulating the cards on his own, so if we kick him out we still have the accomplice to find. You know yourself the first one we look at is the dealer, because...."

"Damn it, Mansfield, quit pussyfooting around," Flint broke in furiously. "Come out and say it. You've decided that because Lia's the dealer, she's got to be the accomplice. You've made that mistake with an honest dealer before and regretted it. Didn't you tell me that?"

"Yes...well, but—"

"Why go after the dealer then? You got rid of the last dealer, but the problem crops up again. That ought to tell you to take a good look at the pit boss, I'd say."

"There wasn't that much to go on the other time. This time there is, and it still doesn't look like it has anything to do with the pit boss. I hate to say it, Flint, because it'll come as a shock to you, but we have reason to believe Ms Andrews and Brasford are not strangers to each other.'

Flint's jaw pulled tight. "Don't tell me about Ms Andrews, Les," he said coldly. "Of course they're not strangers. She and Brasford were engaged. She broke it off."

"You're not serious!"

"Knock it off, Les. I don't mind telling you, my patience is beginning to wear thin."

The manager waited uncertainly to continue. When he went on his manner was cautious but determined. "We've been friends for a long time. Maybe I'm jeopardizing that now, but damn it, Flint, there's something you should know, and I feel it's my obligation to tell you. About this engagement. maybe it's broken, but Ms Andrews and Brasford are still seeing each other. They've had at least two very earnest conversations that I know of in the Golden Urn coffee shop here. I happened to see them there once myself, so it s not just hearsay. The cashier says they've been in together before."

This was his old friend, Mansfield, who was saying these things, Flint reminded himself. He glared at the tall, bespectacled, bookish-looking manager and restrained himself from striking out with the barrage of angry words that crowded into his mind.

At last he said quietly, his voice strained, "I think we'd better bring this conversation to a halt

Les, while we're still friends. I promise you this, I intend to find out what Brasford's game is if it's the last thing I do. In the meantime I'd just as soon we stay the hell out of each other's sight until you can find it in your conscience not to bad-mouth the woman I love. Because I'm warning you that when you do, I find it hard not to say a lot of things we'd both be sorry for.''

His anger at Mansfield stayed with Flint all the way to Lia's front door. When he saw her standing there, his throat swelled with love, leaving no room for anger, no room for words. Stepping inside, he took her in his arms in a fervent embrace as if he had just returned from a long journey away from her.

To FIND HERSELF in Flint's arms, pressed so close to the main artery of his heart she could feel each beat thundering against her breast, was the last thing Lia had imagined would happen when she opened the door. She'd expected to see him cool eyed and formal, with that inexplicable tightness to his face that discouraged intimacy. It was the way he'd been in the odd moments when they were together the day before. His detachment that afternoon at the blackjack table had given her no reason to expect a change.

Maybe it had been a forewarning of the show-down on the marriage question she'd known inevitably lay ahead. But somehow she didn't think so. It had seemed like something sudden and new.

For her own peace of mind she had to know what was at the bottom of it, and she'd resigned herself to a long painful evening of probing talk to close the mysterious distance that had sprung up between them.

She had looked forward to his coming tonight with ambivalence, and had opened the door half-reluctantly. Now to have him walk in and without a word sweep her into his arms, to find their yearning bodies clinging to each other rapturously, answering each other's intimate secrets... Where was the distance now? The rest could wait, thought Lia, and lifted her face to meet his lips in a hungry kiss.

"Oh, Flint, I love you. I'm so glad..." she murmured, her mouth sweet from the taste of his. His hands shaped themselves around the firm curve of her buttocks, pressing her ever closer to him. She responded to the rise of his passion with a swell of sweet hot pain within.

"Oh God." The words seemed wrenched from the man. Slowly he released her and stood looking down, breathing unevenly. "That wasn't the way I...not the first...order of business," he said, his words ragged and forced. He stopped for a moment, waiting for his breath to grow steady. "We...there are things we've got to talk about, Lia, and if—" He broke off with a despairing groan. "Don't look at me like that!" His arms reached out to pull her to him again but she would not allow it.

Did he really think he could charge in here as if he was storming a fort and then break it off suddenly because he'd decided he wanted to talk? she thought hotly, drawing back. Wasn't there something to be said for priorities?

She was locked in his arms again, but the mood was shattered. In her pique and frustration she brought into play a harmless but effective move she'd mastered in a self-defense course she'd once taken and sprung herself from his embrace, leaving Flint to stare at her in amazement.

"I didn't know you were a judo artist," he said with a wry grin.

Lia's flash of temper had burned out. She grinned back at him.

"Not judo. I took a self-defense course once to get dad off my back when I started living alone." Then she asked cautiously, "You want to talk?"

An early-evening chill had settled in off the lake. A fire crackled in the fireplace. Lia led the way into the living room and seated herself in her favorite green corduroy wing chair. To her surprise Flint passed up the companion chair near her and took a place on the love seat facing her across the width of the fireplace.

In answer to the question in her eyes, Flint said, "If I'm to get this out I'd better sit over here. When you're within arm's reach I forget everything but making love."

"Is that how it is at the casino?" she teased.

"Can't you tell?" he asked with another grin. "Why do you think I keep losing my shirt?"

There he sat, his lean athletic body looking strangely out of place on the undersize sofa, gazing at her with something speculative in his eyes. In the next second he'd left the sofa and dropped down to lounge on the floor beside her, half propped against the frame of her chair, eyeing her with a touch of defiance. He looked like some splendid, not quite tamed animal that had deliberately chosen to humble itself at the feet of its master but wanted to make certain the master understood its position, thought Lia with a strange feeling of apprehension.

When he spoke again all the playfulness was gone. There was something ominous in the very blandness of his voice.

"Why didn't you tell me the guy who's been winning at your table—this Toby Brasford—is your ex-fiancé?"

There were no preliminaries. Just the blunt question, and with it came to her a wild feeling of helplessness, a sense of impending disaster, as if her car brakes had suddenly gone out on a downgrade.

Why hadn't she, indeed? The only thing she could immediately think to say to the man looking up at her with no-nonsense eyes was not an answer but another question.

"Where...how...? So you and Toby have talked?"

"We haven't gotten that friendly," Flint said acidly. "Your dad told me yesterday."

"Dad?"

"And before you start blaming your father for telling tales out of school, I might mention he didn't even know he'd said anything that might embarrass you."

"You needn't have said that," Lia told him indignantly. "Dad would cut out his tongue before he'd deliberately embarrass me. It never crossed my mind that he would."

From where he sat on the floor beside her, Flint came up to his feet, the suddenness of the movement breaking the relative calm with which the original question had been asked.

"Damn it, Lia, don't try to evade—"

"I'm not evading. I just wanted to know how—"

"And I want to know *why*! What's going on between you and Brasford that makes it so hard for you to level with me?"

She could see the rising tide of anger in his face, and she wanted with all her heart to turn it back.

"There's nothing between us, Flint. There never was all that much. Besides being one of the best-looking men around, Toby has a kind of dazzling charm when he puts his mind to it that is easy to mistake for substance. I was infatuated at first, and then my dad started a campaign to save his daughter from the evils of Toby Brasford, and Toby became a raging issue—a matter of principle between us. I look back in shame. Where dad was concerned, it's taken a while for me to grow out of a solid state of adolescence, I'm afraid.

"The important thing I'm trying to tell you, Flint, is that it had nothing to do with love. You're the only man I've ever loved, and it took you to show me the difference between what was real and what was not."

"The question was not prompted by jealousy," Flint said stiffly. "I believe you, but none of that explains why you didn't tell me who Brasford was when he first came to the table."

Lia's brow puckered a moment in thought. "I honestly don't know why, Flint, except it was so beautiful between us then. I suppose I didn't want to spoil what we had with the irrelevancy of Toby."

"I just find it hard to believe the guy doesn't have some kind of hold over you, Lia. Otherwise you would have told me when he first came. If you'd done it then it would have been no big deal."

"I know. It would have been easy then, only I didn't, Flint, and it got hard. I thought in a day or two he'd be gone, the way gamblers go, you know. When he stayed on, I asked him to find some other place to play—another casino, another table, another pit—but he stayed. I even asked the pit boss to remove him. You can see what good that did."

She could see the doubt and the look of hurt in his eyes and felt tears well up in hers.

"Don't you believe me, Flint?"

"Oh, I believe you." He lowered himself restlessly into the other wing chair and jockeyed it around to where he could look directly in her face. "But I still don't understand why you went to so much trouble to keep me from knowing who he is. I can't help but wonder what the sleazy swine's presence here has to do with you."

"That's not fair, Flint," flared Lia. "Toby's not a 'sleazy swine.' He was a successful San Francisco real-estate broker when I knew him. He's not a bad person—just weak. Except for the unfortunate fact that where gambling's concerned he's a moral cripple, he's no worse than most ambitious young men on the way up."

"And you're trying to reform him! I suppose that's the reason for all those surreptitious meetings in the Golden Urn. You're still trying to reform him!" Flint accused.

Hanging on to her temper, Lia replied, "*Two* meetings, and they were never meant to be surreptitious. I don't know who's keeping track of my movements, but your reasoning is off. If I ever thought I could reform Toby, it didn't take much reading in psychology to learn that it can't be done, unless the gambler himself wants to. I didn't come up here to look for a cure for Toby. It's just that my experience with him made me want to find out what makes one person gamble purely for pleasure and another because he's compelled by something inside. *That*, Flint, is the only reason I'm here."

"And Brasford? What's he here for? You're sure it has nothing to do with you?"

The outrage that had been building up within her at the accusing tone in Flint's voice boiled over.

"I haven't the slightest idea, but I'm glad he's here," she snapped on impulse. Sorry at once, she tried to make amends. "I didn't mean that the way it sounded. I'm only interested in Toby as a case study. He's the only gambler I've been in contact with long enough to really chart. But I'll be honest with you, Flint. I'm interested in learning how to help Toby and those like him. I'd be lying if I said I wasn't. Anyone locked in to a compulsion is a real challenge to my profession."

"And a real threat to our marriage," said Flint bitterly.

"Meaning?"

"Meaning you're more interested in the blasted gamblers than you are in marrying me. Sure, you love me, Lia, but your damned stubborn intellectual curiosity is stronger than your love. Isn't that right? As long as you've got your own private case study to work on at your table day after day, you'll fight shy of the distractions of marriage. Be honest with me, Lia. Isn't that it? You have no intention of marrying me until—"

In that instant her temper exploded in a fire

storm of words. To her horror they were words she had promised herself she would never say to this man.

"You asked for honest. Well, you're going to get honest. If all I wanted was a case study I'd marry *you*. You want to know why I won't marry you? Because you're a hard-core gambler—another one of those blasted gamblers you vilify. That's why I...won't...marry...you, Flint." She was crying now. The damning words spilled out with the tears, punctuated by shattering sobs.

Flint watched her in stunned silence.

"I love you, Flint...I do...really love you," she sobbed, "but you're a gambler, and there's not a single thing I can do about your gambling...or about...loving you."

"Lia, dearest, listen to me," Flint said, finding words at last and reaching forward to take her into his arms. "Oh, God, Lia, please stop! Listen to me. I'm not a gambler, I swear. You've got to believe me. I'm not."

She fought the arms that tried to encircle her, and the storm within her raged on.

"Leave me alone," she sobbed fiercely. "You're worse than poor...weak Toby. So strong...you were able to quit. For years and years you...quit. And for what? Just to start all over again. I can't stand it, Flint. I love you. I can't stand to watch you do it to yourself."

"Please, Lia. You're tearing yourself apart. Let me hold you...."

"Just...leave me...alone, you...you...*degenerate*!"

Gradually the great sobs that convulsed her body subsided, and she straightened up and rummaged in a pocket for a tissue. Flint, standing helplessly by, a look of dazed horror on his face, dropped to his knees beside her.

"Lia, darling woman, listen to me. I love you," he said softly, but the magic had gone out of the words.

She pushed away his hands, which still tried to hold her, and rose so abruptly to her feet that he lost his balance and toppled against the chair. He was immediately on his feet beside her, but she drew away from his outstretched hand.

"Go away, Flint," she said, her voice still swollen from her tears. "I can't go through any more of this. It was bad enough with Toby, but nothing like now. I love you more than I ever thought I could love anybody. It hurts."

"Listen to me, Lia," he said, but she turned and walked away from him.

"Turn out the light when you let yourself out, please," she said over her shoulder. "I'd rather not see you again. I'm going to bed."

One last time Flint tried to get through the barrier she was building around herself. "Wait, Lia. It's not like you think. If you'll just let me...."

She'd gone only a few steps when she stopped and turned. "Please, Flint, just go while we still love each other." Her voice was infinitely weary and near tears once again. "It's just no good. I can see now I can't be a silent witness to what you're doing to yourself. I'd preach and scold and plead with you until our love turned to hate, and you'd still be a gambler, and I'd be...embittered." She took another step forward then stopped and looked back over her shoulder. "It's been a lovely dream."

She moved across the living room and into the hallway. When she reached the door to her bedroom she didn't look back. With a kind of finality she closed the door behind her.

CHAPTER TWENTY-ONE

HE FOLLOWED HER a few steps and let her go, watching the straight slender back, the head held high like a rose on its stem, with a terrible sense of helplessness. She had never seemed more desirable to him, her eyes puffy and red, her face blotched and swollen from her tears. Every instinct told him to go after her, to break down the door, if necessary; to take her in his arms, to comfort her, tell her there was no need to worry, tell her...tell her what? What could he say that she would listen to, shut off as she was by her wall of pain? Not platitudinous assurances, however loaded with love, and at the moment that was all he was prepared to give.

Nothing short of the truth would reach her now, and he couldn't give her that. Not until he first warned Aaron that he was going to do it. He'd made an agreement with his brother-in-law that he wouldn't tell her. He owed it to Aaron to give him fair warning that he was about to break that promise.

Listening, he could hear her stirring around in her bedroom. He heard the sound of water running and understood with relief that she was all right. The devastating sobs that had torn through her had passed. She had cried herself out and sensibly given herself over to her nighttime preparations. He imagined her standing naked on the pale coral-colored bath rug in the bathroom he knew as well as his own, a foot reaching out to step over the barrier into the shower stall. For a moment he saw in perfect detail the slender rise of her waist up to the firm full breasts, the beautiful swell of her hips, and he wanted desperately to try once more to get through to her. Maybe if he slipped in quietly and she found him waiting to take her in his arms when she came out of the bathroom... maybe if he didn't say anything, just made love to her....

But it was a fool's hope, he knew. He turned out the lights and checked the door to make sure it was locked as he left the house.

His watch showed nine-thirty when Flint reached his penthouse quarters at the Goldorado. He went straight to the phone.

"Aaron? I didn't get you out of bed, did I?" he asked when he had his brother-in-law on the phone.

"Hardly," said the voice at the other end. "Roz is beating the hell out of me at gin. I'm glad you interrupted. She just won a trip to Bermuda."

"Serves you right. I told you never to play cards with a Tancer. Roz wasn't dad's kid for nothing," said Flint with a derisive laugh. "In case you wonder why I called, I thought you should know that I'm going to tell Lia I'm spying for you at her blackjack table.''

There was a moment of silence at the other end of the line. Then Burney asked anxiously, ''Right now? Tonight?''

''No such luck. I just left her, and she's in a state. She wouldn't even let me in the house if I tried to go back to her now, but I'm going to tell her first thing in the morning. I plan to be waiting for her in the parking lot when she comes in for work. I want her to know before she sees me at that table again.''

''Now wait a minute, Flint. You realize, of course, this could blow the whole operation?''

''To hell with the operation! I realize I could blow the only really important thing in my life if I don't tell her pretty soon. You and Mansfield and I have already done enough mischief with all this secrecy!''

He heard Burney clear his throat at the other end of the line.

''What do you mean 'mischief'?'' Burney asked cautiously.

''It's just like I said it would be from the first. She thinks I'm a hard-core gambler...a degenerate! That's what she called me just now. And what else could she think when I show up at her table every day, right along with Brasford?''

''If you hadn't been at that table we wouldn't have known Brasford has graduated from compulsive gambler to card cheat,'' Burney reminded him quietly.

"Right at this moment that doesn't mean much to me, Aaron. I don't really give a damn about Brasford. I just want Lia to know the truth.''

At the other end of the line the throat was cleared again. It was Burney's nervous tic.

"You know, Flint. . .uh. . .Mansfield's got this crazy idea that maybe Lia is working as Brasford's accomplice. I told him he was crazy but. . . ''

Flint sent an expletive hissing along the wire.

"I don't want to hear anything more about that, Aaron,'' he said coldly, bringing his temper under control. "It's not true. I know who Brasford's accomplice is, but it may take me a day or two to get the evidence I need to prove it ''

There was a moment of silence, another throat clearing, then Burney said, "Well, go to it, and good luck. Don't you think the fewer who know about what you're doing, the more likely you are to succeed?''

"Damn it, Aaron. I've got to tell Lia. That comes first. Things can't go on the way they are.''

"It's that important to you?''

"It's *this* important to me, Aaron—Lia Andrews is the only woman I've ever loved. I want to marry her. This stupid gambling thing is all that stands in the way.''

"You've gone this far at the casino. Will another two or three days make that much difference?''

"It's tearing her apart. Tonight she made it quite plain that although it shatters her to do it, she's locking me out of her life. The only reason I'm telling you this, Aaron, is so you'll understand the extent of the trauma she's going through—and I am, too, to a lesser degree. The longer she has to suffer because of my silence, the greater the risk the breach can never be healed."

"I'm sorry I put you through this, Flint," Burney said quietly. "I never really thought that seeing you gambling every day would matter that much to her. I thought she might rather like having you at her table all the time."

Flint answered with a derisive snort. "The fact is, she was once engaged to Brasford and broke it off because of his gambling. Doesn't that tell you something? She's already been down that road, and she's not going down it again."

"Mansfield mentioned she'd been engaged to Brasford. How does she feel toward him now?"

"Nothing special. I gather she wishes he wasn't here but has no real bitterness toward him. She says it was never anything but infatuation on her part, anyhow. She's a graduate in psychology, you know, so she regards him as a case study more than anything else. Deep down inside I suspect she's looking for a way to make him quit gambling."

At the other end Burney sighed. "Well, if you feel you have to tell her, Flint... well, go ahead."

"Thanks, Aaron. I appreciate your feelings."

Again the throat was cleared. "I suppose...
no...of course not...."

"Out with it, Aaron."

"I was just wondering if there's any chance....
You say she still has some concern for Brasford.
She wouldn't feel compelled to tip him off to try
to save him, would she?"

"I'd ask her to promise not to."

"Suppose she won't listen if you ask her to
promise first? Suppose she won't promise, after
you've already told her?"

"Then to hell with the whole business. We'll
just have to take the chance. I've got to tell her."

"Suit yourself, Flint. If you really think delaying it a couple of days would make a difference,
by all means, go ahead and tell her. You're most
likely right. She probably wouldn't tip him off."

They talked a few moments about other mutual
concerns, Flint gave his brother-in-law some mes-
sages for Roz and the children, and the two said
good-night. Flint hung up with a feeling of uneasiness.

Aaron was right. She wouldn't listen if he pre-
faced it with a promise, and if he told her first and
she decided she had an obligation to try to rescue
Brasford by tipping him off....

The worst of it was, he couldn't be certain how
Lia would see it. If she thought Brasford might
land in jail for fraud, Flint had little doubt she'd
feel bound to save him, and there would go the
whole operation.

Much as Flint wanted him out of Lia's life, Brasford was not the real target. He was really no more than an accomplice. The other one was the mastermind. If he wasn't caught now, he would still be at the Goldorado after Toby Brasford was long gone. When everything had cooled down again there would be another accomplice in Toby's place.

The groundwork had been laid. Flint hated the thought of having the real crook go undetected. It might mean they could lose the scoundrel for all time. If he felt things were getting too hot, he could easily disappear into the world of casinos and surface at a later time in Las Vegas or Atlantic City—gambler, dealer, pit boss—and start his scam all over again with new victims on new ground.

Flint was brushing his teeth when the phone in the bathroom rang. He gave his mouth a quick rinse and took the receiver to his ear.

"Flint Tancer speaking."

"Flint, Aaron again. I was just checking with Mansfield. Lia doesn't come in until eleven tomorrow morning. Les thinks it's a good idea for the three of us to meet in his office around nine. That will still give you plenty of time to catch her in the parking lot when she comes in. Les thinks we ought to have a...oh, a sort of a strategy meeting to, well...decide what to do in case Lia...you know...."

"Yeah, yeah. Okay. I'll be there," Flint said

shortly. He hung up and stood staring absently at his own bare-chested reflection in the mirrored wall.

Some strategy meeting! he thought grimly. *They think they're going to talk me into waiting until it's over to tell her.*

Flint had another bad night, hours of fitful sleep broken by long intervals when his head argued with his heart over the problem of telling Lia in the morning or waiting a few days until he had the casino's rip-off artist nailed to the wall.

Long before he was to meet with Aaron and Les in Mansfield's office the next morning, he knew he would not be waiting in the parking lot later for Lia to arrive. There was too much at stake. Telling her would have to wait.

A stubborn loyalty to the cause of saving Toby Brasford from his own weakness could very well send her straight to Toby the moment she was told, unless, of course, Flint could get her to promise not to, and he didn't see how he could arrange that.

Once told, Brasford would warn the mastermind, who would promptly have Brasford banned from the casino on a pretext of counting or cheating. He might even point a finger at Lia as Brasford's accomplice.

It simply wasn't in Flint's nature to let the bastard go on his conscienceless way, leaving a trail of innocent and not-so-innocent victims to take the blame and get out of it as best they could. He'd just have to chance it that Lia would understand when he could finally go to her and explain. He looked ahead to the next few days with no joy in his heart.

LIA STOOD MOTIONLESS, her hand still gripping the knob after she had pulled the bedroom door closed and shut Flint out of her life. How it hurt! She could sense his presence still in the house. She had only to fling the door open and rush back into his arms.

The urge to do so was almost overwhelming, and yet she knew that for all the ugliness of the terrible scene with Flint, she couldn't honestly wish it hadn't happened. Sooner or later everything was bound to have spilled out. It was just as well to discover that she couldn't keep it bottled up inside forever as she'd somehow expected to do. Nor could she wish she hadn't closed him out of her life with such finality. It was better to end it while he still loved her; better for him and better for her.

Had she let the relationship go on, it would have turned into a tired, dreary, mutual dislike. She would come to despise him for gambling, and he to hate her for saying what she could never hold back. There was a sort of bleak comfort in knowing that even in parting they still loved each other. Yet the pain was like the pain from a physical wound.

When she heard no sound from the living room

she wondered if he was still there, or if he had slipped quietly out while she had been oblivious of everything. She resisted the temptation to open the door and see. Moving on into the room, she began to get ready for bed.

A kind of peace came over her in the shower, though her head felt swollen from her storm of tears. She had shut Flint out of her life. Now she must learn to live without him. Until she could leave the Goldorado, where she risked running into him almost every day, she must teach her eyes not to look for him, teach her heart to forget.

Showered and ready to crawl into bed, she wrapped herself in the comforting warmth of her fleece robe and went instead to her desk, where she began to sort and evaluate the work she had done to date on her gambling study. She worked until long after midnight, stopping only once when a terrible feeling of bereavement swept over her and threatened to carry her away.

Leaving her work corner, she stirred up the dying embers in the fireplace and threw on a chunk of wood. She brewed a pot of tea, then carried books and papers and index cards from the desk behind the screen to a game table she had moved in front of the fire. She took solace from the cheerful crackle of the new log as it burned, and she sat sipping her tea absently from a favorite china cup decorated with bachelor buttons, watching the bright fingers of flame lick up the soot-blackened chimney. At length she put down her cup and tackled the papers again.

Shortly before three Lia pushed her papers aside and stood up, stretching and yawning. She'd worked herself into the state of exhaustion she'd been aiming for. She knew she could sleep now, and she'd accomplished what she'd set out to do in her work. Her study at the Goldorado was near enough finished that she could leave whenever she chose. In her preoccupation with Flint, she had perhaps even prolonged it unnecessarily.

She was pleased to find she'd done such a thorough job of canvassing the Goldorado and, on her days off, its neighboring casinos. Some of her recent material was actually repetitious and went over ground she'd already covered. It was time to move on.

She had long lists of names and addresses of gambling people. Amateurs who played purely for fun, professionals who made a sporadic living out of the cards as Flint's late father had done, and compulsive gamblers, none of whom admitted they were. These were the people she had talked to at some length at the Goldorado, the ones who had agreed to follow-up meetings with her later. She would have liked to talk to some of the long-time security people about gamblers they had seen come and go, and to the bellboys and chambermaids who looked after the comforts of the high rollers—maybe even interview a high roller if she had the chance. But she could see no way to do it without tipping her hand, no matter how much longer she stayed on.

Yawning fiercely again, she realized she was ready to fall asleep on her feet, and she moved to the fireplace to close the screen on the dying fire. Gathering up her material, she prepared to stow it out of sight again in her corner retreat, then laid the papers back down on the game table. She was too tired to move it all now. Maybe she'd just leave it where it was and work on it there again. It no longer mattered. Flint wouldn't be around to see them. He wouldn't be coming again. She felt suddenly lost.

As she slipped out of her robe and got into her bed she thought of one last thing she must take care of before she left the Goldorado. Toby.

SHE COULDN'T HELP BUT THINK of Toby the next day. He arrived shortly after she took her place at the table at eleven, and a few minutes later Ed Shields came to the table with a new deck of cards. Thinking of Toby's likely connection with the pit boss, she watched the deck closely as Shields slapped it down on the table in front of her for dealer and players to see. She watched him take up the deck again and break the seal, then mark down the time on the inside of the box flap as he was required to do by the house.

At her distance it was impossible to tell if the seal had been tampered with. Short of snatching the deck up off the table and examining it closely, which would be so bizarre Shields would know at once that something was up, she couldn't tell whether or not it had been tampered with. She wondered if she could get Toby himself to tell her what was going on.

Then suddenly she didn't think of Toby anymore. Flint walked up to the table and sat down as if last night had never happened, except that his face looked drawn and his mouth was tight. Lia exchanged chips for money without raising her eyes to meet his. As she shuffled and began to deal her hands trembled almost imperceptibly from the shock of his presence. She went through the motions of her job automatically, shuffled and dealt, paid and collected, but outrage swelled within her. And all the time something inside her was screaming out at him, *Flint Tancer, how could you? This is a really rotten thing to do!*

Because of his connection at the Goldorado, she'd assumed Flint would continue to gamble there, but she'd taken it for granted he would respect her feelings enough to do his blackjack on the other side of the casino. She was stunned that he would act with no more sensitivity than Toby had.

Flint's appearance had caught her completely off guard, and it took a while before she'd recovered enough to take stock of the situation she found herself in. She knew then she must get away before the whole thing destroyed her. The quicker she began to rebuild her life the better off she'd be. As long as she worked at the Goldorado it was impossible. Once away from the casino she could plunge into the second phase of work on her thesis and forget the pain for long reaches of time. The forgetting would gradually stretch out until the re-membering, when it came, would not hurt as much, and in time, perhaps, it might not hurt at all. But here at the Goldorado there'd be no chance to forget. Not while Flint was within hands reach of her every day. Not with a sensual magnet-ism between them that was almost palpable.

She went through her dealer's routine with no more than half of her mind on it, but somehow she lived through the afternoon without putting her job in jeopardy and without ever meeting Flint's eyes. She couldn't help being acutely aware of his every move, though, and aware of the elec-tric feel of his presence around her.

At the same time the other half of her mind grappled with the question of what to do about Toby Brasford. It was something she was deter-mined to settle before she left. Rick Williams had been on the right track, she was sure, when he sug-gested that Toby was winning with the help of Ed Shields. It also seemed reasonable to suppose that the help was in the form of a deck of marked cards, since Rick had already proven to his own satisfaction that the pit boss had switched decks before. Her problem was to get the proof she needed in order to confront Toby.

It wasn't until late that night that she began to look back on what she knew about Toby from their extended acquaintanceship, and she wondered if she really needed solid proof, after all. From the first time Toby came into the casino she'd seen there was something different about him. He'd seemed moody and insecure despite his usual brashness—not at all the devil-may-care Toby she'd known before. She'd even twitted him about it a bit, but she'd thought it strange, considering he was off on a winning streak, that the normally breezy man seemed so unhappy.

In a flash of understanding, she realized that the reason Toby was unhappy was that he was afraid. If she could get him alone long enough to talk to him.... But not at the coffee shop...someone would see them there. She'd have him come to her place the following night. She could confront him with a flat statement that he and Ed Shields were cheating the casino. Knowing Toby, she wouldn't need any proof. He might even be relieved to tell her. It wouldn't be the first time he'd spilled out a sorry tale to her.

It was her good luck to spot him coming across the casino in the direction of her table the next morning as she was heading there herself to begin her shift.

"Toby, there's something really important I've got to talk to you about, but not here," she said quickly. "Could you come by my house about seven? Here are the directions to get there."

She slipped a folded sheet of paper into his hand and walked away from him, not wanting to be seen with him away from the table. Toby moved into his place at her table a moment later as she took over the dealer's slot. His face looked puzzled, but he gave her a nod, assuring her he would come. A short time later Flint arrived.

The eternal triangle! thought Lia sourly as she shuffled and dealt the cards.

CHAPTER TWENTY-TWO

TOBY KNOCKED AT HER DOOR three minutes before seven that evening and by seven knew what he'd been summoned for.

"You're wondering why I asked you to come here, Toby. I know you're in big trouble, and I'd like to help you as much as I can," Lia said without preliminaries once they were seated across from each other in the living room.

Toby's eyes left her face to focus somewhere over her left shoulder, and his feet shifted uncomfortably.

"I . . . what do you mean? I don't know what you're driving at."

"I think you do. This great run of luck you've been having at my table ever since you came . . . that's not Lady Luck looking over your shoulder. It's Ed Shields."

"Who's Ed Shields?" asked Toby, but the innocence failed to come off.

"Funny you don't remember him, Toby, in view of the fact I saw you together in that restaurant a few weeks ago. To refresh your memory, Ed Shields is the pit boss—the one who's been switching the decks at my table to make sure you win.''

He gave a derisive snort. "You've been reading too many detective stories!"

"We both know that's not true. I'm not saying you're basically dishonest, Toby. I know you too well to think that, but I also know your weaknesses. Ed has got something on you, and he's using you to make crooked money for him."

Toby fumbled in his pocket and came up with a flattened cigarette package from which he extracted a last bent cigarette. With a visibly trembling hand he fumbled again for a lighter, touched the cigarette to the flame and drew hard on it. The damaged cigarette failed to light. He crumpled it angrily then looked helplessly at Lia.

"Got a smoke?"

Lia, who had watched the elaborate delaying action with a growing certainty she was on the right track, held out an ashtray for the refuse he had crushed in his hand.

"Sorry," she said. She had tossed the ball into his court and now sat quietly waiting to see how he would return it.

"You're crazy, you know," he said at last. "You're just sore because I've finally hit on a surefire counting system, and you can't get a line on it."

"I wish that was true. In that case the worst that could happen to you would be to have the manager ask you not to play at our casino anymore.

Look Toby, when Ed Shields finds out someone's about to blow the whistle on his little operation, he's going to throw you to the wolves just like he did the last gambler who worked with him.''

"He *did*?"

"He did. And the dealer, too. He told the manager he'd caught the two of them cheating the house. The dealer had already found out what was going on, but Ed beat him to the draw. He figured the manager would decide he was framing the pit boss to save his own skin, so he didn't even try to defend himself. He quit. Well, let me tell you something, Toby. I don't intend to be Ed Shields's scapegoat, and you don't have to be, either. With solid evidence—''

"Wait, Lia," Toby broke in. The handsome face looked suddenly drawn. "You've got evidence?"

Lia eyed him shrewdly for a moment, then answered him with a seeming irrelevancy. "Your glasses. When did you start wearing glasses, Toby? I notice you're not wearing them tonight.''

His eyes moved again, avoiding hers. His face had taken on a waxy pallor, and a muscle twitched fitfully at the corner of one eye.

"Bright lights...smoke...I wear them just in the casino," he muttered.

"You don't want to go on like this, Toby." Lia pressed on. "You're miserable. I've seen it from the first. You're not by nature crooked, and here you are getting in deeper every day, knowing sooner or later it's going to land you in the worst trouble you've ever been in. Get out of it, Toby. Get out of it while you still can.''

Her words leeched all the bluster and brashness from him. His face seemed to crumble before her eyes. For a moment he struggled to find his voice, and when he spoke it was on a shrill note of panic.

"What am I going to do, Lia? I'm already in over my head!" To Lia's shock he put his head down in his hands and began to sob.

It was not pleasant to witness the complete collapse of the once debonair overconfident Toby. It saddened her but did nothing to weaken her purpose. She was the psychologist now. There wasn't a lot she could do for Toby except steer him toward a course that would at least leave him some remnants of self-respect.

"Would you like to talk about it, Toby?"

It was as if she had pulled the stopper in a barrel. Once the words began to spill out they poured on and on. She couldn't have stopped them had she wanted to.

She knew the story. She had read case histories not unlike it before, but for the first time the principals were people she knew. It gave her a new understanding of the almost predictable path that had led Toby from compulsive gambler to petty criminal.

"What you're telling me is that Ed Shields is blackmailing you with a bad check for twenty thousand dollars you gave him on a gambling debt? Is that right?'' she asked finally.

''He threatened to send me to prison. I had to come in with him on the scam. I've been paying him back from the winnings. I swear, Lia, when I get Shields all paid off I'll give up gambling for good. I can't go through this anymore.''

''What makes you think Shields will give you back your check, Toby?'' Lia asked gently.

Brasford moaned. ''Don't think I haven't thought about that. I've got to *believe* he'll give it back. He could send me to prison with that bad check. What else can I do?''

''You can go to the manager and tell him what's going on. I know the owner, Mr. Burney. He's not a vindictive man, and I'm sure he and Mr. Mansfield, the manager, will agree to be lenient with you if you'll give them evidence against Shields.''

For a moment she thought he was going to give in. A look of hope brightened his face. Then it turned dark again, and he shook his head.

''That doesn't get my check back for me from Shields.''

''I don't think you'll have any problem there, Toby. If I understand it correctly, you were playing on Goldorado money, but the check to pay it back was made out to Ed Shields. I would guess that when Mansfield starts checking he'll find enough wrong with that little maneuver that Ed will be glad to return your bounced check to you and drop the matter.''

"Yeah well, you could be right," Toby said slowly after a moment's thought. "It wasn't exactly on the up-and-up. I thought about trying to bluff Ed with it myself, but he had me behind the eight ball. Mansfield could make it stick. Shields falsified the marker—you know, the note a player has to give the pit boss to get house money—and then I—"

Lia broke in. "Never mind that, Toby. Tell it to Mr. Mansfield. The important thing is for you to do it as quickly as you can, because once the security people decide to go after you it means Shields is already two jumps ahead. It won't be so easy to get a sympathetic ear if you wait for them to close in on you before you tell your story."

He sat on the sofa, his elbows on his knees, his head buried in his hands, a picture of abject misery. Lia was afraid to push.

After a while he looked up at her. "I guess you're right. Just the thought of having the nightmare end makes me feel better. I'll go in and see Mansfield first thing in the morning."

"Just don't talk to anybody about it until you do," Lia warned.

Brasford rose to his feet and took a step toward Lia, who had stood up, thinking he was about to leave. Another step, and he reached out with the clear intention of taking her in his arms. Lia sidestepped him.

"Cut it out, Toby. I didn't ask you here to start anything."

He looked puzzled. "Why are you doing this, then?"

Lia gave him a rueful grin. "Because I can't help it, I guess. I just can't sit by and watch you go down the drain. Because we used to have good times together, and you're really a pretty good sort, except—"

"Except for my gambling!" Toby broke in, showing the first small sign of spirit. "Honest to God, Lia, I believe you still love me. When this is all over I promise—"

But Lia wouldn't let him finish. "Don't say it. You're not going to quit gambling, at least not for me. Maybe never, not even for yourself. And I'm not in love with you, Toby. You may as well get that straight. The truth is, I never was, but I was too stubborn to admit it."

"I don't believe that, Lia. You're just mad because I haven't quit gambling. You'd marry me in a minute if you thought I'd quit."

Why you arrogant. thought Lia, slightly amused.

"There's one thing I haven't been able to figure out," she said as she ushered him firmly toward the door. "Why on earth did you settle in at *my* table?"

"I'll give you one guess. Ed had found out somehow about our engagement, and he wouldn't let me play anyplace else. He figured even if you caught on you wouldn't report it, because of me." There was a sound of smugness in Toby's voice that set Lia's teeth on edge.

"Then he's in for a surprise, isn't he?" she said sweetly, furious at the way she'd been used. There was little doubt in her mind who had told Shields about the engagement. What was she doing here, she asked herself in disgust, trying to carry on a reasonable dialogue with this egocentric, harebrained *ass*?

"Good night, Toby," she said firmly. "You're giving me a headache. Go to wherever it is you go, but for heaven's sake don't open your mouth to *anybody* until you've talked to Mansfield."

IN HIS OFFICE Mansfield turned the last page of a handful of papers he had just finished reading and looked up at Flint, who was seated in a chair opposite his desk.

"Well, it's all there, Flint. It boggles the mind! He was making two or three hundred dollars a day at three-card monte on the streets of New York when he was twelve years old. And listen to this—" he riffled the papers until he came to a particular page "—he was kicked out of three casinos he was dealing for in Las Vegas at different times. Seems he was using some of the sleight-of-hand tricks he'd learned as a kid. A skillful second carder, it says here. As a gambler in Atlantic City they caught him with aces up his sleeve. Now that he's ours, he's using marked cards and switching decks, not to mention the markers he's falsified."

"Looks like your personnel people slipped up there, Les."

"Not really. He came with the place. He was a pit boss when Aaron took over. He'd been around for a while before that, and there were no complaints in his file. Which may partly explain why the place was on the verge of receivership when Aaron bought it," Mansfield said with a laugh. "It looks like I owe you an apology."

"Not me, but may I remind you that you owe Lia one?" Then, seeing the look of genuine regret on the other man's face, Flint assured him, "It's all right, Les. I know you always have our best interests at heart. And as for Lia, she'll forgive you. I wish I could be as sure she'll do the same for me," he finished broodingly.

"I'm really sorry as hell, Flint. . . ."

"Forget it," Flint said, his voice suddenly testy. He sighed and gave his friend a bleak smile.

After a moment Mansfield said, "I suppose now that we know what the scam is, the simplest way to handle it would be to pick up the new deck when Shields lays it down on the table in the morning. You'll be there to do it, and I'll see that a security guard is waiting to relieve Brasford of his glasses at the same time. We'll wrap it up quietly in a few minutes. How does that sound to you?"

"Not good. Not good at all. There are a lot of ways cards can be marked. Invisible ink is only one. Suppose Shields has switched to something else this time. We go around snatching glasses off noses, we could end up with egg on our faces."

Mansfield was visibly let down. "Damn it, Flint, I want to catch them in the act on this. I'm sure it's the glasses, but if you don't think we should...."

"I can't see any way we can find out exactly how those cards are marked without tipping our hand, Les, unless Shields or Brasford tells us, so if you want to chance it, I'm game. I don't mind looking foolish, but I don't much like letting the bloody crooks slip through our fingers. We'll lose them if we're wrong."

"Only one of them. Not Shields, who is the important one," said Mansfield. "Yesterday when I talked to Rick Williams he told me something else Shields has been pulling, and Rick says he'd be glad to swear to it. It seems when he was working in Shields's pit he saw a player come in and get three thousand dollars' worth of chips from Shields one day and sign a marker for them."

"What's wrong with that?"

"What's wrong is that Rick also saw the signed marker, and it was short one zero. When the fellow came to pay the chit he only paid the house three hundred dollars, which was all the marker was for. He cashed in the three thousand dollars' worth of chips Shields gave him, paid off the chit with cash and had twenty-seven hundred left to split with Shields. Rick saw it happen twice again for lesser amounts. You can be sure Shields's cut was at least half."

Flint let out a low whistle. "An operation like that could cost the house a pretty penny."

"It has. Incidentally, you might be interested to know, your Lia's been doing a little sleuthing on her own," Mansfield said after a moment. Flint eyed him with new interest.

"She's apparently trying to find out what Brasford's up to, too. Williams told her about the marked cards, but since she appeared mostly interested in what was going on at her own table, he didn't go into the business about the markers."

"She knows about the cards, though?"

Mansfield nodded and Flint gave a cluck of alarm.

"I told you we should have told her what was going on from the first, Les. She's a very intelligent lady and not easily intimidated. She could just as well as not decide to take off after Shields herself. Shields could get wind of it, and then where would we be?"

"On the other hand, from what you tell me, she might pin Shields to the wall and save us the trouble. Never underestimate the power of a woman, Tancer," said Mansfield with a sly grin.

The idea that Lia was conducting an investigation of her own disturbed Flint considerably. Once he'd gotten over the troublesome hurdle of Brasford's past connection with Lia, Flint had decided the gambler was harmless, but Ed Shields was something else. He had ties with a pair of casino hoods, according to the dossier the security people had put together on him, a vicious twosome who were known to play rough for a fee. He wondered if Lia had any idea what a dangerous game she had dealt herself into.

A chill of apprehension for the stubborn courageous woman whose life had become so closely intertwined with his own caused him to turn back to the security office. He had no real idea how he could have Lia protected, but he would breathe easier if he knew Shields was the only one they would have to deal with.

Leaving the security office a short time later, Flint made his way across the casino toward the hotel lobby and the elevators that would take him up to his topside quarters. He moved with something less than his usual decisive walk. A pall of loneliness hung over him. He dreaded that first moment when he would step into the penthouse to the lovely subtle reminders of Lia that lingered in the rooms. Her fresh sweet scent was as pervasive as the first smell of spring on the air.

He was tempted to stop at a small bar located off the main passageway through the casino for a brandy to lift his spirit and delay the moment when he must open that door, but at the entranceway he hesitated. In the shadows at the far end of the horseshoe-shaped bar he recognized the figure of Toby Brasford. With a grunt of disgust he was about to move on when it occurred to him it was time he made an effort to find out what the gambler could tell him. Though they had seen each other daily at the same blackjack table for some time, they had spoken no more than a dozen words to each other. It seemed possible that there might be something useful to learn from Brasford if he went at it right.

He slipped quietly onto the high barstool that was vacant next to the other man and ordered his drink. Except for a customer on the far side of the bar, they were the only ones there. Flint sipped his brandy, waiting for the right moment to express surprised recognition. Brasford beat him to it. He swiveled in his chair and beetled his brows in a long puzzled look at Flint.

"Don' I know you?" he said thickly, obviously drunk.

"I suppose you do," Flint said amiably. "We've been betting at the same blackjack table long enough to have established an acquaintanceship."

"Oh, sure. Tha's right...I rem'ber you," said Brasford with a nod that momentarily sent him off-balance. It seemed he might not stay in his seat, but he recovered and righted himself. He eyed Flint fuzzily. "Lemme buy you a drink. Yeah, I gotta buy you a drink. Anyone tha's 's big a loser as I was before I got...but I'm not s'posed to tell you about that...." His voice wandered off with a kind of giggle, as if he'd forgotten what he was saying, or forgotten, perhaps, that he was talking at all. He blinked in confusion for a moment, and then, remembering, snapped his fingers in the direction of the bartender, who was watching with obvious concern from his station behind the counter.

"Hey, bartender. . . bartender."

The bartender turned his head away and moved to talk to the single customer on the far side of the bar. Flint, who had barely touched his brandy and had no wish for another, knew that if Brasford had one more drink he would get no talk out of him.

"I've been watching you play, and I'd give a lot to know your system," Flint said. "I've tried a counting system or two myself, but I never come out the way you do."

Brasford eyed him craftily. "Yeah. . . well. . . le's just say I'm lucky. Le's just say that. Okay?"

"I know luck when I see it, and the way you win isn't luck. I'd be willing to pay you a good price for that counting system of yours. I'd keep it under my hat, of course."

The other man stared at him solemnly. It was obvious he was having trouble concentrating on what was being said. His reply was a hiccuplike mumble.

"You aren't trying to convince me you don't have a system?" prodded Flint.

"System?" There was that vacant giggle again. "Yeah. Y'might call it a system. But it won't work for you."

"Why not?"

"B'cause you don't know the pit boss. I need a drink. Hey, bartender!"

"What's knowing the pit boss got to do with your counting system?"

"Who said an'thing 'bout counting? Shields is the system."

"You mean Shields, the pit boss?"

"I need a drink. What the hell happened to the bloody bartender?"

Flint could see he'd better get the matter wound up fast. Brasford was getting further away from rational thought by the second. Another drink and he would pass out. Luckily the bartender was in no hurry to take the order.

He tried again. "You mean the system belongs to Shields, the pit boss? Think you could get him to teach it to me?"

Brasford looked at him coldly through glazed eyes, as if he'd suddenly tired of the game. Flint had a moment of frustration. It was all over, and he still didn't have the answer he'd been working toward.

And then Brasford said, "'S not a system. It's the deck. . . ." He drifted off again.

"What kind of a deck?" Flint prompted.

The gambler eyed him slyly. "I'm not s'posed to tell. Anyway, you don' have the glasses. . . hey, bartender! Get the lead out."

This time the bartender started around the bar to where they sat, but it didn't matter to Flint. He'd gotten what he came for. He was about to move when the bartender motioned that he wanted to speak to him. Flint moved on around the bar to meet him.

"If that drunk's a friend of yours, I'd sure appreciate if it you could get him out of here without any trouble. Otherwise I'm going to have to call a security guard, and they'll have to detain him until he's sober enough to get out of here without killing somebody in a car."

Flint hesitated. He was in no mood to saddle himself with Toby Brasford.

"Okay, I'll see what I can do." He slid back into the seat beside Brasford. "I don't like the bartender," he confided. "Let's go someplace else where we can get a good drink." He grasped Brasford's elbow firmly and started to guide him away. Too drunk at this point to resist even if he had the wits left to do it, Brasford allowed himself to be led unsteadily away. Bearing a good share of the other man's weight, Flint pointed him in the direction of Mansfield's office.

By sheer determination and a lot of luck Flint got all the way into Mansfield's territory before Brasford let out a warning squeak. Flint hurried him the last few steps into the executive bathroom, where the gambler was at once wretchedly, drunkenly sick. Flint left him alone to his misery while he summoned room service for a pot of hot black coffee, which he began pouring down Brasford as soon as the man could swallow. Half a pot of coffee and a few sieges of nausea later, the gambler lay stretched limply on the leather lounge in the reception room with Flint sitting nearby, evaluating his patient's progress.

When he was satisfied Brasford had reached a degree of sobriety where they could have some meaningful talk, he said, "First, I think you have a right to know that I've been watching you play for some time. My name's Flint Tancer. My brother-in-law owns the Goldorado."

The other moaned. Quietly Flint repeated to him what Brasford had revealed earlier in his drunken state. Only for a moment did the gambler try to bluff his way out of it, and then very weakly. He seemed to understand it was hopeless. He was no match for Flint, especially not now. Craven in defeat, he broke down.

"You won't turn me in, will you, Tancer?" he pleaded. "You wouldn't want to ruin a man that way. Lia said if I told Mansfield the whole story he'd go easy on me. Please, Tancer...."

"You told all this to Lia?" asked Flint, suddenly uneasy. "When?"

"Early tonight. She asked me to come to her house, and when I got there she started firing questions at me, and before I knew it I'd told her," he said sullenly.

"You haven't told anyone else, have you?"

"She told me not to. I wouldn't have told you if I hadn't had too much to drink."

"Did you talk to anyone else at the bar before I came in?"

"No." But even as he spoke his face went ashen. Beads of sweat stood out on his forehead and his hands were suddenly palsied. "Oh, my

God,'' he whispered. "He'll send me to prison. He said if I told anyone, he would. He's going to send me to prison, Tancer.''

"Wait a minute, Brasford. If you mean Shields, I'll see what we can do about that later if you do your part. We're not through yet. Who did you talk to? What did you say?'' Flint asked with rising alarm.

"I talked to Ed Shields. When I left Lia I just went to the bar and started drinking. I don't remember anything too clearly after that except Ed came. I remember thinking Ed was the one I especially shouldn't tell. Well, we had some more drinks, and I don't really know how it happened. I heard him say that if I ever told anyone he'd have me killed, and that's when I realized I'd told him what Lia had found out. He'll kill me, Tancer. I know he will. . . I—''

"Shut up!'' barked Flint. "What about Lia?''

Brasford was almost whimpering. "I didn't know how to stop him. . . . ''

Flint reached to where the other man sat slumped forward on the edge of the sofa, head in hands. He pulled him to his feet.

"What about Lia, you bastard? If anything happens to her I'll kill you myself!''

"Shields said he was going to shut her up.''

CHAPTER TWENTY-THREE

LIA SQUARED HER SHOULDERS and walked back
into the living room. The ordeal with Toby, who
had just walked out the door, left her feeling as if
she had been squeezed from a tube. She stopped
and looked around her in a kind of bewilderment,
not sure what she was going to do with herself.
She rejected the stack of books and papers on the
game table in front of the fireplace where she'd
left them the night before. There was still plenty to
be done before she left Sapphire Point, but she
was in no mood to apply her mind to it at the moment. She needed to do something physical.

An unusually warm day had turned into a still
balmy evening with not so much as a whisper of
the usual crisp breeze off the lake. She thought
first of a swim, but the faint sounds of voices and
music from the beach told her it was a night for
Sapphire Point families to picnic. She was simply
not up to being sociable, so she ruled out the possibility of a swim.

She quickly changed into shorts and tennis
shoes, took her racket from a hall closet and headed out for the point's tennis courts. There an auto-

matic server would shoot tennis balls at her until she ran out of energy to return them or coins to feed it, whichever came first.

The courts were empty when Lia arrived, except for a lanky teenager with a good wrist who was hitting his last balls at the server. When he finished he called out to her.

"Hi! You alone? Would you like to volley a few balls with me? I need to work on my serve."

Lia hesitated. The boy's returns were out of her class, but it would give her the workout she was looking for. She had little doubt the boy would dump her as readily as he took her on if he decided she was too slow for him

The first game assured her they were fairly evenly matched. The boy was stronger on the return, but his serves were erratic, and Lia was a faster, steadier, more wily player. If she had waited for him to put an end to the game they might have kept at it all night, but Lia finally called a halt. Perspiring and breathing heavily, she shook hands with the young man, thanked him for the game and trudged back up the slope to the house. There she found that she had left her key to the front door locked inside. Taking the walkway around the side of the house to the deck, she lifted a potted geranium and pulled out a key to the kitchen door. Entering the house, she let the door close and lock behind her. She walked into the living room and slid open the large glass doors to let in the warm night air, then went out to return the key. She didn't go back inside. Laying her tennis racket on the table she dropped onto the cushioned chaise longue beside it. The terrible feeling of aloneness that had threatened to engulf her throughout a day filled with people fell over her like a dark veil now that she really was alone. Even the tennis game with the boy had been a cruel reminder that the things she enjoyed most had lost their flavor without Flint.

It was dark out except for a pale amber arc of light from the gate lamp over the walkway at the end of the house. It cast a faint illumination across the deck, but the chaise on which Lia lay was outside its pale circle. From the shadows she looked out unseeingly into the deeper darkness, hearing rather than seeing the gentle ripple of the lake in the breezeless night.

The twitter of night birds in the trees stirred a memory of that first evening with Flint out on the deck—the misunderstanding and its sweet resolution with Flint's appearance afterward at her door and his preposterous load of flowers.

In an excess of sorrow she had not allowed herself till then, she embraced the bittersweet memories until they ran out, reminding her that there would be no more. Now all she could see ahead of her was a gray world.

One thing she would never have to worry about, she thought wryly, was whether or not she would agree to have Flint's children. She was surprised at how much the thought hurt. That she would never have children with Flint seemed, ironically, a kind of bereavement, almost the greatest loss of all.

Afterward she could never say for sure what brought her to attention—the sudden silence of the night birds, maybe; the creak of a board. She turned her head quickly and there was Ed Shields, stealthily approaching the deck from the walkway. He apparently hadn't yet seen her. His goal was the kitchen door, which he tried to open before hunkering down on one knee to work at the lock with some small tool he carried.

Lia got quietly to her feet, hoping to slip unnoticed through the open glass door, which Shields fortunately hadn't thought to try. If she could get inside without alerting him, she was sure she could make her way to the bedroom phone and call for help without the intruder being the wiser.

As she stepped into the circle of light she had to cross to get there, Shields looked up. He got quickly to his feet.

"I want to talk to you," he said.

"I must say you've got a unique way of paying a social call!" Lia snapped. "Just stay where you are, Ed. You take one step nearer, and I'll open my mouth and scream at the top of my lungs." It was sheer bluff. The people on either side of her were away, and anyone else would assume it was just another sound from the beach. To her relief, Shields made no move to come closer.

He gave a short harsh laugh. "You're just

another mouthy broad to me, baby. I didn't come here to rape you. I came to tell you if you sing to the management or anyone else about what you and Brasford talked about here tonight, you'll wish you hadn't.''

She shouldn't have trusted Toby! She might have known he would go straight to Shields. Now what was she supposed to do?

''Just what do you have in mind, Ed? You don't have a hold on me like you've had on Toby, and somehow I just don't think you're the type of hood who would bump me off.'' She hoped the words sounded more gutsy than she felt.

Shields laughed again. ''Don't be so sure of it, baby. I do like to keep my hands clean, but I've got a couple of friends in the Mafia who owe me, and they wouldn't mind doing it a bit.''

Lia stared at him in astonishment. All at once the whole situation was bizarre. It was so much like a bad TV movie it seemed unreal. If she had been listening to the voice of the psychologist in her she would have known it was no time to laugh. Even so, she might not have been able to restrain herself. It was the threat of the Mafia. Something a little less legendary she might have taken seriously, but to have Shields threaten her with the Mafia seemed so ludicrous she made no effort to hold back the derisive laugh that rolled out.

A sullen anger distorted the face of the pit boss. ''You'd better believe me, you silly bitch. I've a notion to beat the hell out of you—just to remind

you to keep your lip buttoned. You understand?
You see that lake out there? It's a thousand feet
deep in the middle. My men have got a boat with
an outboard motor that will take them across.
Anything they might happen to drop overboard
would never come up.''

Lia was not laughing now. "Wait a minute, Ed.
Let's talk about it...." But he was moving toward her, and she could see a glint of brutal pleasure in his eyes that told her he'd found the idea of
beating her up so appealing he was about to carry
through on it.

"You don't like women, do you, Ed?" she
asked, stalling for time as she tried to decide what
to do. The single vile phrase the man spat out told
her it would have been wiser to have held her
tongue.

As he moved toward her like a beast stalking its
prey, shoulders hunched, taking his time about it,
telling her in ugly terms what he intended to do to
her, she knew he was trying to make her cry out
for mercy, to run. Her instinct was to back away
from him, but tips she had learned in the self-
defense course she'd taken years ago flashed
through her mind. She balanced herself solidly,
feet planted shoulder width apart, one foot slightly ahead, and waited.

"Listen, you dumb broad. If you're worrying
about your pretty face, you can forget it. I won't
give you anything you have to explain like a fat lip
or a black eye. Just a bellyache and a few broken

ribs that'll hurt like hell when you're dealing cards. Just to remind you. Nothing that'll show. Nobody'll know about them but you and me and the doctor that patches you up. And the three of us won't tell, will we?''

Still he moved toward her, and she waited. Not until he was scarcely more than an arm's length away did Lia know exactly what she was going to do. Her hand shot out and closed around the tennis racket on the table beside her. Before it registered on Shields what she had in mind, she called into play her best backhand and brought the hard frame of the tennis racket around in a vicious swing that caught the pit boss straight across the middle of both knees.

With a howl of pain Shields bent over and grabbed his knees. She knew it was no more than a delay, yet she had no stomach for applying the recommended self-defense tactics—the knee to the groin, the uppercut with the heel of the hand to the nose, the finger stabs to the eyes—on an attacker who was already incapacitated. Yet if she gave him time to recover before she moved, she would have lost her advantage. On the other hand, if she left him there and locked herself in the house, he would get away, and the whole scene had been so outrageous, who in the world would believe her?

As she hesitated, the moans of the pit boss tapered off. Swearing, he started to rise clumsily to his feet. Lia knew she had to decide fast whether to try to deal with him again or get out while there was a moment's time. Then, under the gate lamp at the corner of the house, her eyes caught sight of Flint. She held her ground and let Shields come for her. Even as the pit boss lunged, Flint took a flying leap at the man's back. Satisfied to let Flint to the mopping up, Lia stepped aside.

MOMENTS LATER Shields was in the hands of two deputies from the sheriff's office who had been summoned by the security people at Flint's request as he left the Goldorado. They charged onto the scene with drawn guns almost upon Flint's heels.

When they were gone Lia said shakily, "We should do this more often. We make a great team."

"The way Brasford sounded I thought Shields was out to kill you." Flint's voice caught with emotion.

Lia grimaced. "He was going to arrange for the Mafia to do that in case I talked."

"I know all about his 'Mafia.' A three-time loser and one of his prison cohorts. The police picked them up tonight on a charge of conspiring to murder a Nevada businessman. None of them, including Shields, is going to be bothering anybody for a while," Flint said grimly. "When I think...."

"Oh, darling. Don't worry about it. It's all over."

"It was pure hell, Lia, knowing you were in danger...trying to get to you. It was like one of those nightmares I used to have as a kid where I'd be running and I couldn't get anyplace. I'd try to pull myself along by the fence posts, but I couldn't get ahead."

"Flint, I love you so."

"Lia...." Whatever he was about to say was lost as their lips met and clung. They held each other in a kind of desperate rejoicing closeness until Lia, still fired with adrenaline, pushed herself slightly away and drew a deep breath.

Still in the circle of his arms, she said, "Oh, Flint, I'm so glad you came. He was going to beat me up. I didn't know what I was going to do next."

Flint looked at her, amused. "Don't worry. You would have thought of something!" he said.

"No, really! This time you really did save me."

Flint pulled her close to him again with an indulgent chuckle. "Thanks, my darling. Don't think I don't appreciate your trying to make me the hero of this little fracas, but it's no dice. If I saved anyone it was Ed Shields."

"Ed Shields?"

"That was a broken man I tackled. What did you do to him, my love?"

"Oh...that. I...well...." Lia giggled a little hysterically. "I just cracked him across the knees with the tennis racket."

"Well, I'll be damned!" Flint said with a startled

laugh. "I always did say you had a wicked back-hand."

As the unnatural excitement wore off, Flint took her face in his hands and peered into it anxiously.

"Are you sure you're all right?" he asked. "Come into the living room so I can get a good look at you. You seem a little ghostly in this deck light." He guided her through the open doorway and turned on a lamp and looked into her face again. His inspection ended with a satisfied sigh. He enfolded her in his arms and buried his face in the cap of brown curls.

"If anything had happened to you...oh, God!"

"How did you know to come?" she murmured.

"You have Brasford to thank for that, I'm afraid."

Suddenly Lia felt shaky. "Do you mind if I sit down? All at once my legs feel like a pair of old shoelaces."

On the sofa, in Flint's arms again, Lia picked up where they had left off.

"What's this about Toby? I didn't know you two were on speaking terms." There was a trace of asperity in her voice and her words were stilted. In the few moments since Flint had said Toby's name, reminding her of what lay between her and Flint, she had raised her guard against him. Nothing had changed, she thought dully.

In her moment of letdown she felt so defeated and lost she hardly listened to Flint's account of his meeting with Toby at the bar and his own part during the past days in uncovering Shields's illegal machinations at the casino. Then gradually it begin to sift through until she understood, at last, the one thing that mattered. Flint was not a compulsive gambler and never had been.

"Why didn't you tell me?" she asked at last.

Flint hesitated, then he said, "Les and Aaron asked me not to, and finally I agreed. They thought you might be tempted to try to save Brasford's hide by telling him, if you knew. I'm sorry, darling. I'll have to admit I wasn't too sure you wouldn't myself."

After a moment Lia said thoughtfully, "I'm so relieved you're not a compulsive gambler I can't seem to get mad about it. I might have told him. I don't know. I almost blew it trying to help him anyhow. What's going to happen to him now?"

"It's up to him, darling. I'll talk to him tomorrow. He's pretty shaken. If he'll agree to get some professional help and take a life membership in Gamblers Anonymous, I think Burney will agree to give him a break. There'll be no more problems with the bad check to Shields, but we'll hold it over his head as an inducement for him to stay clean. Whether he can quit gambling or not, who knows? There are people in G.A. who've licked it. Mainly it's up to him."

"I know. He doesn't deserve it, but I'm glad you'll help," Lia said quietly. "Oh, Flint, I've been so miserable."

"Tell me about it," Flint said softly, but he covered her mouth with his, and they came together as if they had been apart for a long time. Their hands touched and caressed, as if reacquainting themselves with places that were especially dear; Lia running her fingers across the roughened surface of his face, nipping gently at his ears; Flint kissing her eyelids, the hollows of her throat, molding his palms to fit the curves of her breasts.

"You'll stay tonight?" Lia said breathlessly at last.

"Is that a proposal of marriage?" Flint asked.

Lia sat up and blinked at him owlishly. "Of course it is, but before you answer I'd better tell you I haven't been completely candid with you, either, darling. I've been taking advantage of your brother-in-law. He's actually been paying my salary while I've been doing my fieldwork for a master's thesis on gambling. I was afraid I'd be fired if they knew."

"I wondered why you didn't tell."

"You knew?"

"It would hardly take a man from Mensa to figure out you were up to something more than you were admitting to. If he'd known, I don't think Aaron would care."

"I'm winding the work up now. I'll tell Aaron and give him a proper apology."

Flint got to his feet suddenly and pulled Lia up with him. "Enough talk. We've got better things to do. Let's be on our way."

"On our way where, for heaven's sake?"

"I thought we were going to get married?"

"Tonight? Now?" Lia looked at him and then down at her shorts and tennis shoes in dismay. "Like this? Flint, it's almost eleven o'clock."

"You look fine to me. And you forget we're in the magic state of Nevada where two people can get married any time of day or night."

Lia, about to be swayed, remembered her father. She gave Flint a chaste kiss. "Flint, I can't do it, darling," she said. "We've got to have a wedding.... Don't look so stunned. Just my parents and the Burneys and half a dozen friends to see my dad do what he's been waiting for since the day I was born. I couldn't deprive my father of the satisfaction of giving his daughter away to the right man."

She could see by Flint's eyes that he was pleased.

"You *will* stay tonight?" she asked softly.

"Will I stay? With you? In paradise? Now *that's* an invitation I can hardly refuse."

ABOUT THE AUTHOR

Setting her second Superromance in Lake Tahoe seemed a natural choice for Jenny Loring since the Nevada resort is just a two-hour drive across the border from her home in California. Jenny often visits the Tahoe area—more for the spectacular scenery than the gambling, though she confesses to dropping a few nickels into the slot machines from time to time.

Jenny was destined for a career in the world of romance. Her father, a closet romantic, gave up his law profession and moved his city-bred wife and two daughters to a cattle ranch in Oregon's high-plateau country. There Jenny was born on the most romantic day of the year, Valentine's Day—a birthday she shares with her husband.

After graduating with a university degree in journalism she worked as a reporter and columnist on a California daily newspaper—thus beginning a writing career that eventually led to romance novels.

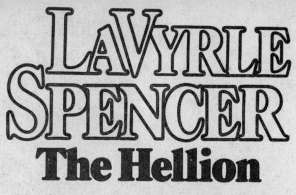

BARBARA DELINSKY
Fingerprints

Carly Quinn is a
woman with a past.
Born Robyn Hart, she
was forced to don a new
identity when her intensive
investigation of an arson-ring
resulted in a photographer's death
and threats against her life.

Ryan Cornell's entrance into her life
was a gradual one. The handsome
lawyer's interest was piqued, and then
captivated, by the mysterious Carly—a
woman of soaring passions and a
secret past.

Yours FREE, with a home subscription to HARLEQUIN SUPERROMANCE™

Begin a long love affair with

HARLEQUIN SUPERROMANCE.™

Accept LOVE BEYOND DESIRE **FREE**.

Complete and mail the coupon below today!
